NUMBER 111

Edited by

John P. Gunnison

© 2010 Adventure House

All rights reserved. No part of this publication may be reproduced or transmitted in any form. If you have purchased this copy without a cover, please report to us from whom you purchased it. Additional copies, as well as library or wholesale discounts, are available through Adventure House, 914 Laredo Road, Silver Spring, MD 20901 or through Diamond Book Distribution Company and Diamond Comic Distribution Company.

The Lost Beasts of Ta'Tamba — Jungle Stories, Winter 48-49. Copyright © 1948 by Glen-Kel Publishing Co., Inc. No Notice of Copyright Renewal.
Nirvana of the Seven Voodoos — Jungle Stories, Spring 1949. Copyright © 1949 by Glen-Kel Publishing Co., Inc. No Notice of Copyright Renewal.

Subscription Rate - $45.00 - 6 Issues - Advertising Rates - Full Page - $75.00.
The publisher has made every effort to contact the present owners of any copyrighted material. Our apologies to those who hold such rights but whom we failed to contact because ownership was unknown or addresses were incomplete. Appropriate credit will be given in future editions if such copyright holders contact the publisher.

Printed in the United States of America

ISBN: 1-59798-272-5
ISBN-13: 978-1-59798-272-6

First Adventure House Edition March 2010

Two more Ki-Gor stories. Two more jungle thrills and chills. Two more stories of The White Lord of the Jungle swing through the jungles of deepest darkest Africa to save his mate, Helene. Although Ki-Gor was not as well written as Tarzan, Ki-Gor had more action and adventure than the other White Man of the Jungle. If the publishers of the pulps knew one thing...it was that you copied whatever formula that worked. Edgar Rice Burroughs proved way back in 1912 in ALL-STORY that a white man in Africa adventure was a big seller and it took the rival pulp publishers nearly thirty years to clone the idea.

THE LOST BEASTS OF TA'TAMBA — Ki-Gor, White Lord of the Jungle, and Brend, boy-emperor of the Stolen Kingdom, battled side by side against the thousand warrior-beasts of Ramfis. Crawling swamp lizards would have had a better chance of victory. But struggling in the claws of Durga-Rama, the fiend usurper, Helene cried: "Ki-Gor, my mate, will save me!"

NIRVANA OF THE SEVEN VOODOOS — No broken, haunted captive lived to flee the jackal-born terrors of Nirvana, land of the red mists, where the gleaming-eyed scientist Krishna ruled by the dread hand of ancient gris-gris. And yet, Ki-Gor, White Lord of the Jungle, dared enter that forbidden kraal, dared try to wrest his mate Helene from its secret power—and even dared challenge the half-human gorilla-men to a battle that could only end in defeat.

Lastly, R.V. Geary's story from SHORT STORIES, "The Fugitive" — A novelette of a challenge that sounded from a remote corner of the African jungle.

John P. Gunnison
gunnison@adventurehouse.com

Durga-Rama snarled a command, and Panthra, the lioness, leaped at Ki-Gor, clawing at his eyes. Ki-Gor tried to shift position . . . He heard Arlenna scream . . .

THE LOST BEASTS OF TA'TAMBA

By JOHN PETER DRUMMOND

Could a thousand crawling jungle monsters stop Ki-Gor's safari to the Stolen Kingdom?

KI-GOR had been watching the strange scene for many minutes. He had seen the black man fall and die with the peculiar foam showing at the corners of his mouth. He had watched the terrified movement of the boy, who had light brown skin and slim, un-negroid features. He had watched the leopardess as she first caught their spoor and crept forward, belly down along the drooping bokongu branch.

So intent had the leopardess been on her prey that she had not noticed the slight stir of air, like the passage of some mighty bird, as Ki-Gor swung in a wide, pendulum arc through the air, one long, supple arm holding a vine. Her eyes had not strayed from the quarry as Ki-Gor dropped lightly to a branch directly above, his well-developed toes giving him sure footing without a steadying touch of his hands.

As the leopard inched forward, Ki-Gor watched with grim intensity, his hand drawing the great, keen-edged hunting knife from his waist. At last the leopard's tail stopped twitching; her body became rigid as it set to spring. He sensed the exact moment and leaped, his tall form plummeting directly in the cat's springing path.

Ki-Gor struck the boy with his back as he fell, knocking him face forward to the ground. The leopardess saw Ki-Gor at the last instant, but she was already launched in the air, unable to alter her course. She twisted, snarling, flinging her feet to strike Ki-Gor's shoulder. It was a movement as fast as the strike of a jungle adder, as fast as the lash of a cobra. But quick as her movement was, Ki-Gor was ahead of it. There was a subtle, lightning shift of his tall, superbly muscled body, a weaving back, a darting movement of his left hand, and his powerful fingers closed on the great cat's throat.

The leopardess was very large——taller, heavier than Ki-Gor himself. From nose to tip of tail she would have measured more than eight feet, and her velvet soft fur covered a massive weight of steel-hard muscle.

But despite that, Ki-Gor held her at arm's length. He seemed to be toying with her, as she herself had so often toyed with baboons before killing them for the pure joy of killing. He held her at arm's length as her forepaws lashed in futile arcs. Then, suddenly, he hurled her to earth, following her down, swinging with the knife.

The next second he was crouched with one knee on her flanks, the long blade driven completely through her chest, pinning her to the earth.

He waited thus until the leopardess was through swinging her paws in death agony. He watched the tension of living leave her muscles, then he removed his knee, jerked the strong hunting blade free, and with considerable care polished the blade on the animal's soft fur.

Only then did he look at the boy.

"I am Ki-Gor," he said, speaking the Congo dialect in a voice that was singularly soft, like the rustle of night wind through ochilla weed.

Brend, the brown boy, backed slowly away, bronze-tipped assagai in his hands, staring at the strange man who stood before him. It had all happened too quickly for his understanding——there had been the man dropping from nowhere, knocking him to the ground; the sudden, sharp struggle between man and clawing beast; the swing of the knife; the death-agony of the leopardess—and now, as a final wonder, here was this man of the light colored skin claiming to be the mythical person called Ki-Gor.

Long ago, Brend had heard of Ki-Gor. In his native valley, far beyond the eastern purple rim, Brend had listened to ivory hunters tell of a great man-animal who called himself thus. However, none of these men claimed to have ever actually seen Ki-Gor, and so he considered it only another story to be told in the hours of night, when the fire burned blue—a story to be followed by tales of Tol-ab, the spotted crocodile, and Skaab, the jeweled elephant who was said to roam the primordial fastness of the White Nile.

And now here was this man, in form like a god, in quickness and strength like nothing he had ever seen, claiming to be the very man.

Ki-Gor laughed, "Why do you stare at me, boy? I am real. Here, feel of my flesh. I am not some shadow of the sun. I am merely Ki-Gor, the man who stood on a limb and watched a leopardess planning to eat you for supper."

Brend remained tense for a moment, hunched forward, the assagai pointed at Ki-Gor's chest. At last the quiet sincerity of the White Lord's voice made him forget his fear. He lowered the assagai.

Ki-Gor then walked to the fallen black and bent over him. He ran his hands over his lifeless muscles, glanced at the still-open eyes, at the flecks of foam at the corners of his mouth.

"This man was poisoned!"

"No, he was not!" Brend fingered his assagai nervously, raising his voice. "I did not poison him. I swear by the gods of my people that I did not——"

"Boy, I did not say you had. You were not terrified of him in life, but in death. Therefore you did not poison him. I watched it all——from above."

Ki-Gor walked through the knee-deep ferns, light-footed as the leopard-cat he had just slain. He laid his bronzed hand on Brend's shoulder.

"Boy——who are you? Where do you come from? I know every native tribe, every cubit of this jungle that is my home. Yet I have never seen a man of a brown tribe such as yours. And this black man ——the tribal welts on his cheeks are strange to me. It must be you have come from a great distance."

THE BOY did not look like a typical African native. His skin had a strange, olive cast. His chin was rather pointed, with a cleft in the middle, his teeth were even and small, his face narrow, his nose thin and high bridged, his hair wavy brown. His face reminded Ki-Gor of the carvings he had seen long ago in temple ruins near the land of Sho-nab, which white men called "Ethiopia."

The lad answered, "My name is Brend. I am from a valley called Ramfis, eight days travel from the rising sun. I do not know where I am or why I was brought here. Only Kal-ab could answer these questions, and he is dead."

"Why would anyone wish to poison Kal-ab?"

"He was not poisoned. For eight days Kal-ab had only the meat he killed, and the fruit we picked. I ate of everything that he . . ."

"Some poisons are slow, and some are quick. The tribes of Bakele have one poison made of white-veil spiders which brings death in the space of twenty breaths, and another poison of dragon toadstools which kills in fifty days. I will wager that your man Kal-ab was poisoned before he left the valley of Ramfis."

Ki-Gor then asked. "What is that tattoo mark on your shoulder, Brend?"

"It is my mark of birth."

"Are all the children of your valley thus marked?"

"Only those of the king's line," the boy answered proudly.

From his first glance, Ki-Gor had guessed that this lad was not of ordinary tribal blood. There are many races clinging to remote corners of the jungle, and such races may have kings and customs dating to eras long forgotten.

"Is the king your father?"

"The king, my father, is dead."

"You were next in line, but you were judged too young by the council of old men——is it not so?"

Brend looked at the White Lord in wonder. "It is so!" he breathed. "Then it must be that you are the real Ki-Gor of whom the ivory hunters told. They said that Ki-Gor moved by magic, flying through the air like the wind, leaping like an arrow of the gods. They said he had eyes that see beyond the most distant horizon, seeing things even in the minds of ordinary men."

Ki-Gor laughed. "I have no magic, Brend. I merely guessed. You see, once, when gored by a rhino, I spent many weeks in a thing which my white brothers call a bed, while my friend, a doctor of the mission house at M'bwela, gave me bitter medicines to cure me. In the end I was cured by an ancient black with a poultice of leaves and bark, but no matter——while there I learned to read. I read a story like yours written in a book. That is all the magic I have——the memory of that story, and the guessing of yours. Now tell me everything."

Brend spoke, "I was born in the valley of Ramfis where my father's people have ruled as kings for more years than a great tree has leaves. My father, King Sandrak, died but a council of chiefs judged me too young to take his place. When I reached my fifteenth year, I could marry the girl Arlenna and rule as king. For two years now it has been so planned."

"There is an old man ruling in your place, Brend?"

"He is not old. Durga-Rama is still young——scarcely five-and-twenty. Why did you think him old?"

"Because the old are more wicked."

"Durga-Rama is wicked although young!" Brend compressed his lips and doubled his small fists. There was in his attitude a hint of the man to be, a glimpse of the royal blood in his veins. "Durga-Rama has always desired Arlenna. He has always wanted to rule. I have been a fool to let him do this to me——let him steal me from the valley. But now what can I do? How can I stop him? He will marry Arlenna and rule in may place."

They were startled by the sound of a woman's voice coming from the jungle's green wall.

"It will not be so."

The boy spun around, staring in amazement as a tall, slim-waisted girl walked into view.

She was beautiful. Her beauty seemed almost fragile at first glance, but there was supple grace and strength beneath her smooth, tanned skin. She wore a strip of leopard fur, leaving her slim waist free, revealing legs that were gracefully long. She came close to Ki-Gor, stood with shoulder pressed against the muscles of his arm.

It could be seen how perfectly they were matched, that she was truly the White Lord's mate, Helene.

A little smile touched her lips. She kept her eyes on Ki-Gor's face, sensing the response of her jungle mate to Brend's story of treachery.

Ki-Gor's muscles seemed tense beneath his tawny skin. They were like drawn springs which had waited too long for release. He noticed Helene looking up at him.

He asked Brend, "You could show me the route back to your valley?"

"You could not find it. Only Kal-ab knew the way."

A tiny man climbed rapidly down a vine and skipped through ferns coming to his armpits. It was Ngeeso, the pigmy chieftain. He cried, "Who is it dares say there is any spot in the jungle that Ki-Gor cannot find?"

Ki-Gor smiled. He again spoke to Brend,

"You say you traveled eight days?"

"Yes."

"Always toward the west?"

"Each morning the sun rose at our backs."

"And on the third day did you see a humped peak through the mists of the north?"

"It was so."

Ki-Gor nodded.

Helene asked, "You have been there, Ki-Gor?"

"I have been to the blue rim of hills which the Spala natives call the ridge of Ngoi. There is a pass which the Spalas fear to climb. They have stories which tell of a fierce race of great apes, and of tall black men who kill them with bronze-pointed assagais." He stepped over, and with a naked toe rolled the bronze-pointed assagai that Kal-ab had carried. "Yes, that is the same place. Ramfis. It has long been known to hunters and traders, though its wealth was not enough so any would brave the danger of trading with its natives. Within five days—six at most—I could be standing on its rocky rim." And he smiled. "If I chose."

Helene could see the sparkle of excitement in the Jungle Lord's eyes, the tense eagerness in his muscles.

"I will never tame you, my Ki-Gor," she said softly.

II

THE ISSUE now decided, Ki-Gor was impatient to start. The valley of Ramfis was a long journey. Even traveling alone it would take him five days. With Brend and Helene along, he would be inevitably delayed. And there was always a risk that the usurper, Durga-Rama, would make Arlenna his wife as soon as Brend was out of the valley.

Ki-Gor whistled twice in a low, vibrant manner, and was answered a few seconds later by a rumbling elephant call from some place back in the deep bush. They could hear undergrowth crashing, the shaking thud of heavy feet, and soon a huge elephant came into view, his trunk swinging like a pendulum between gleaming tusks that would have been worth a small fortune to the ivory hunters of Europe.

Brend trembled and commenced to run,

for there is no beast of the African jungle more feared than a bull elephant such as this, but Ngeeso, the pigmy, streaked up behind the boy and pulled him back.

"Have no fear, brown boy! Behold! It is Marmo. See the man Marmo calls his master?"

Ngeeso pointed with triumphant pride as the huge tusker came to a ground-shaking stop, and sank on front knees before Ki-Gor, curling his trunk for the White Lord's foot.

Brend returned with hesitant step, staring in wonder as Ki-Gor was lifted lightly to Marmo's head. The elephant would have started off, but Ki-Gor's voice, speaking the Swihili tongue, stopped him.

"There are more to follow, thou impatient mountain!"

Marmo sank again to his knees, waving

his wide ears in understanding. He coiled his trunk again, lifting Helene.

"Come, Brend," smiled Ki-Gor. "You are of a line of kings, you must ride in a kingly style."

With Ngeeso jabbing at his back, Brend placed his foot on the curled end of Marmo's trunk, and was lifted aloft.

"And now, boy, I must bandage your eyes," said Ki-Gor.

Helene explained, "Do not be afraid, Brend. We have a secret home that none except the pigmies of Ngeeso's tribe know about. Even though we trust you, Ki-Gor will let no one see the path that leads to it."

Ki-Gor fixed a blindfold of leopard skin around the boy' eyes, and Marmo started through the jungle. Despite his great bulk, the elephant moved gracefully along the narrow footpath. After a couple miles there was a roar of falling water and the feel of spray filled the air. They were nearing the cataracts and rapids of the river.

A trail broke out in a clearing where natives once cultivated cassava, and Marmo waded belly-deep in cane grass. Before them was the river, lashing itself to a white fury over a series of cataracts, then splitting in rapids around an island. The island was narrow, only a few acres in extent, bowered over with huge trees beneath whose vaulted tops only stray beams of equatorial sun penetrated.

From a towering tree of the island to one equally high on the near shore, a bridge of vines had been swung. It looked slim, like a single spider strand at its great height. From below, it could be seen swinging slowly in the breeze that forever blew up this wild stretch of river which had not been looked upon by a half dozen white men.

Helene found the end of a tendril ladder, and climbed swiftly as the others watched from the ground. She reached the bridge and paused, looking down, a tiny figure against the blue sky. She waved, and started with swift, certain stride as the fragile bridge swayed beneath her.

But even such travel was too slow for Ki-Gor. He had speedier ways of crossing to his island. He lifted Brend on his shoulders, cautioning him to keep a tight grip around his neck. Then, as though the boy weighed no more than a ngila monkey, he went swiftly, hand over hand, up a tendril to the high-swinging bridge. There he found a vine rope, tied and ready. He untied its end, pulled back, stretching it tight, stood for a few seconds, looking at the river far below. Then, calling a final word of caution to the boy on his shoulders, he wrapped the vine rope around his left wrist and leaped.

He swung down, down with the swiftness of a diving eagle. Brend screamed and might have fallen, but Ki-Gor seized him with his free hand. The rope was fixed to the exact center of the bridge. They swung like a long pendulum, the swiftness of their passage making wind burn their faces, and their hair straighten out behind.

Then they were no longer descending. They were at the bottom of the arc, flying level with the river, its white-running froth just beneath their feet. And next up, up, until it seemed they would never stop. At the very crest, Ki-Gor laughed, and twisted about his eyes seeking Helene who was only a tenth of the distance across the bridge. And the next second, he alighted at the island end of the bridge, his feet touching the tendril and bamboo walk as lightly as an eagle feather striking water. The crossing had been made in a matter of seconds.

"You are slow, copper-haired one!" he called to Helene. "Why do you choose to imitate the ant instead of the hawk?"

"I choose to live and enjoy our island home!" she answered.

Ki-Gor shook his head in wonder at such an attitude. For him, a vine swinging through the air of the jungle was the last word in safety.

He made his way swiftly to the ground, and followed a neat path of pebbles through an opening in the wall of green. He put Brend down then, and untied the blindfold from his eyes. The path led to a tiny clearing with a small house at one side. The house was made after the white man's fashion of logs and bamboo, with a verandah, and a roof of bundled palm.

They went inside. It had no furniture in the general sense of the term, but it was clean and dry, with numerous couches of fragrant grass, and a hammock of woven vines where Ki-Gor liked to take his ease after one of his journeys that well might encompass a quarter part of the dark continent.

THERE was not a great deal to be done in preparation for the journey. There was no food to take, for Ki-Gor and Helene were adept at finding food anywhere. There were no plans to be made, for the master plan of the expedition had already mapped itself in Ki-Gor's brain. For supper he ate a few strips of pink antelope meat which had been hanging in the cool shadows since the day before, and he spent the hours of evening whetting his hunting blade and assagai point until either would cut hair that was blown against them, and to wrapping new sinew around his mighty strongbow——the bow that no man save Ki-Gor had strength to bend.

Helene watched these preparations intently. "You act like one going to war!" she said, with a tone of alarm.

He nodded. "I have a feeling that I am about to face great danger, to see many strange forms of death. I cannot explain it." He indicated his heart. "It is something that comes to me——here."

They slept, and in the morning they left with blue mist still hanging over the river. The scent of the jungle rose around them——the incredible fragrance of unseen blossoms mingled with pungent odors of fungus and decay. Night prowling animals had gone to their dens, and only a chorus of birds and the inevitable chattering of monkeys interrupted the crystal stillness of morning. Marmo went steadily, following a narrow footpath, the sides of his huge body brushing the narrow, jungle walls, carrying with effortless ease the ones on his back——Helene, Brend, Ngeeso, and Ki-Gor himself.

From time to time, without uttering a word, Ki-Gor would seize a low hanging vine and disappear into the vast ocean of treetops overhead. Marmo would trudge on, never glancing or waving an ear at these strange antics of his master. The others would ride for what seemed a long time, then, unexpectedly, Ki-Gor would appear, dropping lightly to the elephant's back from the overhanging jungle.

That evening, after being gone for longer than usual on one of his mysterious trips, Ki-Gor said,

"There is a clearing ten miles distant on a little trail branching to the north. We will find fresh water there, as well as plantains and bananas."

It seemed incredible that Ki-Gor could have gone so far, even swinging from tree to tree, but after a long hour's travel, they found the camping place exactly as he said.

Next day was much like the first, as was the next, and so on for five days. They were now deep in an unknown jungle where swamp stretched for many miles, and trees with bulbous bases, like giant tulips, grew from the water. Reaching higher ground, they found an ancient footpath striking northeast through the domains of Shuli and Bantu tribesmen. Toward the close of the fifth day, the camel-humped mountain rose at their left, and on the sixth they saw a jagged horizon, purplish and remote through primeval mists.

"It is there!" cried Brend, standing on Marmo's swaying back, dancing on his small feet from excitement. "It is the ridge of Ramfis! Ki-Gor's magic has led us back by the identical trail that Kal-ab followed!"

After sighting the ridge of Ramfis, Ki-Gor hunted the remote back paths of the jungle. He turned over the guiding of Marmo almost wholly to Helene, and spent practically his entire time making long excursions through the treetops, scouting to make sure that the men of Ramfis would not be warned of their approach. For the safety of Brend, and the girl, Arlenna, his coming must be a surprise to Durga-Rama.

That night he chose to camp in a deep ravine where a trickle of cool water flowed from a mossy cleft. In the morning, he awakened Brend, and the two of them set out to survey the country.

They left the ravine and climbed slowly through areas of thicket and scrubby trees.

Half way up the ridge of Ramfis, Ki-Gor sighted the stone and thatch huts of the black guards, who, with their families, lived out their lives near the passes, standing guard chiefly against bands of wild Mahkoor tribesmen who each five or ten years, sent raiding parties down from their country in the sudan of south Egypt.

Ki-Gor squatted in the crotch of a small tree, so perfectly concealed that one of the great apes which frequented the scrub forest passed within an assagai's cast without detecting him. Ki-Gor dropped to the ground a few seconds later, and found Brend trembling from fright.

"Boy, what is the matter?"

"The ape. Did not you see——"

Ki-Gor laughed. "Of course I saw."

Brend was serious, "Even the greatest black warriors fear to meet the great apes. See up above! The guards stay always near the passes. They would not dare venture over where the country is broken by caverns."

"Who are the warriors of your tribe that they are terrified by a colony of apes. Surely——"

"They are not terrified!" said Brend with sudden loyalty. "They have been left alone for hundreds of years because they help us guard against raids by the Mahkoor."

"In other words, the apes keep their place, and the people of Ramfis keep theirs."

"Yes."

Ki-Gor pointed toward the ridge where it was rock-jumble and gnarled trees.

"If we were there, we could see almost the entire valley, is it not so?"

Brend nodded. "If such a place could be reached."

"The ascent does not look difficult and I must see what lies ahead."

"But I told you, the——"

"Yes, the apes!" Ki-Gor nodded. "Perhaps those apes will prove to be our allies before we are through, Brend."

"You do not understand. They are untamed. They make no friends." He looked at Ki-Gor, "You do not intend that we should——"

"Not we. You are going back to the ravine to wait with Marmo, Helene and Ngeeso. I will go up the ridge."

KI-GOR looked at the sun. He had time for the journey before dark.

He paused for a moment to eat a strip of uncooked zebra flesh. Afterward he cleansed himself in the tiny stream, tightened the thong of his strong-bow and slipped it over his bronzed shoulder, made certain that his quiver was filled with heavy, copper-pointed arrows.

The sun was dropping toward the vast jungle of the west when Ki-Gor emerged from the ravine, and trotted with a long, effortless stride up a flank of the ridge to the country pockmarked with trees, and covered with billows of gnarled trees. The wind was wrong, carrying his scent to the hills, but that did not stop him. He must find a safe camp in the ape country, then cross to the valley of Ramfis without delay.

As he neared the crest, he climbed more slowly, the assagai in his left hand.

There were movements——shapes of grayish black moving here and there among the trees, blending in color with the basaltic rocks. Ki-Gor's keen nostrils were distended a little, catching the characteristic unpleasant odor of the anthrapoids. He watched the earth, noting the droppings, and the trails that had been worn by centuries of hairy feet.

The way became steeper. Here and there he scaled sheer-faced escarpments. The rocky crest was now only an arrow's shot above. He sensed the closeness of danger, and his hearing became more acute. He detected soft, rustling movements ahead of him, and behind. There were red-lidded, savage eyes watching from trees, and brush, and rocks, but Ki-Gor walked on, seeming to be as casual and relaxed as ever.

Then there was a different kind of movement. Abrupt. He sensed what was coming, and spun around. A gray-black, hairy form was charging from behind a twisted thorn tree. A huge bull ape. Massive——almost on the scale of a gorilla. As Ki-Gor saw him, the beast roared, rising to his bowed hind legs, throwing high his massive, hairy arms, his yellowish fangs flashing in the dim, evening light.

With a movement of automatic quickness, so fast no eye could have followed, Ki-Gor slid the strong-bow from his shoulder, fixed the notch of a copper-pointed arrow. The bow bent under his mighty arm, and the arrow was driven with the force of a swinging axe.

It was a perfect shot. The arrow entered just left of the ape's frontal chestbone, plunged on to shatter the spine, pass completely through, and bury half its shaft in the rocky earth a dozen strides beyond.

The ape plunged on for three desperate strides. He shrilled a death-cry, and plunged face foremost across the ground. He lay there, chest heaving blowing red foam from his nostrils so close that Ki-Gor could feel his hot, damp breath against his feet.

A garbled chorus of sound went up from the brush around as other apes jabbered, watching their fellow lashing in death agony. Another bull bounded out, and as he rose to charge, Ki-Gor smashed him down with a second arrow. A third ape crashed out. Ki-Gor spun, fixing an arrow, bending the bow. He hesitated, and watched with grim satisfaction as the bull paused, and retreated on all fours with his ugly rump thrust high.

Ki-Gor's arm relaxed. He removed the arrow, dropped it once more into the quiver.

Here and there he caught sight of gray black forms slinking into the deeper shadows. He waited until the sounds of their retreat became faint, and the air was cleansed of the peculiar taint of their bodies, then, moving swiftly once more, sometimes bounding to the crotches of trees and away again, he covered the final three hundred meters to the ridge crest.

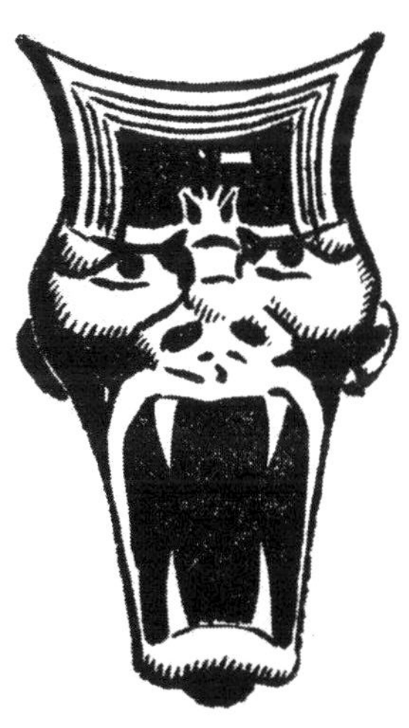

There, after many days, he looked down and saw the wide valley of Ramfis spread beneath him.

The valley was broad and undulating, covered with jungle, broken at intervals by irregular patches of sudan grass. The patches of grass looked tiny from his remote vantage point but Ki-Gor, with his acute sense of distance, knew that many of them were miles in extent. Gigantic baobab trees grew here and there among the sudan areas, and in one clearing, like long-legged spider-creatures, he could see grazing giraffes.

Through the center of the valley flowed a river, its surface gleaming like polished steel in the last reflected light of the sun.

He was tempted to go on, now that he was so close. Instead, he turned back. Helene had been worried by Brend's talk of the savage apes, and he did not want to cause her unnecessary anxiety.

He retraced his steps, the apes giving him a wary distance. Darkness settled, and he covered the final miles with instinct guiding him through the black, jungle night. Helene, Brend and Ngeeso were sitting close to the comforting bulk of Marmo, waiting.

Ki-Gor squatted on the sandy floor of the cave for hours that night, talking to Brend about the valley of Ramfis.

III

LIKE ALL PLACES, Ramfis had its good and bad men. There was the ruling class of brown men who had long ago journeyed up the great river from the land where all is desert. And there were black tribesmen, like Kal-ab. The blacks outnumbered their brown rulers by eight to one, and they were brave fighters, but through superior intelligence the brown men kept them in virtual slavery Across the river, Brend said, a tribe of cannibal blacks called the Batolo had held sway for centuries. Sometimes the Batolo would cross the river and steal a woman or two who were working in the Ramfis yam fields, but generally they kept the peace, for, despite their savagery, they were no match for the well-disciplined army of the Ramfians.

On the sand of the cave floor, Brend drew maps of the valley, the city, and even plans of the bamboo and ironwood houses of the brown men, while Ki-Gor watched intently, fixing each picture in his mind. Brend told much of Durga-Rama; of Arlenna, the virgin; and of his friend, Liike, the high-priest of Isis. He also told of the danger that waited, of the merciless treatment accorded spies, of the great Arab dogs which were kept chained to give alarm when strangers entered the walled city of the brown men, and of the savage lion, Panthra, which Durga-Rama had trained to guard him.

With the first sign of dawn, Ki-Gor left the cave. He walked rapidly down the slope toward Ramfis. As the scrub growth was left behind, and the jungle became deep, he seized a vine and swung to a tree limb. He moved from tree to tree, swinging in easy arcs.

He did not hurry. He did not want to reach the city of Ramfis before dark. For minutes on end he would pause and stand on some high, swaying limb, perfectly blended into the pattern of the jungle, watching for some telltale movement. He could see none.

When evening came, Ki-Gor was close to the city of Ramfis. Hand over hand he climbed the huge branches of a baobab tree, and perched near its top to watch.

All was as Brend had diagramed. There was a large native village of thatch huts, a circular stockage enclosing the more pretentious houses occupied by the brown rulers. He recognized from Brend's descriptions the palace of Durga-Rama, the ampitheatre where gladiators of the black race often fought on feast days, the temples of Isis and Ra with the house of High-Priest Liike standing between them.

He mapped his course. He would scale the stockade on the far side where large trees of the jungle crowded close. Once inside, he would cross to the shadow of the inner stockade which circled Durga-Rama's house, and enter Liike's house from the rear. His chief worry were those great, Arab hounds of which Brend had warned him. They might catch his spoor, and commence howling their alarm.

Darkness settled. He dropped to the ground, passed through the soft, wet earth of a millet field, commenced circling the native city. Tom-toms were beating, and he could see oiled, black bodies dancing around a fire. There were no brown men dancing, of course. They looked with disdain on such pleasures, preferring to lie on reed couches and drink a sweet, pink wine concocted of the juice of sugar palms.

There were watchmen along the stockade. Sometimes Ki-Gor passed within long assagai reach of them, but so silent were his footsteps, so stealthy was every movement, that his presence was not once suspected.

Ki-Gor paused on reaching the far side. It would be easy to scale the stockade when the guards were not watching, but there was always a danger that one of the dogs would scent him and raise the alarm.

He moved back in the shadows of the great trees, planning another course. One of these trees towered far above its fellows. He climbed it, examining the long, ropelike vines that stretched from its high branches. None of them swung with sufficient freedom to suit his purpose, so he cut one and tied it near the end of a middle limb. He grasped the vine, swung himself in a wide, gentle arc. At the crest of his swing he released his grip, sailed clear of the stockade, alighting in the deep shadows far beyond.

He stood close against the inner wall which surrounded the house of Durga-Rama. The guard was a short assagai cast away, standing with his back turned. Ki-Gor started away——stopped. A huge, gray dog emerged in the starlit yard. The dog snarled, lunged towards him, and was brought to a sudden stop by a chain around his neck.

Ki-Gor whisked the strongbow from his shoulder, fitted an arrow, released it. There was a thud as it struck. The dog had commenced to bay, but the sound changed to a whining gasp as he fell.

Ki-Gor waited, back pressed against the wall. The guard was turning, assagai ready in the bend of his arm. He was peering toward the spot where the dog lay. He evidently could see nothing. He probably would not even have investigated had not something else caught his eye.

A tiny man had climbed the stockage

and was balanced on its crest. The guard shouted a word in his tribal tongue and charged forward with assagai pointed. For a second, Ki-Gor did not realize the small man's identity. Then he saw——it was Ngeeso, the pigmy.

"Ki-Gor——you must return. The apes ——there are hundreds of them. We saw them creeping through scrub-brush by sunlight. Even Marmo fears."

Ki-Gor seized the little man, "Tell me, Ngeeso. Is Helene . . ."

"She was still safe when I left. She did not want me to come, but I know danger when I see it, Ki-Gor——"

"You do, indeed, my brave Ngeeso!"

He started back toward the stockade and then saw the guard. The fellow had stumbled over the dead dog and was crouched on one knee, examing the animal. He found the arrow, tried to remove it. It came free only after he had braced his feet and pulled with both hands. He stood with the shaft, staring. He had evidently never seen such an arrow——its copper head the size of a mans palm, its shaft the thickness of the thumb.

"Hoo-ee!" came his shriek of alarm.

Ki-Gor and Ngeeso were moving with swift silence. A patch of starlight separated them from the wall.

A rear gate of Durga-Rama's palace opened. A man stood outlined in the slice of pale light. A thick man with vast shoulders He wore a robe of white cotton and around it a flowing scarlet scarf. He led a massive lion on a leash.

Ki-Gor knew that this man must be Durga-Rama himself, and this lion the mighty Panthra.

Durga-Rama had been drinking wine in the civet-scented luxury of his home. He was so close that Ki-Gor caught the scent of it on his breath. Due to the wine which had somewhat dulled his senses, Durga-Rama might have passed without seeing the White Lord, even though they were so close, but Panthra turned, snarling, lifting one front paw.

"Panthra!" roared Durga-Rama, jerking the huge animal back.

KI-GOR could have killed the lion at that moment with an arrow from his strong-bow, but he still had hopes of avoiding a general alarm. He moved to one side, skirting the wall. He stopped. A dozen guards were coming, assagais and elephant hide shields waving. He turned the opposite way. More guards. Durga-Rama was bellowing orders.

There was only one way. He would have to scale the wall to Durga-Rama's yard. He leaped to its top, thrusting his leg so Ngeeso could seize it and clamber after him.

The pigmy chief caught his ankle, but his fingers slipped and he fell backward to earth. The guards were there. They rammed and fought each other in an attempt to get their hands on the pigmy. He struggled, eluding them along the ground.

"Escape! Escape without me, Ki-Gor!" he hissed.

"No, little friend!" Ki-Gor answered.

He leaped into the mass of struggling guardsmen. It was dark, but he located Ngeeso, still struggling along the ground. Ki-Gor flung men from his way, he bent, seized the little man, and flung him bodily over the heads of the guardsmen.

"Run! Run little chieftain!" he shouted. "You must go to Helene and Brend!"

Durga-Rama had freed the lion, and it came roaring forward, eyes on Ngeeso. He saw Ki-Gor and paused. This, he could see, was his real assailant. This strange white man. The pigmy on the ground could wait.

Panthra faced Ki-Gor, hesitated a fraction of a second with muscles tensed and belly dragging the ground. Then he sprang, fangs hungry for Ki-Gor's throat.

Always before when Panthra had been set on a human quarry, it had been easy. Men always put out their hands, trying to fend him off, but Panthra, with his strong front paws, had swept aside such puny efforts at defense. His leap would carry him on, taking man to earth. His teeth would close on the throat, there would be a crunch of bones, and the man animal would become a limp mass of flesh. That was the real sport for Panthra——to slam the helpless creature, to shake him, the while feeling the good, warm blood running in his mouth.

But this time it was not the same. This white man did not retreat as all the others had. Instead, he had actually moved forward to meet the charge.

Panthra swung his paws to brush aside Ki-Gor's hands. The hands were not as he expected. Only empty space. It threw the lion off by an imperceptible degree. For a ragged fraction of a second he was off balance. He tried to shift the direction of his spring in mid-air. At that moment, a hand came, quick as the strike of a snake, closing like a steel trap on his left foreleg.

Panthra twisted, trying to free himself. He lashed with the other paw. It was the movement Ki-Gor expected——that he wanted.

He seized the other leg, and flipped the great beast over in the air, side-stepped, and slammed him on his back to the hard-packed earth.

For a short click of time, Panthra was helpless. Ki-Gor's hand streaked from the scabbard at his waist, his long-bladed hunting knife making a blue flash in the starlight.

He pounced forward to drive the blade through Panthra's heart . . .

But quick though the jungle man's action was, the ragged second of his advantage was too short. Panthra twisted to his side and struck at the knife hand with a hind foot.

Had the dagger-claws of that foot taken hold they would have ripped skin and flesh from the bones of Ki-Gor's forearm. A subtle shifting of Ki-Gor's body saved him. He was at one side, feeling only the sting of the sharp claws as they brushed him.

He was crouching forward, knife in hand. Panthra snarled and came to his feet. The savage lust of battle was strong in Ki-Gor. He forgot the others, forgot the dozen assagais at his back, forgot Durga-Rama, himself a warrior and strong as an ape.

Panthra retreated, reaching back with slow, tense legs, his mouth snarling open, revealing his yellow fangs. Now, for the first time in his savage existence, he felt fear——fear of the tall white man whose quickness and strength was greater than that of a jungle animal.

Ki-Gor started forward, knife ready—but there was a pin-prick of an assagai point in his back, just over the heart. He stopped short, and stood rigid.

"One move you die!" a heavy voice snarled behind him.

HE did not move. He knew the words were true. Death was only an assagai-thrust away.

He lowered his knife, turned slowly. He could not see Ngeeso. The pigmy must have escaped. Panthra retreated yet a couple of steps, lay on his belly, eyes like yellow coals, tail licking back and forth. Native guards with assagais leveled made a circle. Durga-Rama elbowed his way through, and stood with hands on hips, powerful legs spraddled wide.

"Who are you that you call yourself Ki-Gor?" he sneered.

Ki-Gor did not answer. He looked at Durga-Rama, judging his qualities as they were written in his face.

He was not old——perhaps thirty years. Although short, he was heavy, and as massive of muscle as Ki-Gor himself. His eyes were small, but they were quick and crafty. The assortment of gold and copper ornaments on his arms and fingers told Ki-Gor that the man was vain; his perfume of civet indicated that he fancied himself as a lover; his sneering smile was proof that he thought himself extremely clever.

"Answer me!" roared Durga-Rama. "Who are you to refuse an answer when you are questioned by the king of all Ramfians. And that dwarf who escaped——why did he call you by the name of Ki-Gor?"

The jungle man answered, "Ki-Gor is a legend believed only by fools. I am Bondo, the hunter. I came to your valley seeking friendship, and you meet me with lion's fangs and the points of assagais."

Ki-Gor was not tempted to reveal his identity. It would only lead Durga-Rama to doubling precautions to prevent his escape. The name "Bondo," which was a term of respect given him by Buto tribesmen, would serve well enough for the short time he intended to remain in captivity.

Durga-Rama kept looking at him with his crafty little eyes. He stepped forward, to took the strong-bow from Ki-Gor's shoulder. He lifted it, hooked his forefinger in the thong, and with a heave of his muscles bent it slowly back. Ki-Gor watched with composed features, as though it were an everyday occurrence to meet men with strength to thus half bend his bow.

"It is true that the White Lord called Ki-Gor carries such a bow as this," Durga-Rama said craftily. "It is perhaps unfortunate you are not Ki-Gor, otherwise I might take you inside my palace and feast you. As it is I must lock you in the prison."

"I do not fear your prison."

"Good! And perhaps you will not fear the things I am planning for you——you, the man who would dare swing a dagger at my royal lion!"

He spoke to a leader of the guards in a language Ki-Gor did not understand, and strode over, placed the leash once again on Panthra's neck, and led the animal through the gates to his palace.

The blacks bound Ki-Gor with many strands of grass rope, and thus, with only his legs free to walk he was taken through the gates of the arena.

The guards stopped there, muttering to

each other, keeping Ki-Gor surrounded by their spears. One of their number started away at a run, and came back, carrying a blazing faggot.

He held the light overhead, and Ki-Gor could see a circular wall of close bamboo pickets twenty feet high, and above, the seats where spectators could safely watch the struggles of men and beasts. They turned right to a doorway. The torch-bearer went ahead, lighting the way down a series of damp, stone steps. There, beneath ground, was a passage and a row of little, cavelike rooms with ironwood doors.

The torch-bearer swung one of the doors open on its creaking hinges, guards jabbed assagais in Ki-Gor's back, and he stooped over to enter the room. The door closed behind him. He could hear a thump as the bar dropped in place.

He stood, his head just touching the low, planked ceiling. The room was tiny. Had his arms been free, Ki-Gor judged that he could have spread them and touched both walls. At one side was a shelf dug into the dirt which served at once as a bed and a chair.

Ki-Gor sat down. The torch had been thrust in a crevice of the wall out in the passageway, and through the copper grating he could see a couple of the guards peering through.

He twisted his hands, trying the ropes that bound him. It had not been a skillful job of tying. He could have freed himself had he wished, but there would be no purpose in it with the door locked and guards watching. So he sat still, waiting.

The dungeon was close. Prisoners had been there many times, but in years it had not been cleaned. The bones of animals that had been tossed them as food lay rotting and noisome on the floor.

Distantly he could hear the sounds of the tom-toms, the weird chant of warriors executing the native dances.

After a time, Ki-Gor said to the guards, "Do your people never sleep, or do they dance on forever?"

One of the guards grinned through at him, his strong teeth showing in the fading torchlight.

"Perhaps they dance for your death."

"And when do I die?"

"Tomorrow. Did not Durga-Rama tell you? You will die for the pleasure of his wedding-feast."

Ki-Gor knew he must escape. He must escape quickly. He must somehow get to the High Priest, Liike, to tell him that Brend still lived. Liike was a man of power, and he would use his influence to see justice done.

"And how am I to die?" asked Ki-Gor.

"You will die as Durga-Rama told you. You will fight the great ape Zag in the arena above us."

"What weapons will I have?"

"The weapons your mother gave you when you came into the world. Your hands!"

"Have other warriors fought this ape with their hands?"

The two blacks laughed at this. One of them said,

"Twelve times since the great ape was captured on the ridge there have been warriors turned in the arena with him, and twelve of them made food for the hounds. But a man does not have to win. All he needs do is escape. You see, white man, there is a peeled palm pole smeared with fat. If a warrior can escape, climbing that greased pole, then he is the chosen of Isis and can sit at the right hand of Durga-Rama, and be given the honors of our greatest warrior for one day."

The second guard stamped his bare foot on the floor, laughing, "Ho! Do you think you can escape by that pole, *bondele?*"

"Perhaps I will *kill* this ape of yours!"

And that brought shouts of merriment from both of them.

Ki-Gor asked, "When is Durga-Rama to marry?"

"I have heard he will take the maiden Arlenna to his couch before the sun sets thrice."

"Three days!"

"Ho! There will be much feasting, white man. And you will be part of the feast." This brought new laughter, new assagai pounding as dust rose from the floor. "You will be a fine meal for the hounds, white man."

Ki-Gor sat back, listening to the continuing throb of tom-toms, as the dance went on in celebration of Durga-Rama's approaching coronation and marriage. At last he lay down and slept.

The tiny room was still gray with darkness when he awoke, but rays of reflected light shone through the copper grating, and he knew by that it was morning. He stood, moving his hands inside the rope bonds. He stepped to the massive door, but the guards were still there.

"How is the fighter of lions this morning?" their leader asked, thrusting his ugly, tribal-scarred face close to the grating. When Ki-Gor did not immediately answer, he went on, "I bring you great news, *bondele*. You are to be honored."

"In what way?"

"You are to be taken for final judgmen before Durga-Rama himself."

The guards ranged themselves on both sides of the door, weapons ready. The bar was then lifted, and Ki-Gor walked out.

"How long has Durga-Rama been your king?" he asked in an off-hand manner as he climbed the stairs.

"For three seasons."

"So long?"

"There was another——a boy. A weakling. But he is gone. The gods have been good and stole him away. Durga-Rama has not worn the crown. But he will, after his feast of marriage two suns from now."

"And what if the gods bring this boy king back?"

"You are a fool, and a *bondele*," said the officer, twisting his notched lips, making his nostrils flare over the copper nose ring he wore. "The boy king will not come back. It is the word of Durga-Rama."

IV

KI-GOR was taken outside. His hands were tied, there were guards on all sides of him. The arena gate was open, and a cage of heavy bamboo poles waited. He bent, entered the cage. He sat on its floor with head and shoulders hunched against the low top. The door was closed and double-latched. Four porters lifted the cage and carried him through the town for dancing, paint-smeared natives to see. They spat at him, flung chunks of dirt, followed him back to the gates of the brown men's city.

The cage was carried inside the house of Durga-Rama, up a flight of rude stairs, and inside the private rooms of the usurper.

Ki-Gor peered through the slats of the cage and saw Durga-Rama himself, squatted on a heap of thatch, eating a cassava and palm-nut concoction with his fingers. Behind him Panthra lay crouched, gnawing a joint of freshly killed goat.

The door was opened, and Ki-Gor stepped out standing with a height that made the ceiling seem low. Panthra, scenting the hated white man, roared and lunged forward, his yellow eyes on Ki-Gor's throat. A sharp word from Durga-Rama froze the action, and the lion crouched back, his tufted tail whipping the matted floor.

Durga-Rama wiped his greasy hands on thatch and smiled, showing a set of teeth turned brown by the chewing of betel nuts.

"Bonda!" he said, using the name Ki-Gor had given him. "It is well that such a mighty warrior as you should call on me."

"I was brought in a cage. Did you not notice?"

"My people wanted to see you," said Durga-Rama, picking his teeth with the nail of his small finger. "It is not often that they see a warrior so mighty he fights lions with one bare hand and a knife."

"Why have you brought me here?"

"To tell you of the honor that is to be yours." Durga-Rama hunched his huge shoulders forward, and again showed his betel-stained teeth. "Last night you said the name of Durga-Rama was spoken from the land of the White Nile to the hills of Kenya. Is it not then an honor when you are chosen to fight Zag, the great ape, at my wedding feast?"

"I would fight your coward lion instead."

Durga-Rama bent forward, hand on the hilt of the crescent shaped scimitar at his waist.

"Do not anger me, white man, or you will die like a slave at the fire and your carcass will be thrown in the river to be eaten by crocodiles, or by the cannibals of Batolo."

"You fear me, Durga-Rama, otherwise

you would show your strength by fighting me yourself."

"I fear no man, nor does my lion, Panthra." He sat there, the corners of his mouth drawn down. He reached and stroked Panthra's massive head. The lion received the caress, but made no return show of affection. He had been tamed through fear, not love, and someday he would turn on his master. It was always thus with the great cats.

Durga-Rama said, "I do not toss Panthra into the same arena with every renegade warrior. You will have to content yourself with our fighting apes. They will be savage enough for you, I'll wager. And if you prove a coward, as I suppose you will, there will be a way of escape. There will be a pole, three times the height of a man, that you may climb to the wall." He spoke to his men, gesturing sharply with a greasy hand, "Throw him back in his dungeon."

Again in the dungeon, Ki-Gor sat with his back against the dirt wall, waiting, listening to sounds of natives, drunk on millet beer. He thought of brave little Ngeeso, wondering if the pigmy had escaped; he thought of Helene, of her danger.

A pot-bellied slave of a Bantu came down the steps carrying an earthen pot. A slot was opened in the door of Ki-Gor's cell, and a heap of vile-smelling offal was dumped inside on the dirt floor.

"Your food, Master," grinned the slave, showing rotting teeth.

Ki-Gor took the insult without flinching. He was immovable as a bronze god. He waited in the foul hole as the day passed. He closed his eyes, resting himself so he would be at his best for the ordeal. Sleep came as the stultifying heat of afternoon settled. Then, suddenly, he awoke.

Men were shouting. He could hear tramping feet above. It was the crowd entering the stands that circled the arena. The games were about to commence.

"Get your sleep, white man," grinned a guard through the grating. "You have yet a while to wait. There are to be other fights. Yours is merely the last."

The noise increased. After an extended wait, Ki-Gor heard the sound of warriors fighting with *boo* sticks. There were resounding whacks as the clubs struck home, the cheers of savage blacks, the laughter of the brown men. Following that engagement, a wild boar was turned in with a lancer and killed, and by way of diversion, two drunken hags clawed each other with their fingernails.

The hags were finally chased out and an expectant silence settled. The guard peered through at Ki-Gor. Other faces appeared. The leader of the guards strode down the stairs and came to the door, elbowing his subordinates aside.

"It is your time, Bondo!" he said. "Are you ready?"

"I am ready!" answered Ki-Gor.

V

THE BAR was lifted, and the door creaked open on wooden hinges. Ki-Gor stepped out, arms still bound at his sides.

"Free him!" said the leader.

Two of the guards fumbled, untying the knots. The ropes were unwound, and Ki-Gor stretched himself, shaking the kinks from his magnificent muscles. For a moment there were no words spoken. Guardsmen looked at him in hushed awe. Never before had they seen a man of such proportion, of such strength.

"The king must not be kept waiting for you, white man," said the leader.

Ki-Gor climbed the steps, crossed a narrow passage lined with bamboo pickets ten feet high and lashed across the top, walked through a gate to the arena.

He stood for a moment, allowing his eyes to accustom themselves to the brilliant, late-afternoon sunlight. Then, with a single, sweeping glance, he took in the features of the scene.

The arena was about a dozen strides in diameter, roughly circular, surrounded by a perpendicular wall about three times the height of a man. Above the wall, safe from the highest-leaping beast of the jungle, were the seats of the brown men. Beyond, on a circular platform, the blacks were jammed together in a solid mass, resplendent in feast-day paint and finery.

A roar greeted Ki-Gor as he came into view. Then, as the roar subsided, taunting voices made themselves heard. Bits of food and pellets were flung at him, striking him, bounding to the dust at his feet. He made no sign of having noticed.

His eyes noted Durga-Rama, gowned in a white kuftan with scarlet sash. Panthra lay at his feet, lips drawn back from his fangs, his glowing eyes on Ki-Gor. At Durga-Rama's back was a slave, waving a long, ostrich-plume fan, and at his left, seated a few inches lower, was a girl.

The girl was young—perhaps Brend's tender age. She was beautiful. Even judged by the classic features of Ki-Gor's lovely Helene, she was beautiful. Her skin was brown, with a velvet texture; her eyes were very large, and dark; a thin robe of cotton was drawn around her young figure which was just swelling into the lines of womanhood. She seemed fragile as a lotus leaf.

Ki-Gor did not doubt that this young girl was Arlenna, whom Durga-Rama intended to take to his couch in marriage.

Ki-Gor looked up at her, and for a moment their glances met. He saw compassion in her eyes—pity for the horrible fate that awaited him.

Durga-Rama bent, and spoke to her. He laid his hand on her shoulder, had his thick lips close to her ear. She shrank a little, as though his closeness were loathsome, but she nodded quickly. It was not a pleased smile. It showed that she feared the man, and her fear made Ki-Gor detest him as he had never detested a person before.

Ki-Gor's eyes traveled farther. In scarlet robes of their calling sat the priests of Isis and Ra. One of them, gray-bearded with sightless eyes, sat in an elevated position. This, he knew, was the high-priest, Liike——the man he had come to the valley to see.

If fate went against him, in his last extremity, Ki-Gor would shout his message to Liike. He would tell him that Brend still lived, that he had been kidnapped through the connivance of Durga-Rama, and that someday he would return. But that only as a last resort. For the moment, Ki-Gor looked at the sightless Liike with no sign of interest or recognition.

Ki-Gor walked to the middle of the arena. He folded his arms. His muscles were long; they rippled like the bodies of pythons beneath his smooth, tanned skin.

Two black men ran in, carrying a pole. It was the trunk of a palm, two or three inches in diameter, glistening from a thick application of grease. Quickly they placed it in a hole that had been bored close to the wall. When in place it weaved uncertainly, its top within reach of Durga-Rama's arm. Perhaps it would bear the weight of a man such as Ki-Gor, and perhaps not, but its coating of grease would prevent his climbing it anyway. The pole was merely a bit of torture. It would provide a comic spectacle for the mob if a terrified man were to grasp it and try to climb while the great apes clawed his flesh to ribbons from behind.

One of the blacks made an announcement. The arena was cleared. There was a creak of wooden wheels outside. A dozen slaves and guardsmen were pulling a huge cage. It was rolled to a sliding door, the door was lifted, the cage opened. Ki-Gor could feel the tenseness of the crowd as a guardsman with a long pole poked between the bars of the cage to force out some surly animal. There was a gasp, a cry of pleased anticipation as a huge, gray-black creature lumbered into sight. It was an ape, shaggy and abysmal, turning, limber hands on long arms trailing in the dust.

"Zag! Zag!" screamed the crowd, calling the brute's name.

There was more shouting and poking, and another ape came out. This one was "Gombon," evidently. The two of them remained near the entrance for a while, blinking dull, red-rimmed eyes, growing accustomed to their new freedom.

If Zag saw Ki-Gor, he made no immediate move to attack. Perhaps it took some time for his dull brain to digest the fact that an unprotected man was there. Then he opened his mouth, showing powerful, yellowed teeth, and let loose a gutteral snarl.

One of the guardsmen reached through with a barbed lance, sticking the animal in the back. The pain of the lance infuriated him. He charged, but the weapon was quickly withdrawn, and the huge beast struck the arena wall, making it creak and wave.

THE CROWD shrieked with laughter at the spectacle. Once more the lance, this time from a new direction. Zag beat at the walls with his huge arms in a raging fury, but the second ape, Gombon, merely stood by the gate, rocking back and forth on bowed legs, his eyes on Ki-Gor.

Ki-Gor still stood in the center of the arena. He seemed relaxed. His face was still composed, still arrogant.

In his blind fury, Zag's eyes fell on Gombon. He rushed, and suddenly stopped. Only then did he notice Ki-Gor, He turned, and charged with long arms brushing the ground.

At a distance of two strides the ape slowed, and stretched high his arms. He pounced, swinging them down with a force that would have driven most men to the earth, a heap of broken bones. But when the arms descended, Ki-Gor was no longer there.

At the final moment he had moved aside, shifting with the quickness of a leopard-cat. He slid beneath one of Zag's descending arms. The ape was thrown off balance. He snarled with froth dripping from the corners of his wide mouth, enraged that his quarry had evaporated from the earth in front of him. With an effort, he came to a stumbling stop, veered his huge bulk around, But Ki-Gor was not there, either. Zag's half human voice rose in a frustrated scream, while his claws tore at the coarse, straggling hair at his own chest. And at that second, Ki-Gor saw his chance. He sprang through the air, pouncing with knees on Zag's back, his hands feeling for the great arteries of his throat to close off the blood supply to his brain.

The ape's arms beat the empty air. He turned, flopping blindly like a monster that had lost all sense of equilibrium and direction. He turned around and around, fell to the ground, pawing over his shoulder, trying to free himself of the terrible thing that was holding like a leech to his back.

Zag rose to great heights, flinging his arms high in one final effort. His hind legs seemed very short and bowed, his chest became pointed, his belly sunken. He was all massive shoulders and arms, a horrible, distorted beast, a thing conceived in the mind of an angry god and born in the furnaces of hell. He flung himself backward, trying to crush Ki-Gor against the wall of the arena.

Ki-Gor was jarred, and Zag succeeded in writhing part way free. He swung back, finding the flesh of K-Gor's shoulder with his claws. He raked three shallow furrows from which blood came in quick, scarlet streaks. But the jungle man did not relinquish his advantage. His fingers still probed the soft recesses of Zag's throat.

During this time, the second bull, Gombon, watched dull eyed from a crouching position by the gate. He seemed to have no interest in the fate of Zag. Then suddenly he scented the fresh blood flowing from Ki-Gor's shoulder. It seemed to whet his savage appetites. He roared, and came forward.

The crowd saw him and was in ecstasy. Now indeed would they see the arrogant white man defeated. He would no longer be a conquerer, riding on the shoulders of their mightiest beast. Instead he would fall crushed and mangled with broken bones poking through his bloody flesh. They would see him become a limp and lifeless thing. They would see him tossed about by the two apes until they were tired of playing with him, and finally they would see the starved hounds of Durga-Rama turned inside the arena to devour him.

They watched as Gombon paused with hands uplifted, directly over the back of Ki-Gor. They watched those arms descend and close on his naked back. They cheered as Gombon reared back, the white man in his arms, tearing him off the back of Zag. But what followed after that was so quick that not one eye in the vast assemblage followed it.

There was a flash of Ki-Gor's bronzed body as he twisted. Suddenly Gombon's arms were no longer around his body. Instead he was thrust back, those hairy arms held wide and high by the hands of the white man.

Ki-Gor released the hold, leaped backward, landed on the balls of his feet, knees bent in a crouch. Then he moved sidewise and sprang. His fingers reached, fiinding the eyes of Gombon. A quick twist of crooked fingers, and the ape was for the moment blinded.

Gombon roared, his voice rising higher and higher until it became a shriek. He staggered, arms lashing like some insane monster. He collided with Zag, and slammed him to the dirt of the arena. He plunged on, falling, and collided with the wall, striking it with such force it threatened to collapse.

In their seats above, the brown men were shouting from fear. Danger to themselves—that was a thing they had not reckoned with. Durga-Rama stood, hand resting on Panthra's collar, watching while a scowl twisted his heavy face.

Ki-Gor backed to the middle of the arena, hands resting on hips, stepping nimbly to one side or the other, avoiding the blind rushes of the ape. He waited his moment. Finally the beast was directly between him and the greased pole, standing a full height, hands pawing at his eyeballs. It was exactly the thing Ki-Gor had wanted. He went forward with two swinging strides. He launched himself into air. One foot touched the beast's back, the next rested on his head. From that elevated position he sprang, grasping the grease-slick pole in one hand, while his toes swung on, resting at the top of the arena wall.

For the second he balanced there precariously, looking down on Durga-Rama.

THE USURPER acted quickly. He snarled, and whisked the heavy scimitar from his waist. He leaped forward, swinging the crescent-shaped blade in a mighty arc. It connected with the pole, cutting it in half just beneath Ki-Gor's fingers, and the jungle man fell backward to the deep dirt of the arena below.

Durga-Rama waved his scimitar on high and shouted down to his guardsmen, "Death to him! Death! Death!"

Black guardsmen were swarming near the gate, the metal heads of their assagais rattling together. They peered through the strong bamboo pickets, fearing to disobey the command of Durga-Rama, but fearing more the fury of the savage apes and equally savage white man.

Ki-Gor came erect, and his eyes flashed around the arena. His attempt at escape had been frustrated, and now he could see only death on every hand. His eyes rested on Liike who had stood, and was facing down on the scene, trying to piece it out by hearing alone.

"Hear me, Liike," screamed Ki-Gor, his voice rising over the sounds of the mob.

Liike took a blind step forward. "I hear!" he said in a harsh voice.

"I have come to tell you of the true king of Ramfis! I have come to tell you of Brend, the boy whom Durga-Rama had stolen from the valley and taken to a far jungle to die. He is not dead, Liika! The real king still lives. Someday he will return . . ."

"I hear! I hear!" Liika kept calling.

Durga-Rama leaned over the railing, his scimitar clenched in his hand, an expression of black rage mottling his heavy face. He seemed poised there, tempted to leap to the arena below, to swing his scimitar on the hated white man, to cut off the voice forever with its damning accusation against him. But his fear of the great apes was too strong. Suddenly he remembered Panthra. He spun around, cut the leash with a whip of the scimitar, snarled a command in the beast's ear.

Panthra did not hesitate. He saw the hated white man below—and this time there was no sharp knife to strike at him with cobra quickness.

Panthra launched himself into air. A shrill scream from the throat of Arlenna reached Ki-Gor's ears. He turned, and there was Panthra, poised above him.

Ki-Gor moved aside—one of those lightning movements that had saved his life so often in the past. Panthra saw him, but he was unable to change the course of his spring in mid-air. The huge lion struck earth on all fours, spun, started to lunge. Again Ki-Gor was gone. Cleverly he had shifted position, placing Zag between him and the lion.

Zag saw the big cat, and writhed back from fear. Sight was coming back to Gombon's eyes, and he saw Panthra, too. The two of them fled, chattering their terror. Simultaneously their weights struck the arena wall. The bamboo bent, creaking. It wavered a moment. There was a sharp, splintering sound as one of the outside supports gave way, and following that a roar of collapsing wood mingling with the screams of brown men and black.

A section of the wall had collapsed. The wall had served as a main support of the overloaded stands above. The stand slumped forward, pitching its mass of humankind toward the ground.

For a second the way was open. It was Ki-Gor's chance to escape. He sprang through, reached the gate, ran to the central path of the brown men's city.

Only one guard was there. The guard recognized him, and after a momentary hesitation, charged with his assagai lifted high. He set himself, and drove the spear at Ki-Gor's heart. But his quickness was no match for that of the jungle man's. Ki-Gor sidestepped, felt the bronze head of the assagai burn past his chest. His hand streaked down, seized the shaft, and with a powerful twist, sent the black warrior rolling head over shoulders to the ground.

The guard came to one knee, shrieking the alarm, but no one could hear him through the pandemonium that seethed through the arena. He still had a weapon —a short-bow, and quiver of tiny, poisoned arrows. He fitted an arrow in the thong and drew back, aiming at Ki-Gor's heart, but at the same moment, moving infinitely quicker, Ki-Gor's long arm came down, driving the assagai The copper head of the assagai flashed once in the late, afternoon sunshine, aud cut the warrior through the middle, pinning him to earth. The cry of terror that rose from the warrior's lungs ended in a death-gasp.

Guards were running from their posts around the arena now. They came a moment after their companion had fallen. For a second they paused, staring at the tall white man as they would stare at some evil spirit protected by the armor of the gods.

Ki-Gor did not turn and run. The fear they felt of him would have vanished had he done so, and an arrow, or a carefully aimed javelin would have cut him down. Instead he planted his feet wide, and his voice rose in a wild jungle scream of triumph.

"Aye-ya!" he cried, beating his chest with forearm and fist. "Hear me! I am Ki-Gor, beast of the jungle!"

Many times they had listened to the tales of Ki-Gor, the great white lord of the forests, and now that mythical being had assumed flesh in all his terrifying proportions, and stood facing them. Ki-Gor kept one arm upraised as though ready to call down the thunder of the gods, while he backed slowly toward the ironwood gate of Durga-Rama's palace.

The strength of that gate would have defied Ki-Gor's strength, but he did not need to open it. With a vaulting spring backward he reached the top of the eight-foot wall. He crouched there, looking at the blacks, and still no weapon was lifted against him.

Durga-Rama had by now broken free of the terrified mob in the arena. He charged from the gate, trampling men and women. He saw Ki-Gor poised there and shouted,

"After him, you cowards!"

When his men still did not move, he roared with rage, and charged them with his scimitar. He cut down two of them with the first savage swing. He rushed on, scattering the guards before him.

"That man is Ki-Gor," he bellowed. "You hear me?—Ki-Gor! He has come to conquer you and murder your women. Death to Ki-Gor. Hear me! I will give a brown maiden to any black who will bring me his head."

Ki-Gor dropped to the inner court while he was speaking. The sound of Durga-Rama's bellowing seemed distant there. He reached the door. It was barred. He drove into it, shoulder first, and it collapsed beneath his power. Five strides took him the length of the great hall; three long leaps, and he was up the stairway. He burst inside the private rooms of Durga-Rama. Only a slave was there—a woman, sprinkling fresh thatch over the couches.

Ki-Gor saw his strong-bow hanging on a peg, his quiver of arrows nearby, his long-bladed hunting knife sticking in a pillar.

Guardsmen were inside the front door. He could hear them in the courtyard, too. Durga-Rama was issuing orders, organizing pursuit.

Ki-Gor fixed quiver and knife at his belt, slipped the strongbow over his shoulder and climbed to the top of a thick, bamboo pillar supporting the roof. He held himself aloft with locked legs, and dug his way through the thick layer of palm thatch.

ONCE OUTSIDE, he crouched, looking at the scene below. Over there was the arena with its seats half collapsed. One of the great apes was plodding across the street of the native village. Durga-Rama could be seen waving his scimitar, ordering his guardsmen to surround the house.

For the time no one noticed Ki-Gor, crouched on the ridgepole above. He stood, and ran along the narrow apex with the same ease that he would follow a tree limb in the forest. He speeded his step near the end of the roof, and with a bounding leap he launched himself in air.

He seemed poised, like a bird in flight. He sailed out a long distance, and then down, down. It appeared that he would surely impale himself on the pointed poles of the stockade. He didn't. He cleared the stockade by inches, and ran toward the encroaching jungle.

No one was in striking distance except a native archer. The fellow sprang to a perch overlooking the stockade, his bow and poisoned arrows in his hands. From over his shoulder, Ki-Gor saw him. Still running, the jungle man fitted an arrow to the string of his strong-bow, turned, and drove the arrow. It winged true, smashing the native backward as though he was struck by a war-axe.

The vine was there as it had been left the night before. Ki-Gor seized it, and swung far out, alighting on a branch. He swung to another vine, and another. In a matter of seconds he was beyond their sight in the leafy bowers of the jungle.

VI

THROUGH the cool of approaching evening he went, with the breeze fresh against his face. The sun sank like a ball of vermilion through the overhanging mists of the jungle. By dark the area of large trees was left behind. He was forced to travel a footpath. He was on the scab-growth of the hillside when darkness settled.

Here, on higher ground, the scent of the great apes became strong. It continued so as he neared the cave. A sudden fear knifed through him. The apes should not be this close if they had any great fear of Marmo.

He speeded to a run. A gray shape loomed before him, shaggy and truculent. An ape. The animal saw the jungle man and retreated, crashing through scrub-brush.

Ki-Gor went on, bounding in long strides from rock to rock. He reached the crest. There, only an assagai cast away, was the big rock which marked the mouth of the cave.

He came to the black portal. No fresh spoor of ape there, so he took a deep breath of relief.

"Helene!" he called. "Do you hear me, Helene?"

No answer. Only the rolling sound of his voice, echoing from the rock walls.

"Helene!" he shouted more loudly.

There was a stir of movement, a sound of hurrying footsteps. It was not Helene. It was such a sound as a small man or boy might make. A form took body in the gloom—Ngeeso.

'Ah, Ki-Gor, thou hast come!" cried Ngeeso in the pigmy tongue. "I escaped as you told me and came here. They were already gone. I followed their trail into the valley, and then came back in hopes you would escape and meet me here."

"You did well, Ngeeso. Tell me, at what sun did you arrive?"

"At midday."

"And how old was the trail?"

"Only a few hours."

"They will be safe, Ngeeso. With Marmo, they will be safe."

They left the cave and traveled through night blackness down the rocky hillside, finally coming on Marmo's tracks in soft earth a long arrow shot away. A moon came from clouds, and it was easy following the spoor along the zig-zag path through scab-bush.

But in the deeper jungle no ray of moon penetrated. Blackness was complete. Ki-Gor put Ngeeso on the ground and walked slowly, bending forward, guided as much by his sense of smell as by sight. For an hour it was thus, with the men feeling their way.

"One would need the nose of N'goi, the hungry leopard, to follow such a spoor," Ngeeso muttered.

"Patience, little man."

"What have you found, Ki-Gor?"

"Nothing, but I have a sense of Marmo being near."

Ki-Gor whistled softly, the two familiar tones. Instantly there was a responding movement in the deep brush. A crash, a thunder of heavy feet shaking the earth.

"Ha! He is there, the mighty Marmo!" Ngeeso shouted.

Ki-Gor kept talking in a quiet voice, "I am her, Marmo. I am here, thou moving mountain"—and his words, in Shahili, guided the great beast to his side.

Marmo loomed a deeper shadow in the dark. He stopped and reached forward with his trunk, finding his white friend's shoulder, curling it around him with slave-like adoration.

"Where is Helene?" Ki-Gor asked him.

The elephant had no power of speech, but his intelligence was exceeded by no animal of the jungle, save man himself. He understood the question Ki-Gor put, and did his best to answer.

Marmo lifted his trunk high above, trumpeting with a quiet, high-pitched sound. He stamped his feet, rocking his massive bulk to and fro.

"She left thee. And the brown boy, he left too. She told thee to wait for her here!"

Again Marmo rocked, accompanying the movement with a fanlike waving of his ears, signifying agreement.

"She left at mid-morning, Marmo. You have stood here through the hot hours. She feared that they would see your bulk, those guards of Ramfis, and so she chose to go forward without thee. And now she has not returned as she promised, and thou, poor, patient beast, did not know what to do."

"What will *thou* do, Ki-Gor?" asked Ngeeso. "You have not taught your mate to be earth-bound. You have taught her to travel swinging through the trees like yourself, and up there none can follow."

"She would not travel by trees with Brend along. We will find their spoor along the footpaths."

He went on, slowly as before, but any spoor left behind was now too faint. He sat down with his back against the trunk of a Bokongu tree and waited until at last the gray of dawn came up from the east.

He started again, watching for the signs he had taught Helene to always leave as guidance An hour passed, and there was none. He wondered if she had taken the tree route with the boy riding her shoulders. The girl had developed superb strength under the tutelage of Ki-Gor, and she loved, when left alone, to attempt to equal the feats of her jungle mate himself.

He rounded a bend in the little used footpath, and spied a sign of the kind he had been looking for.

A bit of *nogi* vine had been broken off, woven in a circle, and left hanging on a twig level with Ki-Kor's eyes.

He seized it, examined it. It was wilted from yesterday's sun, so she had hung it there shortly after leaving Marmo. There were eight twists used in making the circle, indicating that he intended to travel eight arrow shots, following a circular course toward Ramfis.

Ki-Gor tossed the message twig aside and hurried forward, traveling the footpath in long strides. Ngeeso tried vainly to keep up, but ended by riding on one foot in a bend which Marmo made in his trunk. After a distance of two arrow shots, Ki-Gor found another twig similar to the first. He was standing, examining it, when he glimpsed someone down the footpath. It was Brend.

The boy was exhausted. He was torn by thorns, the soles of his feet left bloody marks in hard-baked earth of the path. He saw Ki-Gor and ran the last few steps of the distance. He fell to hands and knees, weeping from exhaustion and thankfulness.

Ki-Gor lifted him in his arms, "Boy! Tell me about it, boy."

"They have captured her, Ki-Gor," he wept. "I could do nothing to save her, Ki-Gor. She told me to escape. I wandered all night through the jungle without knowing where——"

"Who captured her? Brend, talk to me! Who——"

"The men of Durga-Rama. They captured her last night at dusk when we tried to approach the wall, searching for you. It was my fault, Ki-Gor. I thought we would be safe, but there were so many guards——"

"They were looking for me, Brend. But tell me about Helene!"

"She was carried off and I could do nothing to stop them. I escaped on my hands and knees into the jungle. Am I a coward, Ki-Gor, that I did not——"

"No, Brend. You are not a coward. You could not fight them all. You did right in coming to me."

"But Helene will die."

"She will not die, Brend." Ki-Gor put the boy down and went on, speaking half to himself. "She is worth more to Durga-Rama alive, and therefore she will live. Perhaps the tyrant will use her to force me back to his city. Or perhaps he may want to make a trade—Helene for you, Brend."

"Ki-Gor, I will give myself up. If I do that, then Durga-Rama will free her."

"No, Brend. There would be nothing gained by you giving yourself up. We have only one course open to us. We will ride Marmo through their wretched gates and rescue her!"

VII

THE MORNING BEFORE Helene had ridden Marmo along the valley trail as far as she dared. Brend was along, and he cautioned her that it was Durga-Rama's habit to keep lookouts posted on the main jungle trails. As it would be difficult for any watchman to overlook the spectacle of two persons riding an elephant, Helene left Marmo in a little--used side path, and went on toward Ramfis with Brend, traveling afoot.

Brend said it would be best to circle through the deep bush and approach the city from its river side, where a grove of towering trees grew down near the stockade.

It was a long journey, longer than she had anticipated, and darkness was settling when they came in sight of the city.

From a distance they could hear the noise of shouting men, baying dogs, and the thunder of elephant-hide drums. Helene looked questioningly at Brend.

"Those are the alarms," he said. "It must be they are searching for someone, otherwise the hounds would not be loose."

"Perhaps Ki-Gor?"

"Perhaps."

Helene forgot some of her caution. She started along the path, her lythe, tanned body moving with sinuous swiftness. Suddenly she stopped. She could sense danger ahead. There, in that patch of wild coffee, was a movement, a tremble of glossy leaves.

She seized Brend's shoulder, and started back. A crackle of twigs in that direction made her draw up a second time.

She looked, but she could see nothing. Only the dim, surrounding jungle. Yet she was certain that many eyes were watching her.

She backed slowly, her small assagai leveled before her. A whisk of air sounded directly above. She leaped aside, expecting the deadly arrow of a blow-gun. Instead, a wide loop of grass rope settled over her naked shoulders, and snaked tight, locking her arms against her body.

She struggled, trying to bring her assagai into play. It was useless.

"Brend!" she screamed. "Run, Brend. They must not capture you. You must return to Marmo. Tell Marmo what has happened. He will find Ki-Gor."

A second rope descended, and a third. She was helpless. Brend had vanished. She could hear the crackle of underbrush as he scrambled along. Black men had appeared from every side, their leader bellowing in a coarse voice, telling them to capture the boy. They were after him, smashing through the tangle, stabbing with their long assagais, firing poisoned arrows at him by sound.

In a few minutes they gave up and gathered around Helene, jabbering to one another, staring at the strange sight of a captive white woman.

Their leader, a thick-chested man named Mokotto, issued a gutteral command. An assagai was pointed at Helene's spine, and she was made to walk across a stretch of cassava and millet to the gate of the city.

They paused with her at the door of a large wood and bamboo house.

"Wait!" Mokotto said to her, speaking a variety of Bantu. "I will tell Durga-Rama."

He climbed the stairs and saw Durga-Rama sitting cross-legged on a heap of thatch, drinking palm wine. At sound of the footsteps, Durga-Rama locked up and scowled, his face seeming very large and greasy by the light of the smoky fat-lamp that burned near his knees. When the black man paused to bow, he scowled the more. He cast away the dregs of wine and barked,

"Speak, fool!"

"Great Durga-Rama!" cried the black dramatically. "I have captured a woman."

"What woman?"

"I do not know."

"If she is some black wench, then——"

"She is not, Lord. She is white."

"White!"

"Like Ki-Gor who fought the apes in the arena this afternoon, this woman is white. And she is beautiful."

The scowl faded from Durga-Rama's thick face. He poured more wine from an earthen vessel, lifted his cup and smiled, showing his brown-stained teeth.

"So you have captured a woman of the whiteness of Ki-Gor. I have heard it told that the White Lord had a mate. And this must be the one. That is good. Come, my strong Mokotto, and let me reward you."

Mokotto hesitated, looking at the copper bracelet Durga-Rami was going to give him. Evidently he had not said everything that was on his mind.

"Have you gone deaf? I said to come for your reward."

"I am not deaf, my Lord. There is something more. Please do not be angry with me——"

"Out with it!" Durga-Rama thundered.

"There was another. The brown boy—Brend."

"He was with Ki-Gor's mate?"

"Yes. But he escaped. It was not my fault, Lord——

Durga-Rama quieted him with an abrupt gesture. He looked dark, and cursed under his breath.

"Perhaps it is well," he muttered at last, and the guardsman took a deep breath. Durga-Rama would rather have Brend escape than be brought aliv into the city. There had been mutterings against him since the disaster of the afternoon. Even over the rumble of elephant drums he could hear the funeral chants as the blacks wailed the deaths of relatives who had been crushed in the arena. And now this meddler — Liike — was organizing something against him. So it would be worse if the boy were there, a figurehead to rally around.

He tossed the copper bracelet and said, "You have acted wisely."

"And the woman, my Lord? You will see the woman?"

"Yes, the woman!" A grim smile played with the corners of Durga-Rama's hard mouth. Bring her before me. I would see if she is like the white man."

DURGA-RAMA was happy over this new turn of events. A few minutes before he had grimly contemplated the thought of Ki-Gor returning with the lawful king, and now, like a gift form Isis, this woman had fallen into his hands. With her he could do much. She would be worth more than a hundred assagais against the jungle man. Perhaps he could even force this Ki-Gor to take Brend into the forest and brain him. He chuckled, contemplating such a thing. Indeed, that would be the supreme jest!

He bent forward, his face close above the grease lamp, watching as the woman was thrust through the door. He could not see her for a moment because of the guards, then they stepped aside, and he fastened his piglike eyes on her body.

Durga-Rama had looked on many women, but he could not restrain a little exhalation of pleasure at the loveliness that was here revealed before him. Indeed, she was beautiful. She was tall, her skin a light tan, like Ki-Gor's. She was clean-limbed, slim-waisted, supple. Durga-Rama put down his cup, and heaved his great bulk erect. He walked toward her with a heavy shuffle, viewed her from several angles, inspecting her body with the critical eye of a slave merchant. He laid his hand on her shoulder, and smiled when she shrank from his touch.

"You are Ki-Gor's mate?" he asked, speaking the tongue of the Congo which he knew the White Lord himself understood.

She did not answer, and he went on, as though speaking to himself.

"You, you would be a worthy mate for Ki-

Gor. Tall, and strong, and beautiful. Many men would be glad to have such a woman as you. I know of markets where you would bring a price of two hundred goats —and I certainly could use two hundred goats." He chuckled at that, showing his brown teeth.

He walked close, running appraising hands down her arms, examining the slimness of her naked waist. Then he went back to his couch and sat crosslegged, fingering his straggle of whiskers.

"Leave me!" he said to the blacks. "Wait outside the door." When they were gone, he spoke on to Helene, "Ki-Gor is strong. But strong men sometimes become weaklings—for a woman."

"What do you mean?" Helene cried unexpectedly.

Durga-Rama tossed back his head with a brutal peal of laughter.

"Ha! So you *do* understand my words! It is as I thought." He lifted the wine cup to his lips and drank without taking his eyes off her form. "Yes, strong men are turned into sheep by women. And so will it be with Ki-Gor."

"You have him in your prison "

"Then you do not know?" Durga-Rama made a wry face at the memory of what took place that afternon. "For the moment, Ki-Gor has escaped us. But *you* will bring him back."

"I do not know where he is."

"But you know where he will go."

She met his gaze defiantly.

"Yes, you know. And here is what I would have you do. I would have you send him a message by one of my men. Tell him that you can go free and unharmed —provided he sends me a package."

"Package?"

"Yes. A package." Durga-Rama gulped more wine. "And in the package, I must find the head of Brend."

"You're insane."

"No, I am not insane. I am a king. And I plan to remain a king." He laughed at her. "Come, do not put horror on your face. Ki-Gor has killed many things for you—then why should he not kill once again? Why not this worthless child?"

Durga-Rama clapped his hands, and the guards returned.

"Nungo, you will carry a message for me."

The man called "Nungo" bowed.

"You are to go to Ki-Gor——" The amazed expression which crossed Nungo's face made the usurper pause. "Yes, you fool, to Ki-Gor! Why do you put on that look of a she goat?"

"He will kill me, Lord."

In sudden rage, Durga-Rama leaped to his feet. "Is it better to die here?" he shrieked.

Nungo saw the scimitar swing at the last moment. He tried to retreat and bring his lance into action, but the weapon was too long. Its end rammed the wall, and the keen edge of the scimitar struck. Nungo went down with a rattle of death in his throat.

Panthra, who lay in shadow behind his master, came snarling forward, lured by the scent of warm blood, but Durga-Rama seized his leash and held him back.

"Mokotto, take this coward's body and throw it to the hounds."

Durga-Rama returned to his seat, drinking wine until Mokotto came back.

"Who will now volunteer to carry the message to Ki-Gor?"

"Send me, Master!" pleaded Mokotto. "I would have offered myself first had you given me the chance."

"I may need you for another task. Burra, you will carry it." He turned to Helene. "Tell him where Ki-Gor is to be found."

"I do not know."

"I have ways of helping you to remember. Ways that are quick, and ways that are slow."

"It will do no good to torture me. I do not know where Ki-Gor is. We were searching for him when your men captured me."

"What should I do with you, woman?" he asked.

"Free me!"

DURGA-RAMA roared with laughter, "When I have no further use for you —then perhaps I will free you." He spoke to his guardsmen, "Take her to the little room, and watch that she does not escape. Perhaps she has learned some of Ki-Gor's tricks."

"She will not escape, Master!" said Mokotto.

"Mokotto, I would have a word with you —alone."

Durga-Rama waited until they were all gone except the ugly Mokotto.

"You have always been faithful to me, Mokotto," he said.

"Always, my Lord."

"I have given you rich rewards, Mokotto. When Lungo would not sell his maiden daughter to you last rainy season, it was I, Durga-Rama, who gave her to you and the cost was nothing."

"I am grateful, my Lord. I am the lowest creature of the forest, and you are a god riding on——"

"Enough of that! We are much alike, Mokotto. We are both merciless, both ready to use our knives on the side that is best for us. Good. I like you for that, and not for your double-ended tongue. That is why I am going to give you even richer rewards than ever before. A brown woman for your wife—you would like that, Mokotto"

The black man's eyes gleamed rapturously.

"One of the temple virgins?"

"Perhaps! Were it not for that blind priest, Liike. He would never give a virgin from the temple of Isis to a black man. So you see, he is a thorn in my flesh as well as yours, Mokotto."

"What would you have me do?"

"I would have you dip your knife in Liike's blood. Tonight. It should not be difficult. You are chief among the guards, and you will be admitted anywhere."

"Liike will be dead before that shaft of moonlight moves the length of your foot along the floor.!"

Durga-Rama watched as the thick-chested man felt the edge of his machete and stalked from the door. When he was gone, the usurper grunted and spat. A brown maiden for his bed! A temple virgin! Even Durga-Rama would not dare give such a woman to a black. Mokotto was a fool—but he was an excellent assassin. Most assassins are fools, for wise men hire others to do their butchering for them.

He poured wine, and sent for his spy, a sneaking, parrot-faced brown man named Lotob.

"What word have you?" asked Durga-Rama.

"No more than I have already given you."

"Have you been asked to join the conspiracy against me?"

"No."

"Nor will you be. They do not trust you, Lotob. They suspect you are my friend. But keep your ears open, anyway. Find out the names of those who are meeting with Liike. I would know the one I am to execute when the uprising is killed."

VIII

LOTOB LEFT, and Durga-Rama sat on his thatch couch, deep in thought, Panthra was at ease, watching with unblinking eyes. Now that he was alone, Durga-Rama stroked the lion's thick mane and talked to him.

"You are my friend, Panthra. My only friend. We are alike. You alone I can trust."

Panthra fixed him with savage intentness. There was no expression in his eyes —no affection. Only a crystallized hate for all the race of men.

The lamp flame wavered and became small as its font of grease was consumed. At last it blinked out, leaving only reddish coal, and a wisp of acrid smoke. Durga-Rama did not call the slave to replenish it. He sat in the dark, watching the shaft of moonlight creep across the floor until it had gone the length of a man's foot. It was time for Mokotto to return with word that Liike was dead.

He did not come. The moonlight crept on. No sound in the large house save for the bare feet of guardsmen patrolling the hall. He cursed. Mokotto could expect no mercy if he came creeping back with an excuse. Durga-Rama had one way of dealing with failure. The man would die on the blade of the scimitar, just as Nungo had died an hour or two before.

The sound of a heavy thud, followed by rapidly retreating footsteps drew him to the tiny, barred window. He looked out, but the shadow of the wall was very dense. Guardsmen were gathered out there, jabbering excitedly. They carried something around the courtyard, inside, and up the stairs. Panthra sniffed, and roared to his feet.

Durga-Rama pulled him back as they rapped at his door.

"What is it?"

"It is Mokotto. He is dead."

Durga-Rama flung the door open. A reflected light from the lower room shone on Mokotto's distorted face. He had died not swiftly, but on one of the breaking wheels of the torture chamber. The conspirators had captured Mokotto, and tortured the truth from him.

"Where did you find this carrion?" he snarled at his men.

"He was thrown over the wall, and the men who did it ran before we could tell who they were."

Another spoke, "They were of the king's race." By that he meant they were brown men.

Durga-Rama sent them away. He strode the room, hand closed on the hilt of his scimitar.

The sands were running out for him. He knew that. His friends were few, his enemies many. The enemies had sent him back Mokotto's corpse as a warning. That indicated that they considered themselves strong enough to act. But Durga-Rama was not yet beaten. He had a few friends—those who were growing fat from his kingship. And he had another lot in the game of fate—the power of his black guard, thirty of the strongest warriors of Ramfis.

He sent for them, the thirty, and they arrayed themselves across the room, oiled bodies gleaming in the semi-darkness. He strode the length of the line, and grunted his satisfaction. He issued an order to a slave who brought a casket of copper ornaments. He distributed leg and arm bracelets, rings for fingers, ears and noses.

"You are my men!" he said abruptly when the casket was empty. "I have made your bodies beautiful with copper. I have given you the pick of native maidens for your wives. As long as I am king, these things and more shall be yours. If another should kill me and be king, your wives and riches will be taken away, and you will be spit on like slaves."

The men shifted uneasily, knowing that Durga-Rama was speaking the truth. He went on.

"Tonight, or tomorrow I will need your lances—to kill some swine." He laughed at this crude joke, hefting his heavy scimitar. "Some swine who walk on two legs and call themselves the race of kings. You will wait below. See to it that no man, brown or black, enters my courtyard."

These guardsmen gave Durga-Rama temporary security. For tonight at least he would be safe enough. And by tomorrow he would find help elsewhere. He knew now that he would not use the white woman to bargain with Ki-Gor. He would use her in a trade with Chong, chief of the cannibal Ta'tamba tribe from across the river.

Chong had two hundred warriors. They were not trained like his own guardsmen, but they were warriors, nevertheless. A hundred of them, added to his own guard, could smash any insurrection that Liike could launch against him. And the loan of a hundred warriors would not be a high price for Chong to pay for so desirable a woman.

Durga-Rama called Nunabba, the guard he had placed in charge of Helene.

"Bring the woman to the river gate. I will meet you there."

He made ready for the journey, dropping a tiny, poisoned dagger inside his kuftan, wrapping an indigo cloak high above body and face. He passed through the river gate, and found Nunabba and Helene waiting for him.

"Where are you taking me?" Helene demanded, wrenching at the ropes which fastened her wrists.

Durga-Rama walked close, smiling, breathing repulsively into her face.

"I am taking you to meet your future mate."

"My mate is Ki-Gor! He will——"

"But I have looked, and looked without seeing him. What good is a mate who skulks like a jackal, fifty arrow shots away?"

Helene was led along a footpath through the darkness of the jungle. In a short time, the deep sound of the river became audible, and they caught sight of moonlight shining from its wide, flat surface. Across could be seen the dark shores of the Ta'tamba domain.

They waded through reeds and stagnant water until Durga-Rama found two concealed dugout canoes. He ordered Helene and Nunabba into one of them, leaving instructions that they should await his return, and set out alone, driving his paddle in mighty sweeps, riding the crocodile-infested waters toward the far shore.

He drew up in an overhung cove where an elephant trail came down to the water. It was still sometime before dawn, so he chewed bethel nuts and waited. With daylight gleaming from the water behind him, he left the canoe and walked up the trail. The jungle was dense for a while, with hundreds of monkeys watching from the tangled branches above, then it broke away, and he entered a wide area of clearing.

Here a few cassava and yam fields had been scratched away from the encoaching orchilla and elephant weeds by crude implements of forked wood. There was a stretch of cane grass higher than his head, and emerging from that he caught sight of the cluttering huts of a village with roofs of thick thatch looking like toadstools.

Durga-Rama had visited the village only once, and that years ago while on an expedition to punish the cannibal Ta'tambas after they had stolen two women from the Ramfian yam fields. On that occasion, of course, the village had been burned,but this one, built on its ruins, was from all appearances the same.

He walked rapidly along the path. Smoke haze rose slowly through the humid, morning air from the fires where women were baking millet cakes on hot stones. There were no lookouts. He was first noticed by a crowd of naked children who ran beside him, coming close to feel the fabric of his indigo robe. Durga-Rama did not glance to right nor left. He seemed oblivious to their presence. When one of them, a boy of six or seven, tripped and fell in front of him, Durga-Rama merely trod over him and left him wailing on the ground.

He entered the duty path which wound like a crawling snake between two rows of thatch huts, passed a mud-roofed house from which rolled an odor of putrefied gri-gris, and came to what was evidently the chief's house—one somewhat removed from the others, sitting on a slight rise of ground.

He was stopped at the door by a guardsman who confronted him with a leveled assagai.

"I would see Chong!"

The guard retreated. He was a coward despite the ferocious appearance of his face which was twisted around a skewer of ivory thrust through his nose.

"Wait! I tell Chong," he said in his gutteral language.

He lifted the drape of skin covering the low doorway, and bent double to go inside. He was gone the time it takes a man to breath fifty times, then he emerged and spoke,

"Chong wait inside."

"Lift the drape for me!" snarled Durga Rama, his hand closing on his scimitar.

With a surly motion, the man obeyed. Durga-Rama entered, and stood for a moment. The hut was dark after the bright, morning sunlight. Uncured skins of zebras, giraffes and jungle cats covered the dirt, giving off an odor of dry decay. Four squat women of the tribe were crouched in the deeper shadow along the wall, while a tall, bandy-legged Poltuni wench occupied a favored position on a skin-covered heap of thatch. In the center of the hut sat Chong himself.

Chonk was large and round-shouldered. He had once been muscular, but some of the muscle had now dissolved into fat from the easy life he led. His face was broad and flat, his skin oily, his head shaved and gleaming like polished ebony.

"Durga-Rama!" he said, not offering to rise.

"You are honored by my visit," growled the usurper.

Chong waited. All his life he had hated these men of Ramfis, and that hatred showed in his face now. But he feared, too, and he was curious about this unprecedented visit. Durga-Rama went on,

"I come to tell you of a woman, Chong. A beautiful woman." With a contemptuous twist of his lips he looked around at Chong's wives. "This woman, she is not a short, bow-legged wench like those with which you have contented yourself. This woman is tall, and white, like a vision of the gods. Her hair is like copper. Her waist is so slim your two hands would pass around it, and yet her hips and breasts are full as the rising moon. Such a woman would be worth the whole of your wretched kingdom, Chong."

Chong's eyes gleamed with interest in the midst of his flat face. He was a fancier of women. He had always dreamed to have for himself such a one as Durga-Rama described—perhaps a maiden of the race of Ramfis.

"Where is this woman?"

"She is near."

"In the village?"

"Sit down, and hear me out. Hear how you may have her for yourself to keep in your hut until you are tired of her."

"What is this woman's name "

"The name is no difference. You may name her as you please."

Chong's eyes shifted nervously. The expression of longing left his face, and a twist of animal fear replaced it. He wondered why Durga-Rama would part with such a woman, and now he guessed.

"I have heard that the White Lord called Ki-Gor is roaming the jungles of Ramfis. Ki-Gor has such a mate as you tell about."

"What care you if she is Ki-Gor's mate?"

"Ho!" Chong beat the dirt with his knuckles. "I have heard of this Ki-Gor. He would come to my village, and hurl lightning bolts with his strong-bow which is said to be thick as a man's leg and long as the neck of a giraffe. He would——"

"You coward fool!" Durga-Rama spat among the dusty, rotting skins on the floor. "Your liver is yellow, and you have a woman's breast where your lion's heart should be. Listen, while I tell you the truth of this Ki-Gor: We ourselves captured him. For us he performed in a cage like a captive baboon. We spat on him, and he cringed from terror. Then we freed him, and he ran skulking into the jungle. I myself saw this mighty bow you tell about. These arms of mine drew it back and shot an arrow. You have been listening to the tales told by the ivory hunters, and they have always been the worst liars in the universe."

It did not occur to Chong that Durga-Rama himself might be lying. Chong was a simple-minded man only a little removed from the apes, and up to this time, each promise and each threat of the men of Ramfis had been carried out.

Durga-Rama said, "Of course, if you do not want this glorious creature for your couch. . ."

"What is her price?"

"A miserable price, or else you could not pay it. I only ask the loan of one hundred warriors for the space of two suns."

"What would the great king of Ramfis need with one hundred warriors?"

"What do you care of my need as long as the woman is yours?"

Chong became crafty. "It is true that the men of Ramfis have taken to wetting spears in each other's blood?"

"Make up your mind about the woman before I take her for myself."

"Our yam fields are low and sour. But the fields on high land across the river grow fine crops. The ancient men of my tribe tell me it has ever been thus, yet the people of your tribe are rich and do not need all their fields. The hundred warriors I will lend you, and I will not complain if half of them die in your battle, but you must give me those fields closest the river, and you must also give me the woman."

Durga-Rama finally agreed as Chong wanted it. He would send Helene when the hundred warriors were delivered to his command. After the issue at Ramfis was settled, the warriors were not to return across the river, but would be allowed to build huts on the area of fertile grassland along the river's western bank.

Durga-Rama laughed to himself as he retraced his steps across the low-lying domains of the Ta'tambas. This Chong he detested. When the insurrection was put down in Ramfis, he would reorganize his guard and slaughter the warriors who had built huts. Afterwards he would cross the river in force, and retake Helene for himself. A white-skinned woman such as Helene would be worth many pounds of copper in bartar with the Arab slave merchants in the north.

Helene was with Nunabba, still bound, still sitting in the canoe. He smiled and said to her,

"I have good news. You are to be a queen—a queen of a cannibal village. You will belong to Chong in trade for one hundred warriors. It is not every woman who is valued at so high a price."

Helene gave no sign of having heard Durga-Rama's words. She sat very straight, looking across the vast stretch of river.

AT THE MOMENT she was helpless, her hands tied securely by the grass rope. There was no point in struggling or pleading. But she would not always be so helpless. Inside the breast of her leopard-skin bodice was tucked a tiny dagger. The dagger blade was scarcely longer than her middle finger, and it folded cleverly inside a golden case shaped like a scarab. Long ago Ki-Gor had found it in the valley of tombs and given it to her. Today, when she was handed over as wife to Chong, the scarab dagger would serve its deadly purpose.

They waited as the morning sun became hot. At length, five dugout canoes so loaded with warriors their sides dipped water, came in sight and crossed the broad stream, avoiding mudbars where swams of crocodiles lay with backs exposed like stranded driftlogs.

The warriors came ashore, naked save for shields, breechclouts, and decorations of feather, copper and cowrie shells. They were armed with assagais, crude bows, and black-headed poisoned arrows. Durga- Rama bellowed a command, and they lined up for his inspection.

When he was through, the guard who had been at Chong's hut came up and said, "Chong told me to bring the woman."

Durga-Rama nodded a trifle regretfully. "Yes, the woman. Nunabba! bring the white goddess who is the wife of Chong!"

The warrior stared at her white beauty as she walked towards them through water up to her thighs. They did not take their eyes away until the canoe carrying her was a small streak far across the water.

"Come!" barked Durga-Rama. "Let us get to the fighting, and afterward I will show you the fields where you will grow rich and fat."

Helene felt slightly sick when she was thrust through the low doorway to Chong's hut. Hot, putrefying odors struck her. She stood near the wall, her eyes peering through gloom. She made out a squat, heavy shouldered man sitting crosslegged on a zebra skin. His forehead was low, his intelligence obviously little above the apes. He was staring at her, jaw relaxed.

After a while he sucked his breath. He came forward.

"You are beautiful," he said. "More beautiful than . . ."

She recoiled from his touch.

"Do not fear me!" he breathed. "I will not beat you like my other wives. I will not scar your smooth skin. You will grow used to me. I am——"

"You are a fool!" she said, trying to make her voice coldly contemptuous.

He stopped. "I a fool? I am Chong—"

"Yes, you are a fool. Did he not tell you I was Ki-Gor's mate? Do you not know that Ki-Gor will carry death to any man who touches me."

"But Ki-Gor is gone, fled from the wrath of Durga-Rama."

"Ki-Gor left the people of Ramfis in terror, with dead men being wailed in every hut. And soon he will return to find me, and the man who harms me will die like a pig with a jevelin through his heart. You are a fool, Chong, or you would free me and save yourself."

Chong's dull eyes became shifty. He rubbed his large, shiny hands together, considering the wrath of Ki-Gor.

"No." He finally said. "I have traded a hundred warriors for you. Is the price not big enough to make you mine?"

"He will kill you with bolts of lightning with his strongbow."

"Agh!" Chong made a wretching movement and spat. "He will do nothing. This is but woman's talk to frighten me. Did not Durga-Rama himself say he had shot Ki-Gor's bow? Are not his arrows but twigs of the assagai tree? I am Chong, and I do not fear him. Let him come seeking you on the elephant men say he rides.

I will make a pitfall and line it with pointed stakes, and I will capture them both."

"You are a fool, Chong. Ki-Gor will leap your pitfall——"

"No. Not even Ki-Gor. The pitfall stands in the passage between two swamps. Men may cross, but an elephant will break through. They will not escape."

Chong grinned around at his ugly wives who were crouched outside, peering through the door.

"Is not my new wife beautiful?" he chuckled, rubbing his hands.

IX

AFTER HIS MEETING with Brend, and hearing from his lips the story of Helene's capture, Ki-Gor left the brown boy and Ngeeso riding on the elephant's broad back, climbed to the high treetops overhead, and swung swiftly from one to the other by means of their ropelike vines. In this manner it took only a few minutes to catch sight of the city.

There were no beating of pursuit drums, no crowds gathered in holiday spirit with bodies bedaubed in paint. Ki-Gor stood on a small branch, close to the swaying top of a lofty tree, and for the space of a hundred breaths his eyes studied the city of Ramfis.

Through the rising heat waves which distorted the picture he could see a cluster of black men near the temple of Isis. He could tell they were warriors by the repeated glints of sunshine on the bronze tips of their assagais. By Durga-Rama's house, another group of men were deployed. There seemed to be no fighting going on, but he could tell that some sort of trouble was brewing.

He gave a grunt of satisfaction, though his fine brows were still drawn together as he puzzled his course. He did not know whether to go openly, or by stealth. To charge in on the back of Marmo, might lead abrupt action by Durga-Rama. He might in his rage plunge a dagger into the heart of Helene. On the other hand, delay did not suit Ki-Gor's impetuous spirit.

He reached for a vine, wrapped one leg, and slid toward earth. He stopped, swinging through air like a pendulum, while his eyes noted something else. A file of warriors wound its way toward him along the footpath. He listened as their voices came closer. They were talking to one another in the guttural language of the Ta'tamba tribe from across the river.

Ki-Gor first thought they were seizing a moment of civil war to make an attack on the city, but when the column came closer, he saw that their leader was not of the degenerate cannibal tribe. The leader was Durga-Rama himslf, regal in a robe of indigo, scimitar flashing at his waist.

Ki-Gor slid down the vine, and dropped with cat's-paw lightness to a thick branch overhanging the footpath.

They passed directly beneath him, so close he could have touched the points of their assagais.

One of the warriors had fallen a trifle behind the rest. He limped, and finally stuck his assagai point down in earth, and bent over to remove a briar from between his toes. Ki-Gor did not move. The warrior stood, and hurried forward to catch his fellows. He did not glance above. He walked beneath the limb, and Ki-Gor swung down, hanging by bent knees. His hands darted, and they closed on the cannibal's throat.

He lifted the fellow from the ground and held him, feet lashing with the desperate impotence of a man on the gibbet. Ocassionaly Ki-Gor's fingers relaxed so the warrior could suck air into his tortured lungs. At length the sounds of the column died away. Ki-Gor released his grip, allowing the man to fall in a crumpled heap on the ground. He lighted beside him and waited for consciousness to return.

The warrior finally sat up, and blinked terrified eyes at the strange white man.

"Do not kill me!" he gasped. "Do not kill. Me only poor warrior. Me——"

"I will not kill you if you answer my questions."

"I am the lowest of the low," he chanted in one of the fetish tongues, making signs over the gri-gri pouch at his waist.

Ki-Gor made an impatient movement, "Where were you being led by Durga-Rama?"

"I do not know. Chong, our chief, he say we fight. He say we kill who Durga-

Rama say. He say we get rich land on river——"

"Have you seen a woman with skin like mine? A woman whose beauty is like the sun?"

The warrior drew in his breath with a sucking sound, rolling his eyes back in their sockets. After this dumb-show, he pointed to the river with his elongated lower lip.

"At dawn, master, I see the white goddess. Her skin like master's skin. Her ——"

"Where is she now?"

"Perhaps they have taken her to Chong's village."

The sudden rage of the white man which followed these words made him lower himself belly down in the footpath.

"It was not my will, Master. I was——"

Ki-Gor seized him by the scruff of the neck, lifted him to his feet.

"You will lead me to this Chong?"

"Yes, Master!"

Ki-Gor started back, keeping his captive running ahead of him until at length he caught sight of Marmo.

Marmo came to a halt, and at Ki-Gor's command held his trunk for the cannibal black to mount, but the fellow fell on his knees in fear of the great brute, and no urging from Ki-Gor could make him walk a step closer. Finally Ki-Gor said a few words in Swahili, and Marmo wrapped his trunk around the man's trembling body, and lifted him to his back.

Guided by Ta'tamba, they soon reached the swampy edge of the river. It was a wide and turgid stream, brown with a cargo of sediment gathered from the black heart of Africa. Here and there were mudbanks with bushes clinging to them, and dotting their edges were the slimy bodies of crocodiles.

"Forward!" said Ki-Gor, barely hesitating at the brink. "You have crossed such rivers before, O Marmo!"

THE BEAST TRUMPETED softly in answer to these words from his beloved master. In a moment he was belly-deep in ooze among the rushes of the shore. He struggled on, slowly, like some huge ant caught in a sea of heavy syrup. At last the slow current of the stream rippled along his broad sides, his back sank almost from sight, and he swam.

Ki-Gor slid from his head and struck out in the lead, his knife in his teeth as protection against devilfish and crocodiles, watching for whirlpools and shallow stretches where quicksand might trap the great brute. He passed close to mudbanks with the eyes of crocodiles fastened on him like god-forgotten eyes of prehistoric monsters.

At midstream, one of the reptiles, larger than the rest, slid from a bar and swam towards him with a swift, sinuous movement.

Ki-Gor speeded. He did not wish to be delayed by a fight. The crocodile drove for him, snapping at his feet. A quick roll by Ki-Gor made the attempt miss him. He kept the knife in his teeth, and trod water for a few seconds while removing one of the heavy arrows from his quiver and breaking it in half.

He waited, missing no move of the crocodile, remaining suspended in order to tempt its speedy return. The crocodile rolled over, disappearing. Only a riffle of distortion on the surface of the water served to mark his progress. Swifter it came, and swifter. Suddenly the long head broke water, eyes on Ki-Gor, mouth open showing the jagged fangs. The mouth was ready to close and cut Ki-Gor in two like a mighty scissors.

Marmo saw and trumpeted shrilly. There were mixed screams from Brend and Ngeeso. Ki-Gor did not move to place himself out of reach. Instead, at the final moment, he twisted forward through the water, and as the jaws snapped shut he thrust the broken half of the arrow, wedging it to prop open the reptile's mouth.

With a quick sweep of his arms, Ki-Gor was away, avoiding by inches the lash of the crocodile's tail.

The huge amphibian turned over and over, beating the water to a brownish froth, shaking his head, trying vainly to free his jaws from the torture of the arrow. But it was propped there as solidly as Ki-Gor's strength could thrust it, and the harder he fought, the deeper sank its keen point in the roof of his mouth. Around him the froth turned pinkish from blood, and suddenly the reptile rolled over with muscles trembling. The arrow point had worked through and found his brain.

Downstream other crocodiles were showing an interest, tasting blood in the water. They slid from their resting places and came in dozens, but Ki-Gor had reached deep water, and was swimming with powerful strokes toward the shore.

He waded through shoulder-high rushes, and found an elephant trail showing the marks of new travel.

"Is this the way?" he asked the Tamtamba.

"It is the way, Master."

The trail led through low-lying jungle where the air was heavy with odors of fungus, miasma, and the damp-rot that clings like leprosy. Orchids grew in fiery splendor suspended from trees, their roots absorbing moisture from the steamy atmosphere, but animal life seemed to be lacking. It was not a good country, this domain of the cannibal blacks.

In time, the trail led to the edge of a swamp where trees stood with half their root systems above water, reaching down like clutching hands. There was a second swamp at the left. This one cut in until the footpath followed a shoulder of land only forty or fifty paces in width.

Marmo suddenly drew up, lifting his trunk in a manner which showed there was something close that did not meet his approval. Ki-Gor saw him, but his hurry was too urgent to pause. He ran ahead, senses drawn to a fine point, while the elephant lumbered in a half-gallop behind.

Ki-Gor's eyes were keen along the ground to pick up a warning spoor, and they roved the solid jungle walls for the tiny leaf movements that would be his warnings of ambush.

The warning came. Perhaps there was no real movement. Perhaps it was only an instinct passed down from the primitive that lays dormant in all civilized men, but had been reborn in Ki-Gor through his years in contact with nature.

He leaped to one side. Up there the glossy leaves trembled. Whether it was a man or lurking leopard he did not know.

Marmo came on, slowly breaking his speed. Ngeeso was leaping back and forth on his head, jabbing him with his short assagai.

"Stop him, Ki-Gor!" he shrilled in his pigmy tongue. "Stop this foolish mountain.. They have set a pitfall for him."

Ki-Gor could not see the pitfall from his position on the ground but it was plain to Ngeeso above. A pit had been tunneled beneath the footpath, leaving the original beaten earth in a fragile bridge over the top. The bridge of earth was thick enough to support several men, but the elephant would have plunged to his death on the pointed hardwood stakes that most certainly were driven below.

Marmo came to a stop at the final instant, setting his feet as the edge caved away. He trumpeted in a high scream, rearing back to his haunches. The ground still crumbled, but the great animal rolled to his side, spilling his human cargo back among the bramble of thorns. For a second he lay there on the brink, then he rolled, taking small trees down as he went, and thus gained the assurance of solid earth.

Ki-Gor saw all this from the side of his eye, for at the same moment Ngeeso shouted warning of the pitfall, an arrow whisked by so close its bit of feathered tail brushed the flesh of his arm.

For a fraction of time the ambusher was barely visible through the leaf-tangle. Ki-Gor's muscles responded like automatic mechanism. With stunning swiftness the strong-bow came from his shoulder. An arrow was fitted, drawn, released. The bowstring twanged with a bass sound, and like an echo came the thump of metal arrowhead as it struck through the bony framework of a human chest. A man uttered a wild, wavering scream and plunged head foremost from his place atop a limb.

ANOTHER POISONED ARROW stabbed the earth nearby. Then a dozen of them, winging in a shower. But like the arrows of most native archers, they were woefully inaccurate. Ki-Gor did not try to answer any but the first. He swung up among the branches, bounded crouching along a limb as thick as a man's body, and in a matter of seconds was looking down of his would-be killers.

So quick and silent had been the maneuver that most of them thought he had simply vanished in air. He balanced with toes holding the smooth bark, drew a half-dozen arrows from his quiver, and in rapid succession he loosed them.

Two of the Ta'tamba fell before their companions realized where the hail of death was coming from. They screamed in terror at the great white man poised above, his hand loaded with winged destruction. They dropped their weapons and fell scrambling to the ground.

They were gone, and Ki-Gor expected no further trouble from them. He turned his attention to Marmo, shouted in Swahili, and the elephant trumpted in answer. Ki-Gor gave the word which instructed him to go right. He obeyed, crashing a way through the undergrowth. He followed the soft edge of the swamp safe from the deadfall, and climbed once more to the footpath beyond.

Ki-Gor swung rapidly from tree to tree, watching the country ahead. The jungle ended, and he looked across a broad park area, dotted here and there by poor yam fields. Beyond the fields were the round-topped huts of the Ta'tamba village.

He waited until Marmo came near, and dropped to his head. He crouched on knees, urging the huge beast to greater speed, guiding him with the point of an arrow.

Marmo had not taken time to lift Brend and Ngeeso once more to his back. Ki-Gor could hear the voice of the pigmy coming to him from the edge of the jungle.

"Wait for me, Ki-Gor!"

But Ki-Gor did not wait. Ngeeso and Brend would only be a hindrance. The ambushers had already fled across the yam fields and were in the village, shouting the alarm.

On reaching the one street of the village, Ki-Gor urged the elephant to a charge. Warriors were running from huts, having seized their lances and their painted leather shields. They saw the thing that was charging down on them, drew up for a moment's consternation, and fled for cover like mice scurrying from a falcon. One of them rose from a pit beside the path, poised a javelin, and hurled it.

The weapon flew true, sinking its point in Marmo's thick hide, but whether or not the beast even felt it was a question. He ran without flinching, while the long shaft whipped back and forth, hanging by its barbed point.

Ki-Gor stood, balancing himself on Marmo's pitching head. He struck himself on the chest, and lifted his strongbow high, and his voice rose in a cry as it did that night on the ridge when he killed the great ape.

Fifty arrows and javelins were ready to be loosed, and out of such a shower it would be a miracle to ride unscathed. But his name seemed to take the fight momentarily out of them, and in these brief seconds of respite, the jungle man guided his elephant up the footpath to the large hut he correctly supposed was the hut of Chong.

He could have charged into the hut and left it a heap of tangled rubble, but he feared for Helene who might be inside.

He leaped to earth, tore the skin drape from the low doorway, and strode inside.

Helene screamed as she saw him. He could see her only vaguely as his eyes accustomed themselves to the gloom. She started for him—stopped. A man rose between them, a huge beast of a man with bowed legs and the chest of a gorilla. He had tripped and fallen, and his hand was clutching his chest, his fingers glistening with blood.

The man was Chong. Helene had struck him with her tiny, scarab dagger, but he was built on a more massive scale than most men, and the short blade had failed to reach his heart.

Chong looked at Helene with dull eyes, then he spun to face Ki-Gor. After a stunned moment, he realized who the god-like white man was.

"You!" he muttered through his heavy lips. "You—Ki-Gor!"

"Yes. I am Ki-Gor."

"Do not kill me!" he whined. "I am your friend. I will tell you of your enem. Durga-Rama. Listen while I tell——"

As he spoke, Chong backed slowly across the hut. He reached the wall, paused there, hands feeling behind him. Ki-Gor stood, waiting, with only his knife in his hand. His bow was on his shoulder, the arrows in the quiver. For the moment it appeared to the crafty Chong that he was quite helpless.

With a swift movement unexpected of a man of his weight, Chong whipped an assagai from the wall behind him, swung it high, and drove it at Ki-Gor's naked chest.

But Ki-Gor was ready for this snake-like move. He pivoted to one side, hitching his body from the way as the shaft fanned past and disappeared through the wall of the hut.

He pounced forward, knife lifted high. Chong could escape to neither side. The wall was at his back. He seemed prepared to meet the rush, then he flung himself backward, striking the heaped robes with his shoulders, legs doubled.

Ki-Gor stopped as Chong's legs uncoiled, but not in time to avoid their impact. They sank into his groin.

The blow was brutal, and for a moment the jungle man was staggered. He recovered his balance, and once more advanced. Chong was ready for him now. He had found a weapon, a native machete with a blade two feet long.

Chong swung the heavy knife with both hands gripping the handle as if it were an axe. But Ki-Gor was himself now. He shifted his body just enough to make the deadly stroke miss. In missing, Chong staggered off balance.

Ki-Gor pounced. His left arm was up as though to guard. The knife in his right hand was ready. Chong managed to regain his balance. He rolled the knife in his hands, and swung it back. Ordinarily that maneuver would have kept an assailant at a distance, but Ki-Gor moved with startling rapidity.

He avoided the knife's murderous point, and sprang, his left hand darting to seize Chong's wrist.

For the second, Chong was helpless as though in the grip of a steel trap. He wrenched once, and that was all the time that was given him. The knife swung up and descended with speed faster than sight.

Chong was struck. He rolled over his toes and plunged face foremost, raising a cloud of dust from the floor.

HE WAS DEAD as he fell, pierced through the heart. Ki-Gor looked at him without regret, without pity. He had killed through necessity, through the operation of the only law he understood—the law of the wild. He turned, and Helene ran to his arms, pressing her soft cheek against his chest, wetting his bronzed skin with tears of thankfulness.

"You are unharmed?" he asked.

"Yes, Ki-Gor."

The scarab dagger was still open in her hand. She closed its slim blade and slipped it inside her bodice.

"You stabbed him, Helene?"

"Yes."

"But you did not kill him." Ki-Gor smiled. "I am glad. I would not want even the blood of a swine on your hands."

He held her for a moment, then he put her away and stepped from the door of the hut. He had been inside for the time it takes to breathe sixty times, and the tribesmen had overcome their first amazed terror and were organizing themselves into a sort of army. In a few moments the air would be filled with their deadly little arrows, so it would be wise to leave quickly.

Marmo was waiting. Ki-Gor issued a command, and the great beast bent his knee for Helene. When she was safely on his back, Ki-Gor vaulted beside her.

The Ta'tamba warriors saw him and loosed their arrows at long range. Twenty or thirty of them had taken positions among the huts at the lower end of the village, waiting to fire their shafts as Ki-Gor and Helene rode by.

Marmo set off at a heavy gallop. For a while it seemed that Ki-Gor would take the beast directly through the deadly gauntlet, then he uttered a command, and Marmo turned sharply to the left.

Huts stood there in a solid line with scarcely room between them for a man to pass. Marmo did not hesitate. He charged directly at the nearest of them. He tossed his head and trunk high, smashing the flimsy structure. Ki-Gor pulled Helene flat beside him so as not to be swept off among falling debris. There was a crunch of rending bambo, a roll of dust from the moldy thatch, and the hut collapsed, with terrified natives darting away like ants from an uprooted hill.

Marmo went on, plunging shoulder deep in cane grass on the soft ground that separated yam fields and village. He trod deep ooze, swung back in the direction of the footpath.

At the edge of the village, warriors were dancing, waving assagais in impotent rage. One of them followed on the run, catching up as Marmo was slowed by the heavy ground. He dropped to one knee, and drove a poisoned arrow from his bow. Most of the Ta'tamba were pitiful in the use of bow and arrow, but this one, through skill or accident, fired straight toward Helene's back. With a rapid movement, Ki-Gor thrust his elephant-hide quiver in the arrow's path, and the leather stopped its vicious little point.

Ki-Gor balanced himself, set an arrow in the string of his strong-bow and shot the warrior through. He fell, threshing the earth in death-agony, and sight of him was sufficient to discourage the rest. In a few moments more, Marmo had carried them out of range. Brand and Ngeeso were waiting halfway across the fields. Ki-Gor paused for them, and continued at an easy pace toward the river.

X

DURGA-RAMA marched his Ta'tamba warriors directly to the river gate of Ramfis. No one seemed to note their approach. It was only a few strides from jungle to gate, and the gate was concealed from the rest of the town by his house and the collapsed arena.

There was no watchman on the gate. With the help of two brawny warriors he broke it down.

Once inside he could hear the sound of shouting men. A battle was in progress. He ran past the stockade of his house, and drew up suddenly as an arrow drove its head in a picket close beside him. He retreated in cover of the stockade, then climbed and thrust his head cautiously over its top to survey the scene.

Five of his black guardsmen and as many of the enemy force lay dead in the open space in front of the gate. There must have been a hand-to-hand struggle, after which the other guardsmen had taken refuge behind the stockade where they were standing off the attacking Ramfians with arrows.

He shouted a few words of instruction down to his barricaded men, and a cheer came from their throats. He had returned! They had been on the point of surrendering with a plea for mercy, but they had no thought of surrender now. To their minds, the leadership of Durga-Rama made them invincible.

Durga-Rama retraced his steps. He paused, hands on hips, to look at his Ta'tamba warriors who were chattering excitedly to one another, barely restraining the impulse to retreat. He quieted their tongues with a sweep of his arm. Beast that he was, he was a natural leader, otherwise he would never have secured a concerted attack from such a draggle-tailed army.

"Forward!" he bellowed. "Death to those few wretched ones hiding by the temple!"

His manner showed only contempt for the enemy. By his confidence the Ta'tambas assumed they had before them only the slaughter of a dozen or so. With sudden enthusiasm they shouted their war cries and rushed forward.

Durga-Rama waved them past. As they rushed into the open beyond the wall, his finely trained guardsmen emerged from hiding, whipping a sudden fury of arrows to keep the revolting army under cover.

The Ta'tambas swarmed along the path. The onslaught was unexpected. Liike's men, who had taken cover near the temple, saw them at the last moment, rose to meet them. Fighting was close, assagai against assagai. One of the cannibals, seeing it was not a slaughter of helpless men as he had anticipated, broke and ran. His action coud have caused a stampede among his fellows, but Durga-Rama saw the danger, leaped forward with a long stride, and cut the man in half with one mighty swing of his scimitar.

"Death to the man who retreats!" he bellowed.

The Ta'tamba feared him more than they did the enemy. In a moment the struggle had so engulfed them that the possibility of retreat no longer existed.

It was fight or die, and they fought like cornered rats. For a while it was thus, with the battle see-sawing.

Above the uproar, Durga-Rama could be heard ordering his guardsmen from the courtyard. They came running, and formed a close group, three abreast, as he had trained them. He waited the correct moment—the moment when the apex of the battle was reached, when a sudden onslaught would tip the balance one way or the other.

The moment came. His soldier's instinct perceived it. "Forward!" he cried.

His guardsmen came in a solid array, bristling with leveled assagais. They cut the battle in two segments, then turned and tore the heart from the Ramfian army. When the enemy tried to retreat to the temple of Isis, a group of archers who had formed the middle men of the column shot them down with a shower of arrows.

This completed the rout. Every man tried to save himself. Liike, the blind priest, was led from the door of his temple.

"After him! Death to the high-priest!" roared Durga-Rama.

A couple of his guardsmen charged around the temple, but they were cut down by javelins. A little group of brown men formed a knot around Liike, protecting him until they reached the far wall. Perhaps thirty of the revolting army reached that wall and escaped. They paused for a while, trying to reform a line, and then retreated slowly toward the protecting cover of the jungle.

Durga-Rama left an order for the wounded enemy to be executed, encamped the Ta'tamba forces in the native village, and posted his black guards along the walls, The city thus firmly in his control, he went to his quarters to refresh himself with wine.

He rested through the hot hours of afternoon with Panthra at his side, then he arose, annointed his massive body with civet perfume, and donned a robe of silk for which he had once traded two young female slaves to the Arabs of the north.

He looked at himself in a mirror of polished silver, and grunted satisfaction. He was handsome enough now to win the love of any woman. For a moment he regretted that it had been necessary to trade Helene to that swine of a cannibal chieftain, but a victim of Arlenna's young beauty came to console him. He smiled in contemplation. He had waited long for this day. He had watched Arlenna grow to womanhood, he had longed for her these many years, and now, this very afternoon, he would take her for wife.

He struck a triangular bronze gong four times, and Kadala, a big-boned slave woman, entered and bowed.

"Kadala, go to the house of Aknor, and tell them I would have you prepare their daughter, Arlenna, for the marriage feast."

"You would have me bring her here?" asked the woman in a coarse voice.

"My tepoi will meet her at the door of her house. She will be carried down the street of the native village as is the custom. We will drink the marriage cup in the temple. Then you will bring her here."

"Yes, my lord."

Durga-Rama issued more orders—orders for feasts to be prepared, orders for casks of wine to be opened in the native village. This completed, he paced the room, pausing frequently to look from the tiny, barred window at the house of Aknor.

ARLENNA had concealed herself in terror while the battle was going on. Finally her nurse, an old slave woman named Raga, came with word that the battle was over, and that Liike's forces had fled.

"I heard the voice of Durga-Rama—was he among the fallen?"

"No, he still rules the city."

Alenna was not cruel, but she prayed for the death of Durga-Rama. She detested the man and feared him. Many times she had dreamed of being made ready for marriage to Brend, but marriage to Durga-Rama seemed like a nightmare.

Raga patted her hand, "But your brother, Relknes, escaped."

This news brought Arlenna some assurance. She came from her room and passed the time by plucking the silken strings of a *kobnoor*.

There was a sound at the door, and Raga went to answer it. She ran back and looked at Arlenna with what seemed like terror in her eyes.

"Raga! What——"

"My child! It is now—today!"

"What are you talking about?"

"Kadala has come."

The significance of her words gave the girl a sinking feeling. Kadala's arrival could mean only one thing. The marriage would be this very evening. It would be Kadala's task to perfume her body, and make her ready for her master.

"No," said Arlenna, backing across the room. "Tell her I am not here——"

Raga shook her head. "No, child——"

"Save me, Raga. Keep her out there while I leave by the back way."

Raga hesitated. She feared Kadala, but she loved her young mistress.

"Go then. Run!"

Kadala strode to the draped door of the room. Raga seized her and tried to keep her from entering.

"You must wait——"

"I do not wait. I come from Durga-Rama, the king. Did I not hear the sound of a *kobnoor* being played?"

Kadal flung the old woman aside and strode in. She glimpsed the girl through the flimsy, bamboo partition and rushed after her. Kadala seized Arlenna by the wrist and led her in. The girl wept, and tried vainly to free herself, but Kadala's strength was like a man's.

Kadala was a slave, but not a slave in mind. She was strong, and domineering, as the leading slave of a tyrant is likely to be. She had Fulani blood, and hence considered herself superior to these brown men of Ramfis, and her bondage had turned that feeling into hatred. She especially hated this girl with her soft cheeks, and her eyes that seemed ready to dissolve into tears.

"You will come!" she said, bowing as a slave must. "I am here to make you ready for your marriage."

Arlenna tried to say something, but her throat was constricted and no words came. Kadala looked at her cotton robe.

"You cannot go to the tepoi of your lord in such a garment as that!"

Raga, the ancient slave, had fled. Kadala shouted until another slave woman appeared. "You! Tell me, has this girl no other robe than this thing of cotton? Has she no robe of purple so she will be made beautiful in the eyes of her new lord?"

"She has a robe of blue——"

"Then bring it! Bring it before I have the dogs of Durga-Rama turned loose on you. And when you return, bring also the oils of palm, and some scent of musk."

Arlenna stood with eyes closed as Kadala annointed her according to the Ramfian custom. Her hair was brushed with pulverized red mica until it sparkled with a thousand facets, then the blue robe was draped over her shoulders, fastened close around her throat.

The task finished, Kadala strode to the door to look for the tepoi. It stood on the ground with eight powerful blacks waiting to carry it on their broad shoulders.

The tepoi was large and ornate. It had a canopy of purple silk, curtains of white gauze. There were bangles and ornaments of copper and cowrie shells. Its handles were made of carved tusks.

Arlenna hestitated at the draped entrance, but Kadala followed, urging her. She lifted the curtain and crawled inside.

The interior was a couch, strewn with Arabian pillows. She sat for a while, but the ceiling was low, so she reclined on one arm. Things were visible through the white gauze as through a fog. She recognized the brown men who had not fled after the battle, she saw the blacks drunk on sweet wine, resplendent in barbaric finer.

The tepoi moved with a gently swaying motion as the blacks carried it along. It paused, and was lowered to the ground. She wondered why—then she saw Durga-Rama coming with long strides, sunlight flashing on his bright, silken robe.

He parted the curtains. She was conscious of his strength, of the massive bulk of him. She smelled the civet and oil with which he had smeared his body, and it made her sick. He came inside, and the drapery fell.

OUTSIDE, people were cheering, but the sound seemed far off, like a part of a nightmare. Arlenna forgot time and place. Her only sensations were fear coupled with loathing for the man who was lying, so close to her.

On one elbow he rested, body relaxed and moving easily with the swing of the tepoi. He looked at her for a while, then he reached with his broad hand, its width almost as great as Arlenna's slim body, and laid it on her shoulder.

"I treasure you even above my crown, Arlenna." He waited for an answer, but the girl merely lay there, fixing him with her wide eyes. "You are beautiful, Arlenna. You will be the first among all my wives. You will bear me a son, and that son will reign as king. It is a great honor to be the bride of Durga-Rama."

When still she said nothing, the usurper twisted his strong lips in a smile. "You have not caressed me, Arlenna."

"No!" she whispered. "Please——"

"I will wait. Soon the magic waters of the altar of Isis will touch our lips, meaning that we are mates."

The tepoi was carried to the edge of the native street, then borne back to the temple of Isis

Durga-Rama stepped from between its draperies, carrying Arlenna in his arms. He took her through the door toward the altar where incense was still smoldering though the priests had fled. He filled a golden chalice with water and held it to the girl's lips. She sipped once, and he quaffed the remainder. He slammed the chalice down and wiped his lips with the back of his hairy hand, and he looked at her with an added possessiveness. By this act, the ancient laws of Ramfis said she was his.

He bore her back to the tepoi and left her there. As the custom of Ramfis willed it, she would be taken to the rooms of her husband to wait, while he celebrated his marriage in flagons of wine with his chiefs.

The sun dropped from sight, and darkness crept in from the jungle, covering the city. There were not many of the brown men left, most of them having joined the rebellion, but these cheered the tyrant, and drank his health.

The drinking finished, he strode to the courtyard of his house.

There he paused to inspect his guardsmen. Ten of them were patrolling the stockade.

"There is need of extra caution," he said. "That coward army of Liike's may sneak back like jackals in the dark. Or perhaps Ki-Gor himself, looking for his mate whom I sold to the Tamtamba. Watch for them, and let no one disturb me. You hear?—no one!"

He climbed the stairway to his rooms. Panthra was guarding the door. The lion rose, fixing Durga-Rama with his savage eyes. Durga-Rama opened the door, taking the beast inside with him. He stood for a moment, looking around at the room as it was revealed by the flickering grease lamp. Arlenna was there in her robe of blue silk, sitting on the edge of a skin-covered pallet. He closed the door, dropped its bar of ironwood in place, looped Panthra's leash to a peg. Then, with heavy lips twisting in a smile, he advanced toward his bride.

"My dear!" he said, looking on her, "My dear, I have come to you. Do not fear. I can be cruel, but I can be gentle . . . to those who are beautiful . . ."

XI

CROCODILES still lay on mudbars, but they were too drugged by the heat of the afternoon to move when Ki-Gor and the others recrossed the river.

Ki-Gor called a halt at the far shore, and the party rested. Helene sat with her hand closed in the hand of her jungle mate. Today there was something bothering her, and Ki-Gor, with his keen perception, noticed it.

"What is it, Helene?" he asked.

"It is Brend," she said in a voice that the boy could not hear. "Have you forgotten that he is in love, too?"

"I have not forgotten. But neither can we fight Durga-Rama in the open, by ourselves. Tonight I will make another journey within the walls. Perhaps this time I will be able to plan a course of action with Liike."

For a time Ki-Gor lay stretched on a tree limb, sleeping in the manner he had grown used to when a boy. He awoke with long shadows creeping through the jungle. Helene and Brend had already made out a supper on bananas and a variety of small breadfruit they had found growing in a bower of okume trees. But such foods were not the kind to satisfy either Ki-Gor or the pigmy chieftain, Ngeeso. They shared a man's craving for meat, and in a few minutes hunt they had found it—a tiny, moloko antelope which Ki-Gor empaled on an arrow. They ate the fresh, red meat, and it gave them instant strength—lasting strength of the kind Ki-Gor well might need before that night was finished.

With shadows settling over the jungle footpath, they again made their way toward Ramfis.

As was their custom at such time, Marmo served to carry all except Ki-Gor, who ranged ahead, watching the jungle to make certain that no trap had been laid.

Ki-Gor had been gone for a considerable time, and Helene was lying on her back, watching the branches above, expecting momentarily to see him come dropping from nowhere, when suddenly Marmo came to a stop. Ki-Gor was standing in the path, holding an old woman by the wrist.

"Can you talk to this woman, Brend? I found her running from the direction of the city, and she will say nothing in a tongue I can understand."

"Raga!" cried Brend, sliding down Marmo's broad side. "Why, this is Raga, a slave in the home of Arlenna. Rago, do you recognize me? I am Brend!"

The old slave woman almost wept when she saw him. "They said you were dead. Durga-Rama told Arlenna you were dead . . ."

"But I am not dead. Here, I will let you see for yourself I am no scorcerer's vision. Feel my flesh, Raga!"

The old woman ran her dry hands over his arms, muttering tearfully all the time.

"What are you doing running through the jungle at night, Raga?"

"Aii! He has taken her from us!" she wailed. "That evil woman whose soul has been eaten by the *jin,* she came for her this afternoon——"

"Tell me the one she came for!"

"For Arlenna. That Kadala came, and said I must annoint Arlenna's body so she would be ready to go to Durga-Rama. The girl begged me to help her escape. I tried. I tried, Master, but that sorceress Kadala was waiting. She would have killed me. She would have thrown me to the hounds and had the flesh torn off my ancient bones had I not run from her. I crept from the gate while they were carrying out the bodies of those who fell in the fighting ——"

"Then there was a fight?" asked Ki-Gor who had now picked up the peculiarities of the slave tongue.

"There was a fight, Master!" she said, backing from fear of him, for she had seen him battle in the arena, and still regarded him as some strange avenging messenger of the gods.

Ki-Gor said, "There was a revolt, and Durga-Rama broke it with his own guards and a hundred of the Ta'tamba—is that not true?"

"Yes, Master!" she whispered, thinking him more than ever a god.

"Has the marriage feast been yet?"

"They would have now drunk the marriage potion."

"And Arlenna was to go to him immediately?"

"It is the custom for a bridegroom to drink wine with his warrior friends until nightfall."

"But nightfall is still not here!" said Ki-Gor grimly, his hand closing powerfully on his hunting knife. "Perhaps with the help of twilight and the gods, there is yet time."

"What is your plan?" asked Helene, sliding from the head of Marmo to stand beside him.

"We cannot give the maiden to that beast. I will go in alone——"

"Not alone, Ki-Gor. I cannot let——"

"Yes, alone. It is the safest way."

When he spoke in that manner, Helene had learned the futility of argument. She knew, too, that in such matters, Ki-Gor was invariably right.

He turned once again to the slave woman, "How many were killed in the battle?"

"Perhaps ten of Durga-Rama's men, and twenty of those who followed Liike."

"And how many of Liiffe's men escaped?"

"As many as the fingers and toes of two men."

"Forty. With the help of Marmo and myself, those forty should be enough."

"And me, Ki-Gor. Do not forget Ngeeso!" said the pigmy chief, trying the points of his sharp little arrows.

Ki-Gor nodded, "And *you,* my brave Ngeeso!"

"But they are gone!" wailed Raga, beating knuckles against her old, flat breast. "They are gone, and Ramfis is lost."

"Gone in what direction?"

"Across the fields toward the high ridge."

"Brend, you know the trails of this valley. You will go with us to the edge of the clearing. From there you will circle alone, and follow the trail left by the army of Liike. Helene and Ngeeso will stay in the jungle while I find an entrance to the city. With good fortune your army will return, and with the help of Marmo we can drive that hireling army of Ta'tamba cannibals into the river."

KI-GOR tossed Brend to Marmo's back, and in a few minutes they could see the big dancing fires of Ramfis through the gathering twilight. Tom-toms were beating, and voices came with a high-pitched chant, indicating that the blacks were celebrating the marriage of Durga-Rama. Several guards could be seen pacing back and forth along the wall surrounding Durga-Rama's house. Upstairs, lamplight shone with a reddish glow through a tiny, barred window.

In accordance with Ki-Gor's instructions, Bren started off at a swift trot to circle the clearing. Helene and Ngeeso waited beside Marmo. Even the mighty tusker seemed ill at ease, as though he, too, wondered how Ki-Gor would gain entrance without falling victim to the sharp assagais of Durga-Rama's guards.

Ki-Gor disappeared for a moment, then came in sight again on a branch above. He climbed higher and higher until he was close to the swaying top of the tallest baobab tree. There he found the vine he had fixed the evening of his first visit, and tested its strength.

With the end of it in his hand, Ki-Gor swung slowly, higher and higher, toward the wall, and far back in the bowers of the jungle. At the apex of his swing, he could have released his hold and sailed over the stockade wall of the brown men's city as he had done before, but tonight, with guards thick around Durga-Rama's courtyard wall, such a leap would not be sufficient. He must not only gain entrance to the city, the leap must place him on Durga-Rama's house itself.

He hesitated for a while, waiting for the twilight to thicken. When night descends, there is a flickering moment of neither light nor darkness, a moment when a man's eyes will tell him things he does not believe—a time when darkness in a heavy layer along the earth, with a flare of light still lingering along the western horizon. That was the moment for which Ki-Gor waited.

The moment came. He leaned forward, judging the course of his swing. His feet left the branch. Down he went, the vine swinging through air. He was an uncertain blur through darkness as he lifted his legs at the bottom of the arc to avoid the tops of low bushes. He swung up and out, far over the wall. With timing developed by years of jungle travel, he judged the exact fraction of time, and relaxed his hold. He seemed poised, a dim object against the dim sky, then he plummeted down, and his feet touched the thatch-covered ridge-pole of Duga-Rama's house as silently as the velvet paws of a leopard.

Ki-Gor moved stealthily along the ridgepole, shifting his weight as though the house were some delicate scale, and he feared tipping its balance. It was not the sound of his passage across the soft thatch which he feared would be noticed below—it would be bits of grass sifting down to tell of his movement.

He found the place through which he forced his way the evening before. It had not been patched. A ragged bit of light showed from Durga-Rama's rooms. He laid full length, peering down. Nothing was visible except an area of floor covered by woven raffia mats, but he could hear sounds of footsteps approaching along the stairs, the complaining squeak of wooden hinges as the door opened. Something about these sounds told him it was Durga-Rama who had entered.

Ki-Gor heard the sudden drawing in of Arlenna's breath. Then Durga-Rama again,

"Do not fear me, my dear."

Ki-Gor could tell by the shadows that she was retreating from him.

He lowered his head and shoulders through the opening in the thatch, and for the first time caught sight of Durga-Rama and the girl. He had seized her by the wrists, and twisted until her lovely young face was drawn with pain. She sank kneeling before him.

Panthra snarled, and slammed the end of his leash, his nostrils having warned him that Ki-Gor was near. The sound broke Durga-Rama's preoccupation. Still gripping the girl's wrist, he turned to see what had disturbed the lion. Ki-Gor knew he must act.

He went head foremost through the roof, caught a bamboo beam flipping himself over in the air so that he landed on his feet, crouching.

Durga-Rama snapped the girl by her arm, flinging her at Ki-Gor. It was a brutal, unexpected movement.

Durga-Rama seized a long-handled battle-axe and swung it high.

KI-GOR had no time to draw his knife. He moved close. The axe swung past his head, he caught the handle on his shoulder. With a quick movement, he seized the big man by wrist and the front of his robe, lifted him overhead, and hurled him across the room.

Arlenna screamed, eyes on the door. Ki-Gor saw the lion at the same instant. He had cut his leash with his teeth, and had launched himself into air, fangs bared for Ki-Gor's throat.

They collided with the wall, and Ki-Gor went down with Panthra straddling him.

Ki-Gor kept his grip on the lion's throat. Their strength was balanced. Then slowly, by infinitesimal degrees, the jungle man's superb muscles made themselves felt.

Ki-Gor thrust the lion back to the length of his arms. With a twisting motion, he rolled over. He snatched his knife that had fallen to the matting, crouched, the blade ready.

Panthra let out a raging snarl. He located Ki-Gor, and did not hesitate. He sprang again, and quick as a released arrow, the knife came around.

Ki-Gor leaped, straddling his back. He braced his legs, lifting the animal in the air. His knife swung up and descended. Panthra stiffened, and then fell backward at the feet of the jungle man, blood coming in rapid spurts from the wound.

Durga-Rama had now risen to one knee. The scimitar was in his right hand, his eyes were on Ki-Gor. He twisted his lips in a smile, keeping his little swine eyes on the knife in Ki-Gor's hand.

"We will throw aside our weapons as I count thrice, agreed?"

"It is agreed."

At the word "three" he made a movement as though to toss away the long scimitar. His quick, crafty eyes saw Ki-Gor's knife start through the air. But instead of dropping his own weapon, Durga-Rama merely let it roll in his hand, and then recaptured it with a practiced motion.

One step Durga-Rama advanced—two. The time was right. He sprang, swinging the scimitar with a horizontal stroke—the same powerful stroke that had chopped the retreating Ta'tamba completely in half that afternoon.

But Ki-Gor was no longer there. He had vanished like some genie seen in a witch-doctor's fire. The scimitar sang through the air, its heavy weight whipping Durga-Rama around.

He fought for balance, and he saw Ki-Gor, crouched, hand between his knees, gripping the knife.

Durga-Rama backed towards the door. Triumph had left his eyes. There was only fear there now—the primeval fear of death. He reached behind him for the ironwood bar, but Ki-Gor moved, and Durga-Rama dashed along the wall to avoid him.

"Help me!" he bellowed to his guards. "Hear me down there! A white devil you have let in! Break the door and help me!"

Men commenced shouting below. Bare

feet thudded the stairs, assagai points rattled along the wall. Someone tried the door and found it barred.

"Break in the door, you fool!" bellowed Durga-Rama, moving along the wall like a caged hyena. "It is Ki-Gor! Dropped down on me from the roof while you dogs were sleeping."

More guardsmen were coming. Ki-Gor could hear them jabbering to one another. They flung themselves against the door, but for the moment its timbers held firm.

An assagai stood against the wall. Ki-Gor seized it, held it poised. Durga-Rama, believing it was to be hurled at him, plunged for cover. Ki-Gor laughed. He would not kill the man with an assagai. It would be too easy. He would kill him with the knife. Instead he aimed the shaft at the door.

That assagai stopped the others from smashing the door, but they could fire poisoned arrows through the rent it had torn. Durga-Rama was still on the move. He saw his chance as Ki-Gor leaped to avoid an arrow, and charged, swinging the scimitar like an axe.

For a fragment of time Ki-Gor caught the blade on the guard of his knife. He stepped aside as the scimitar swung toward the floor. Then he leaped in, striking for Durga-Rama's heart.

Durga-Rama saw the blow coming. He twisted a trifle, trying to avoid it. The blade struck, but it missed his heart. He let fall the scimitar and reeled across the room, clutching his breast.

Ki-Gor did not stop to finish him. No time for that. The black guard saw his shoulder turned and commenced smashing in the door. He saw Arlenna, held his arm for her. She came to him. For a moment he held her close against his perfect body, and he could feel her sweet, warm breath against his arm. Then he sprang, reached a rafter, and swung with the skill of a great ape, hooking it with his legs, still holding the girl with one arm.

Panthra, his life blood pumping away through the chest wound, dragged himself up, his untamed eyes fastening themselves on Durga-Rama.

Durga-Rama had captured him as a cub. Through fear, the lion had come to recognize him as master. He paid him obedience that the man mistook for love. But there is no space for love in the heart of a great cat. Durga-Rama was down with warm blood flowing between his fingers, and he was master no longer. The hate that had always lurked in Panthra's heart flamed now unchecked. With his final resource of strength, he sprang, setting his terrible fangs in Durga-Rama's unprotected throat.

Ki-Gor swung close to the ridgepole, helping the girl through the roof opening. Flames were already turning the room into a furnace. They roared with new draught as the guardsmen smashed open the door.

Then from the edge of the jungle came the high-pitched trumpeting of Marmo—the charging cry of the African bull elephant.

Ki-Gor waited as flames licked closer, holding the girl so her body would be protected from arrows. It was a few seconds before the guardsmen realized what was thundering towards them. The outer stockade crashed beneath Marmo's avalanche of muscle. Light from the burning house shone on his sweeping tusks.

At that moment, with every eye drawn away, Ki-Gor lifted the girl and sprang to earth. He placed her behind him, whipped the strong-bow from his shoulder, and drove arrows in a deadly stream as guardsmen fell over one another to escape the wrath of Marmo.

Ki-Gor caught Marmo by one of his fan-like ears. The beast stopped. Helene and Ngeeso were on his back, and he wanted them to take no chance with poisoned arrows from the guards who had fled to the native village.

The house became a torch, sending its flames higher and higher. Then it slumped, and as quickly became only a heap of coals.

Brend came a few minutes later, leading Liike's army at a swift trot. His men paused a few strides distant, still fearing the White Lord although Brend called him friend.

"Arlenna? What of Arlenna? You have saved her . . .?"

"We have saved her, and the usurper is dead. I think you will have little more trouble in Ramfis."

THE SUMMER'S NEW & IMPROVED PULP CON!

PULPFEST 2010

JULY 30–AUG 1

RAMADA PLAZA HOTEL
& CONFERENCE CENTER
Columbus, Ohio

Western Story Magazine

CAPTAIN FUTURE

BLACK MASK

Featuring

WILLIAM F. NOLAN
"LOGAN'S RUN" CO-CREATOR & "THE BLACK MASK BOYS" EDITOR

90 YEARS OF BLACK MASK MAGAZINE
OF MAX BRAND AT WESTERN STORY

+ THOUSANDS OF YOUR FAVORITE PULP MAGAZINES!
+ PAPER COLLECTIBLES! HARDCOVERS, PAPERBACKS, MOVIE POSTERS, ART and VINTAGE COMICS
+ EXPANDED DEALER ROOM & PROGRAMMING! MORE PULPS, MORE PANELS, MORE EVERYTHING!

VISIT PULPFEST.COM FOR MORE INFORMATION, REGISTRATION AND UPDATES

OR FURTHER INFO OR TO BE ADDED TO OUR MAILING LIST, PLEASE WRITE TO JACK CULLERS,
72 CHEATHAM WAY, BELLBROOK, OH 45305 • OR VIA EMAIL AT JACK@PULPFEST.COM

Ki-Gor clutched at the man-ape's furry throat. He swung the dagger up, tried to ram it home. But the ape snorted a rasping oath and kept boring in. Suddenly, Helene screamed . . .

Nirvana Of The Seven Voodoos

By John Peter Drummond

No broken, haunted captive lived to flee the jackal-born terrors of Nirvana—where Krishna, the strange, gleaming-eyed scientist, ruled with the dread hand of ancient gris-gris. And yet Ki-Gor dared enter that forbidden kraal, dared try to wrest Helene from its secret power—and even dared challenge the proud, half-human ape-men to one last, hopeless battle . . .

INCH BY INCH, THE GIANT figure in the leopard skin crept forward through the waving prairie grass. The fierce tropical sun beat down mercilessly on the mighty shoulders, but a fresh easterly breeze cooled the bronze forehead. Ki-Gor froze momentarily and hugged the ground, as a chorus of snorts and the thud of many sharp hoofs stamping the turf told him that the quarry he was stalking was getting uneasy. Ki-Gor cursed the inadequate little spear beside him, his sole weapon. It was a small, flimsy assegai the Pygmies had given him, and it was all but useless in the important business of hunting game. Not heavy enough to throw, not strong enough to kill anything bigger than a jackal.

But, weapon or not, game had to be killed today. Ki-Gor was hungry. His nostrils twitched and his mouth watered as the breeze bore to him the scent of his prey, the herd of white-throated gnu—wildebeeste—the giant antelope of the East African plateau. With infinite caution he raised his head and peered through the swaying grass tops. Fifteen feet away, a young, full-grown buck stared suspiciously upwind toward the rest of the herd. He was nearly five feet tall at his thick shoulders, and the coarse, matted hairs of his mane fell over but did not conceal the cruel horns that dipped downward from his forehead, then upward and outward.

It was going to be no easy task to subdue this creature barehanded, but Ki-Gor was desperate. He and Helene had not eaten meat for over a week, ever since they had left the friendly back of Marmo, the elephant, at the edge of the Congo jungle to trek on foot, ever eastward through the grassy uplands of East Africa. There had been game in plenty, but Ki-Gor had been remarkably unlucky in his hunting. Five times he had patiently stalked plump gazelles, only to be cheated out of his prey at the last minute by roving packs of wild dogs. On two other occasions, he had lain hidden, after dark, beside water-holes, hoping to make a kill undisturbed by the dogs who would be asleep. But each of those times he had found himself dangerously close to a half dozen lions, who apparently had the same idea. That many lions was too much competition, and Ki-Gor had gone back to Helene empty-handed, and with a very empty stomach.

Hardly breathing, Ki-Gor slid forward another six inches through the grass. He must get that buck. For if he and Helene did not eat pretty soon, they would be so weakened from fasting, that they, too, would fall prey to some prowling carnivores, and their bones would bleach on the wind-swept veldt. Closer and closer to the gnu, the jungle man crept. If only I had a fire-stick, Ki-Gor thought—rifles, Helene calls them. They have a potent magic which kills at incredible distances. But he had no rifle, only the toy spear of the Pygmies, so that he must be close enough to the gnu to be able to reach it in one spring. Once the herd discovered him, even his powerful legs could never overtake them.

Closer and closer, Ki-Gor crept, muscles tensed for action. Suddenly, the herd upwind of him grew ominously silent. Something had disturbed the gnus. Was it he? Had they discovered him? Again, he raised his head to peer through the grass stalks. No, it wasn't he the antelopes were worried about. They were all facing away from him, muzzles raised, testing the air. A few does danced about nervously, ready at any second to break into a headlong gallop. Ki-Gor decided it was now or never.

Gathering his feet under him, he crouched on his haunches for one precious moment. Then, noiselessly, he sprang. As he did, the entire herd jumped forward. Ki-Gor's leap carried just short of the young buck's back—and the buck was going away. Desperately, Ki-Gor clutched at a flying hind hoof, and held on for dear life. The buck went down with a crash. Instantly Ki-Gor leaped for its head and seized a horn with each hand. The buck lunged upward, sharp hoofs scrambling. The horns were levers in Ki-Gor's hands. Using all his mighty strength, he twisted the shaggy head viciously around. There was a tearing sound, and a snap. The gnu sank to the ground trembling—its neck broken.

"Wa-a-aghrr!" shouted Ki-Gor in triumph. At last! Here was food—meat, a plenty.

"Wa-a-aghrr!" came an almost identical roar from behind him.

KI-GOR whirled around and beheld a huge, grey-maned lion crouched not twenty feet away. Its dull eyes and gaunt, mangy sides showed it to be a very old lion, slow-moving and probably toothless. Back home in the jungle, the aged beast would have presented no problem to Ki-Gor. But here on the veldt, there was no cover, and Ki-Gor's only weapon against those great raking claws, was the Pygmy spear.

The brute looked hungry. Evidently it had been unable to knock down any of the gnus as they galloped to safety, and now it intended to take Ki-Gor's prize away from him. Stealthily Ki-Gor picked up the light spear and gripped it. Hungry man and hungry beast glared at each other across the fallen body of the gnu.

Then, with a strangled roar, the old lion sprang. Ki-Gor poised—waiting. And, as the lion hit the ground in front of him, Ki-Gor jammed the spear down the red, gaping maw. At the same time, he made a twisting leap, just missing a murderous swipe from a heavy front paw. The lion thrashed its great head in agony, and quickly snapped the slender haft in two. But the spearhead remained imbedded far down the beast's gullet. A torrent of blood poured out of the lion's mouth, and it staggered away, coughing and shaking its head.

Ki-Gor watched it until it disappeared in the tall grass, then he turned his attention back to the motionless form of the gnu. He knelt down with a smile of satisfaction. It was a fat young buck. Its meat would not be tender, eaten fresh, but it would have a fine flavor, and it would be nourishing. Ki-Gor debated with himself whether to attempt to carry the big antelope back to the camp where he had left Helene, or whether to cut it up on the spot. A foreleg in each hand, he tested the weight of the animal. He shook his head. Strong as he was, it would be too great a load to carry the distance of over a mile.

Suddenly, the smile of satisfaction died off Ki-Gor's bronzed face, to be replaced by an expression of troubled concern. How was he going to cut it up? He could have used the blade of the Pygmy spear to carve off some slabs of meat from the gnu's flanks, but—the blade of the Pygmy spear was far down the throat of the dying lion! Ki-Gor kicked petulantly at the body of the gnu. After all his patience and his care in bringing down the antelope, he was now to be cheated out of eating it. So near, and yet so far.

His lips drawn back in a snarl, Ki-Gor reached down and once more seized the animal's forelegs. Whether he could cut it up or not, he wasn't going to leave it behind for the dogs or the lions to eat. He heaved upward and rolled the animal over. As he did, he saw something glint in the antelope's thick mane—something which reflected the sunlight. A brown hand swiftly explored the thick, matted hairs behind the horns. With a shout of triumph, Ki-Gor extricated a flat piece of metal. It was the wide, shovel-shaped blade of a Bantu assegai. A few splinters of wood in the hollow socket at the rear end told the story. Some black hunter had had much the same experience as Ki-Gor had had with the lion. Except that in this case, the blade of the spear, instead of piercing the thick hide of the gnu, had merely become caught in the thick tangle of hair in the creature's head. The antelope had got away, carrying the spear in it mane, and eventually the haft had worked loose, or broken off.

Ki-Gor wasted no time conjecturing about what had happened to the haft of the spear, however. He whetted both edges of the broad blade, energetically, on a smooth stone, until he had them razor-sharp. Then he set to work skinning the antelope, after which he began carving great strips of meat from its sides. As he cut each slab free, he placed it on the spread out hide. When he had finished, he gathered up the ends of the skin, slung the bundle over one shoulder, and headed across the veldt toward a thin column of smoke which represented his camp. In the antelope-hide bundle there was over twenty pounds of meat.

Helene Vaughn looked up with a quick cry, as Ki-Gor walked into the little thicket where she was crouching over a little fire. She was carefully feeding it twigs to keep it alive.

"Ki-Gor!" she exclaimed, "You brought home something!"

"Yes," said Ki-Gor, subduing a complacent smile that rose to his mouth. "See? Meat. Antelope." And he dropped the bundle on the ground beside Helene.

"Oh! Ki-Gor, that's wonderful," she said, in heartfelt tones, "I can hardly believe we're actually going to eat meat again. Did you have much trouble?"

"No trouble" said Ki-Gor loftily. "It

was easy. There was a lion, but it was a very old lion."

"Oh, dear!" Helene sighed, "I suppose if I stayed in Africa long enough, I'd get used to the casual way you treat leopards and lions and things. But right now, it scares me out of my wits just to think of it."

"I'm strong," Ki-Gor said, simply, as if that explained everything.

"You certainly are Ki-Gor" Helene said, with an appreciative glance at the jungle man's magnificent shoulders, "but just the same, I'm glad you have agreed to come back to your own people with me."

KI-GOR got up abruptly and busied himself with preparations for the long-deferred meal. He didn't like to be reminded of his promise to leave the jungle and go with Helene to find some outpost of civilization, whence they could be guided to the coast and eventually to England. Up till a few weeks ago, Ki-Gor's world had been peopled only by the wild animals, the savage Bantu tribes, and the occasional Pygmies of Africa's Equatorial Forest. He knew that he was somehow different from the black men and the Pygmies but as far as he knew, he was unique. Only the dimmest memory of his missionary father remained to him, and through childhood and youth he had defended himself single-handed, and by his strength and intelligence, survived.

Then one day, Helene Vaughn fell out of the sky practically at his feet. Her red hair, white face, and strange clothes were just as incomprehensible to him, as the red monoplane which she was flying, and which had cracked up. But, instinctively he protected her, even though he didn't know quite why. Gradually Helene's conversation had brought back the English he had once spoken as a little boy, before his father had been slain by a tribe of Bantu. With the bridge of a common language established, Helene had explained to him the astonishing facts that there were many people in the world like him, that they lived far away across the water, and that he belonged to the tribe called English. After days of argument and pleading, Helene had persuaded him to go to his own people, although he was mightily distrustful of the idea, and would have much preferred to stay in his jungle home—provided, of course, that Helene stayed with him. But, in a weak moment, he had given in to Helene's pleadings, and now here they were, camped in a little copse on the veldt—on their way to his own people.

The setting sun hung low as Ki-Gor held strips of antelope meat on a forked stick over the little fire. He was already a little homesick for the dark, brooding jungle. A man knew where he stood back there, with great friendly trees to climb, and yards of strong vines to swing on from one tall trunk to another. Out here there was only the thorn boma, and the fire to protect them from the nocturnal prowlers, and with sunset there came an uncomfortable chill in the air.

But the meat was good. Ki-Gor and Helene thrust strip after strip in the open flames, and devoured them hungrily. Finally, Helene gave up with a happy sigh, and lay back feeling stuffed. But Ki-Gor kept on. He was making up for a lot of meatless days, and like all men of the jungle, he gorged himself.

The sun had long since set, and the sudden African night had settled down over the veldt, when he reluctantly discovered that he couldn't eat another mouthful. He got up with an effort and scoured around collecting a supply of fuel to last through the night. It was an ominous night, moonless and even starless. Even his keen eyes were unable to see far into the inky blackness outside the ring of fire light. The back of his neck crawled uneasily. It was a night to be especially alert for unwelcome visitors, and yet his eyes were uncontrollably heavy. Drowsy though he was, he arranged the thorn boma with great care, and stocked the fagots close to the fire. Helene was already sound asleep. He stood for a moment looking down at her upturned face. He recalled an English word she had used several times, when together they had watched a rosy sun come up in the east and shed its warming rays over a calm world. She had said it was "beautiful." Then you, Helene, Ki-Gor said to himself, you are beautiful—like the sunrise.

He squatted on his haunches beside her, and tried to keep himself awake by whittling a handle for the assegai blade. Presently, in the middle of a stroke, his head nodded and fell forward. Still squatting on his haunches he fell into a deep sleep.

He woke up with a guilty start and stared around him into the impenetrable blackness of the night. What had made him wake up, he didn't know. But a deep-seated sixth sense within him told him that somewhere in the darkness, some unseen danger was lurking. The little fire was almost out, only a few embers left glowing redly. Without relaxing his watchful glare, Ki-Gor reached out and dropped some dry fagots on the coals. In a few seconds a rewarding flicker of flame mounted and lighted up the ground inclosed by the boma. Helene stirred and turned her face away, but did not wake up. With the increased light, Ki-Gor peered carefully in all directions but could see nothing. He tested the still night air with his sensitive nostrils. He thought he caught a faint whiff of a familiar smell, but he was inclined to disbelieve the evidence of his nose. It was gorilla-smell.

IT couldn't be gorilla, Ki-Gor told himself. The only place he had ever seen gorillas was far away on the West Coast. And during the last ten days, as he and Helene had trekked eastward toward the great mountains of East Africa, he had not come across the slightest evidence that pointed to the presence of the giant apes. He tested the air again, but the elusive smell had gone. Ki-Gor stood up and stared out into the night.

Suddenly his keen eyes caught a faint glitter of reflected light. Somewhere out there, a pair of cruel eyes were watching the boma. Quickly, Ki-Gor piled more fagots on the fire, and as the flames leaped higher, he strained forward trying to make out the outlines of the creature that belonged to that pair of eyes. After a few seconds, he was able to distinguish a huge mass from the surrounding darkness. Whatever the animal was, it was enormous. Suddenly the mass moved, and slowly approached the fire. The blood ran cold in Ki-Gor's veins. It was a gorilla!

Ki-Gor reached down, shook Helene's shoulder roughly, and seized the blade of the assegai. He wished with all his heart that he had finished making a haft for it.

Slowly and purposefully, the gorilla moved forward, until he stood right at the edge of the boma. As the firelight illuminated his hairy outlines, he looked to be by far the biggest gorilla Ki-Gor had ever seen. And then suddenly it struck Ki-Gor that this was no ordinary gorilla. This hulking creature looked man-like, and yet at the same time, subtly more bestial than a true gorilla. His little eyes glittering wickedly, the man-ape seemed strangely unafraid.

A frightened gasp from behind him told Ki-Gor that Helene was awake.

"Ki-Gor!" she whispered, "What does that monster want?"

"I don't know," Ki-Gor muttered, "but don't be 'fraid. Maybe he wants antelope meat."

Ki-Gor bent down without taking his eyes off the gorilla-man, and tossed a slab of meat past his head. The gorilla-man paid no attention. And then as Ki-Gor straightened up, the fang-toothed beast deliberately picked up one of the loose thorn bushes that made up the encircling boma, and flipped it expertly aside. As Ki-Gor gazed in astonishment, another bush went the same way, and the gorilla-man shuffled confidently through the opening straight toward the fire.

His spine prickling, Ki-Gor stepped back a pace and shifted his grip on the assegai blade. Then, with a wild yell, he leaped high into the air and forward. He launched a mighty kick with both of his powerful legs straight at the gorilla-man's murderous face. The gorilla-man grunted with the force of the pile-driver blow and rocked backwards on its heels.

Ki-Gor landed lightly on his feet and instantly struck with the assegai blade in his right hand. It was a lightning thrust, the sharp blade slashing at the monster's throat. The gorilla-man backed away with a growl and swung a thick, hairy arm with incredible speed. But Ki-Gor dodged the crushing blow, and countered with his blade at the vast abdomen. The beast howled with rage and pain and backed out of the boma. A thin trickle of blood began to flow from the folds of its throat.

Stealthily, Ki-Gor reached down and seized one end of a long fagot, the other end of which was blazing in the fire. With a swift motion, he flung the burning brand straight at the gorilla-man's head. Again the cruel-faced beast gave ground with a howl, and frantically brushed off the flaming fagot.

As he did, Ki-Gor charged him. Twice the sharp blade bit deep into the hairy arm, and again Ki-Gor dodged out of reach. But the man-ape appeared to have had enough. Growling horribly, he retreated to the edge of the ring of light shed by the camp-fire. There he stopped and slowly beat his breast. Ki-Gor walked coolly toward him, and the gorilla-man turned and ran out into the darkness.

Determined to be rid of the beast for good, Ki-Gor gave chase. But the gorilla-man was amazingly fast, and before he had gone very far, his massive body was swallowed up in the inky blackness of the night. Ki-Gor stopped about a hundred yards from the camp and stood listening. A distant thudding told him that the beast was still running.

Ki-Gor turned reluctantly, and started back to the camp.

Suddenly a wild scream rent the air. It was Helene.

"Ki-Gor! Ki-Gor! The gorilla!"

A HUNDRED yards away, by the light of the camp-fire, a mammoth figure was carrying the struggling girl out of the boma. A wave of sick horror swept over Ki-Gor, and he sprinted toward the camp-site. How could I have been so stupid! Ki-Gor thought bitterly. Apparently the gorilla-man had circled away in the darkness, and returned to kidnap poor helpless Helene. Faster the jungle man's feet flashed over the turf. The man-ape was running too, in the opposite direction—with a terrified, shrieking Helene under a hairy arm.

Sobbing with rage, Ki-Gor put all his strength into an effort to catch up with the brutish abductor. But the man-ape had a few seconds head-start, and by the time Ki-Gor flashed by the camp-fire, was out of sight in the velvet blackness of the night.

Ki-Gor drew up short and controlled his panting long enough to listen. Ominously, Helene had stopped screaming. But the sound of feet drumming over the ground gave Ki-Gor an approximate direction the beast was taking. He plunged forward.

Full fifteen minutes Ki-Gor ran, stopping now and then to listen and to sniff the air. But the thud of the gorilla-man's feet seemed to come from different directions each time, and the still air. heavy with the rank ape-smell, gave no clue as to which way the monster had gone. It was like looking for a needle in a haystack, to find anything in the pitch dark of the plateau.

Finally, Ki-Gor had to admit that the gorilla-man had—temporarily, at least—escaped him. He sat down on the grass, for a moment, to think. What was to be done? And what was happening to Helene? Why had her screams stopped so abruptly? Was it because—Ki-Gor hardly dared ask himself the question—was it because the giant ape had killed her? Ki-Gor ground his teeth, and growled savagely, deep down in his throat.

Suddenly, a tiny puff of wind caressed the hair at his temples. Ki-Gor sprang to his feet, nerves taut, and sniffed it avidly. Faintly, there came to his nostrils a woodsy smell, the smell of trees. More faintly still came the gorilla-smell. Ki-Gor loped upwind. He knew he was going north-east, toward a towering range of mountains, whose slopes were covered by the only trees in any direction. Ki-Gor had noticed that before the sun had set. Undoubtedly, the man-ape was traveling that way. It was the type of high open forestland that gorillas liked.

Ki-Gor pushed on steadily and swiftly through the night, following the elusive ape-smell. But, as the minutes went by, he seemed to come no nearer to the object of his pursuit.

Gradually, the outlines of a mountain range began to take shape, ahead of him and to his right. Almost imperceptibly, the sky began to grow a little paler, and the darkness all about, to dissolve. Ki-Gor found that the grass was giving way to tall shrubs, and that here and there, tall trees reared skyward. He kept on, upwind and upgrade.

After a while there was enough light for him to see the ground fairly clearly. The jungle man then turned abruptly to his left, and began a wide circle, eyes to the ground, studying out possible gorilla tracks. For an hour he traveled that way without discovering the spoor he was searching for. He returned to his starting place and commenced another wide circle to the right. Still, there were no gorilla-man tracks, and Ki-Gor hurried his steps, sick with disappointment and apprehension. His mind was so clouded with fear for Helene's safety that he almost didn't see the twig broken off the flowering shrub close to the ground.

But, all of a sudden, the slight gorilla smell seemed to increase. Ki-Gor stopped and studied the ground around him. Then he saw the broken twig, and dropped to the ground beside it. A moment later, he stood up, his upper lip drawn back off his teeth in a silent snarl.

Unquestionably, the gorilla-man had passed that way.

Swiftly the jungle man followed the spoor, eyes glued to the ground, nostrils flared. In a very short time, he realized that not one gorilla-man had made that track, but two!

That was how Helene's kidnapping had been accomplished! The first ape had decoyed Ki-Gor away from the camp long enough for the second one to rush into the boma and carry off the girl. The jungle man gripped the blade of the assegai, vengefully, and hastened on.

The sky was rosy with approaching dawn, and the upgrade was getting steeper, when Ki-Gor halted. He had made another uncomfortable discovery. The trail of the two gorilla-men had separated, going each in a different direction. The jungle man was face to face with a horrible dilemma. One of those two half-human animals was bearing the limp form of Helene—*but which one?*

Ki-Gor could do no more than guess which trail to follow. He chose the one which went straight up the mountain side, and quickened his steps.

II

HE was rewarded, in a short time, by a noticeable strengthening of ape-smell in the air. Apparently the giant gorilla-man had grown careless of pursuit, and was loitering along, picking nuts and fruit along the way. Ki-Gor raced uphill in an agony of suspense. Would he be in time? Was Helene still alive? Was this the man-ape who had kidnapped her?

The sun was coming up red, as Ki-Gor halted on the edge of an open space on the mountain side. His heart sank. Upwind of him, sitting in the middle of the open space was a gorilla-man. But nowhere was there any sign of Helene. He had followed the wrong beast.

A burning desire for revenge swept over Ki-Gor. If this shaggy monster had not actually abducted Helene it had at least assisted in the operation, and Ki-Gor determined that it should die for it.

He crept closer to the great man-ape, unnoticed.

The gorilla-man was sitting, shoulders hunched apathetically, licking a fore-arm. The coarse hairs of its chest and abdomen were caked with dried blood. Evidently it was the same animal that Ki-Gor had fought the night before.

Relentlessly, Ki-Gor crept forward, until he was behind the gorilla-man, though still down-wind from him. Then, silently, he sprang.

The weight of his body hitting the gorilla-man's back flung it face-forward on the ground. He pounced on the thick hairy brute stood up unsteadily on its hind legs gai blade. The beast heaved and screamed with pain, and reached a huge black hand over its shoulder. Ki-Gor was plucked off and hurled twenty feet away, as if he were a terrier.

He lay stunned for a moment, then began to collect his senses as the gorilla-man slowly reared itself off the ground. The brut stood up unsteadily on its hind legs for a moment, gave a terrible roar, and started toward Ki-Gor's recumbent form. But, blood was gushing from the wound in the neck, and its short legs suddenly buckled. Before it could reach the helpless Ki-Gor, the gorilla-man's evil little eyes glazed, and it wavered and fell in a crumpled heap.

Ki-Gor picked himself up, made sure none of his bones were broken, and approached the fallen gorilla-man warily. There was no doubt about it, the strange monster was stone dead, its jugular severed. In death it looked more simian than in life.

The jungle man's blue eyes flashed. He uttered a bellow of triumph, and started back down the man-ape's trail. He was going back to pick up the spoor of the other monster, the one who was carrying off Helene.

But his triumph was short-lived. His nose was assailed by a strong smell of Bantu. A moment later he was surrounded by a dozen or more tall, well-formed blacks, armed with broad-bladed assegais.

"Stay, O strange inkosi," said the tallest one in halting Swahili, "and tell us how it is possible that you could thus slay the fearsome brute, single-handed and without a fire-stick."

"Nay, stand aside, black men," Ki-Gor answered, "I have no time for idle chatter. There yet is another gorilla-man I must slay—a murdering beast that is carrying off my woman. I must find him before he kills her—if he has not already done so."

"Indeed, inkosi," said the tribesman, "that is a dreadful story. This other gorilla-man, then, is not far away?"

"That I do not know," said Ki-Gor, "I must first pick up his trail which I left before sunrise. So, let me pass."

"Nay, inkosi," said the tall black, "if the gorilla-man bearing your woman has that much of a head-start, then indeed, you are on a fool's errand."

"What do you mean, black man?" said Ki-Gor, sternly, "I will catch him and I will kill him, as you have seen me do with this other ape up the hill."

"It is this way, inkosi," the tribesman said patiently, "when you catch up with the man-ape bearing your woman, you will find not one man-ape but hundreds. By now, he has undoubtedly carried her into the Land of the Living Dead. The entrances to that Land are guarded by hordes of these ferocious gorilla-men. And it is said that these man-apes, furthermore, are not wild man-apes, but trained beasts who obey the wicked commands of some mysterious human."

"O cowardly black man," said Ki-Gor, "chicken-hearted Bantu, why do you tell me old woman's stories like that? There is no slightest word of truth in what you say!"

"I am no chicken-hearted coward," replied the tribesman, stoutly, "I am as brave as you, O strange inkosi, and I tell you truth. Many from about here have been kidnapped by these hulking gorilla-men and carried into the Valley on the other side of the mountain. If you do not believe me come with us in friendly fashion, back to our village. Our chief speaks N-glush fluently, and he will tell you of this dread place."

KI-GOR stared long and hard at the tall black man, and his heart sank. There was the ring of truth in the man's voice.

"Lead on," he said, gruffly.

As the little party wound down the mountain side, Ki-Gor watched the blacks around him, narrowly. They were Bantu, his traditional enemies back in the Congo jungle. But there was a difference. These men were taller, better looking, prouder than the forest blacks. In spite of himself, Ki-Gor trusted them a little.

Although the story of a mysterious Valley guarded by gorillas sounded almost too fantastic to believe, Ki-Gor suspended judgement until such time as he could talk to the Chief.

After a considerable trek, the party neared a good-sized village which was enclosed by a large stockade. They went through a gate and proceeded straight toward a large house that stood in the middle of the village and dominated all the other huts. Strangely, Ki-Gor felt no fear for his safety. In fact, he hardly thought about it. Uppermost in his mind was the desire to hear about the strange valley from the Chief, himself.

The door to the large house was guarded by two warriors with assegais. The men with Ki-Gor spoke rapidly to them, and they turned and disappeared into the house. A moment later, they reappeared, and behind them towered a huge, bull-necked negro, with alert little eyes, and an oddly humorous face. His clothes, a white shirt and white shorts, set him apart from the others—he was evidently the chief—He spoke at once, in a rolling, rumbling basso.

"Man, it's sure good to see a white face ag'in—" then he stopped, and his little eyes blinked in astonishment at Ki-Gor's leopard-skin loincloth. "Say, you is a white man, ain't you? American? English?"

Ki-Gor in his turn blinked with astonishment. He had never before heard a black speak what sounded like English. He studied the Chief for a moment, then said, "Yes. N-glush. I am of the N-glush people."

"I thought you-all looked kind of English," the Chief rumbled, "Underneath all that tan. Whut-all's yo' idea? Back-to-nature stuff?'

Ki-Gor had not the slightest idea of what the Chief was saying, even though he recognized most of the English words. So he said nothing. Then the Chief spoke again, nastily.

"Nem-mind, Boss, let it go. I'm kinda fergettin' my Southe'n hospitality, standin' yere askin' questions. C'mon in an' have a bite of breakfast."

He smiled and beckoned the jungle man into the house. Gravely Ki-Gor followed him.

He regarded the table and chairs with suspicion, but sat down at the Chief's invitation.

"Well, now, I'll tell you who I am," the Chief began, "'n' then you c'n tell me who you are. I'm the head-man around yere, but I ain't been yere but about a year. My name is George Spelvin, and I come from Cincinnati. I been a Pullman porter, an' a ship's cook. I jumped ship one day in Mombasa, and took myself a little walk. An' first thing you know, I'm head-man of the M'balla. It's a full-time job, but they're real nice folks, an' I like it. Only now and then, I git a little homesick. Tell me where you-all come from."

Ki-Gor thought for a moment. He was thoroughly bewildered by the flow of English from the Chief, very little of which he comprehended, but he kept a grave face.

"I come from far over there," he said, finally, pointing to the west, "from the dark jungle. One day a woman, a white woman, came out of the sky in a red bird-machine. She told me I was of the N-glush, and that I must go with her to my own people. So we left the jungle and traveled this way for many nights. Last night, two gorilla-men came to our camp. While I was fighting one of them, the other one carried my woman away. I trailed them through the night, but this morning the tracks separated, and I followed the gorilla-man who did not have my woman."

"An' you caught up with him, my boys told me," said Chief George Spelvin, "and really polished him off."

"I killed him," Ki-Gor corrected, "and now I must find the other gorilla-man and take my woman away from him."

"Um," said George, "that's real bad. I'm sorry to say this, but I'm awful afraid you ain't goin' to see your woman, again. There's some awful queer doin's over th' other side of the mountain. I don't know just what it is. But these yere great big gorilla-men comes around in pairs and grabs people and carries 'em away and don't nobody ever see 'em again."

"WHERE do the gorilla-men carry those people?" Ki-Gor demanded.

"Over th'other side of the mountain is all I know," George replied, "There's a story around yere about a queer kind of place over there, where there's a man who's kind of King of the gorilla-men. They say the big apes kidnaps the people, an' then they is just slaves in this place for the rest of their lives. They never come out, once they is carried in."

"Then I must go there quickly," said Ki-Gor, "and take my woman away. She must not be a slave."

"Man, you haven't got a chance," George said, earnestly, "I went over the east shoulder of the mountain, once with some of my boys, and we come out on to the entrance of a deep rocky canyon. The boys told me that was the entrance to the Land of the Livin' Dead, and there was a whole lot of the biggest gorilla-men I ever see layin' around there. I just said

'C'mon boys,' an' walked away from there. I once went two rounds with Dempsey 'fore he was champ, but I don't believe in messin' around with no gorilla."

The jungle man stood up, blue eyes flashing

"I am Ki-Gor, Lord of the Jungle," he said, "and I am going into the Land of the Living Dead, and take my woman away from the gorilla-men, no matter how many they are. Give me a boy to guide me to that entrance, I am going now."

"But, Mr. Ki-Gor," said George, "you ain't got a chance. One man can't lick an army, no matter how big or strong he is."

"I will find a way," said Ki-Gor.

"Say, you must set a great store by your woman," George said, with an admiring shake of his head, "is she English, too?"

"Her name is Helene" said Ki-Gor. "She has a white face and red hair, and she says she is of the the tribe of 'Mericans."

"An American girl!" George shouted, "Wait a minute! That's different! Hold on, now, we can't let them apes take an American girl into that awful place."

"You know her tribe?" Ki-Gor asked, curiously.

"Know 'em!" cried George, "I'm American, myself."

"But you have a black skin," Ki-Gor said, blankly.

"Don' make no difference," said George, stoutly, "I'm jus' as good an American as anybody else. An' I suttinly don' aim to leave another American lay in the Land of the Livin' Dead, I don' care *how* many gorillas is guardin' the place."

"You mean you will come with me?" said Ki-Gor.

"I do," said George, emphatically, "an' moreover, we'll take my army along. As head man of this yere M'balla tribe I c'n call out about seventy good fightin' spearmen. I got a rifle and a Luger of my own with plenty of bullets. I'll let you use the rifle—"

"I don't know how to shot a rifle," Ki-Gor interrupted, "Give me some assegais."

"Mr. Ki-Gor," said George, "someday, I'm going to set down and really ask you-all some questions about yourself—when I got more time. Right now we better get goin'."

The huge negro stood up and bellowed some orders. Feet padded out of the house, and a moment later, a great drum began to throb.

"C'mon out and watch this," George said, "I got to give the boys a fight talk."

Outside, in the open space in the middle of the village, men, women and children were assembling. They came running from all directions, and squatted on the ground, arranging themselves in a wide circle. Into the middle of the circle, George strode, carrying his giant frame like an Emperor. The excited crowd ceased its chattering and fell silent under his commanding gaze. Then George's deep voice rolled forth in the rapid dialect of the M'balla.

He had hardly begun before he was interrupted by cries of anguish and terror from all about him. He whirled about and raised a threatening hand, and the crowd quieted down. Then George launched into an impassioned oration.

Presently the crowd began to sway and murmur. As George's emotions mounted higher and higher, the responsive murmur grew louder and rhythmic. And finally, when he wound up his oration at fever heat, the men of the M'balla leaped to their feet shouting and brandishing their assegais.

George made his way through the howling gesticulating mob over to Ki-Gor.

"Well, I got the ahmy lined up," he said, "They didn't like the idea so good, at first, but I talked 'em around. In about an hour we-all'll be ready to go beat up on the gorilla-men, an' see whut kin' of a place this yere Land of the Livin' Dead is."

Ki-Gor and George Spelvin, Chief of the M'balla regarded each other with mutual respect. In spite of the fact that each one was a complete puzzle to the other. Together they went into the Chief's house to plan their strategy.

WHEN the little army filed out of the village and headed eastward toward the mountain, each warrior, at Ki-Gor's suggestion, carried a long, throwing spear, in addition to the short stabbing assegai. Ki-Gor's reasoning was that if they met gorilla-men in any quantity they could do considerable preliminary damage with the throwing spears at long range, before they closed in on the powerful brutes.

George carried his rifle in his hand and the Luger holstered on a belt. Over each shoulder he had draped a bandolier with ammunition for both weapons. Ki-Gor wore a long knife in a scabbard strapped around his waist, and in each hand he carried a broad-bladed M'balla assegai.

After a half a day's brisk climb, the swift African dusk caught the party still several miles short of their destination. They made camp on a bare shoulder of the mountain, taking care to build many bright fires, and detailing plenty of sentries. They had no intention of allowing themselves to be surprised by a night raid of gorilla-men.

The night passed without incident, and before sunup the little army was on its way again, climbing once more. Ki-Gor noticed that many of the strapping M'balla warriors seemed to be less than enthusiasttic over the expedition, as they drew nearer to the high, mountain gateway to the Land of the Living Dead, and its dread defenders. But if Chief George noticed it he gave no sign of it.

The line of march lay down hill for a while, down the eastern slope of the great mountain. But still in front of them was an even higher mountain, or rather, range of mountains. High up in a niche between two peaks, George said, was the Gateway. Soon the M'balla army skirted a rim, and started on the final upgrade. A nervous silence settled down over the party, and the rate of speed noticeably slackened. As they toiled higher and higher up the mountain side, the vegetation began to thin out a little. Tall trees gave way to more stunted growths, and odd-shaped bushes, twisted by high winds.

And a hot, dry west wind baked the bent backs of the M'balla.

Suddenly the party came in at right angles on what appeared to be a well-worn trail. It was a strip of bare, hard-packed ground, six feet wide, that twisted up the slope, flanked on either side by high banks. Ki-Gor crinkled his nose.

"Gorilla!" he said, laconically.

George nodded and detailed two of the M'balla to go up the trail as scouts, in advance of the party. Then, he growled an order over his shoulder and led the little army forward.

They had not proceeded far, when the two scouts came tumbling down the path, faces grey with fear. They immediately started babbling about gorillas, but George hushed them with a stern command, and with Ki-Gor, took them off to one side, out of earshot of the rest of the M'balla. Then, he listened to the scouts as, eyes rolling, they described what they had seen. The Gateway, which was hardly more than a thousand yards away, up the trail, was fairly swarming with gorilla-men. They had evidently scented the approaching M'balla, and reinforcements were pouring out of the narrow opening in the natural rock bastion.

"You have done well," George commented, and turned to Ki-Gor. "This ain't goin' to be so easy, Mr. Ki-Gor. I think you-all better take this yere Luger. There ain't no trick to usin' it. Jest point it like you'd point your finger at somethin', and squeeze this yere little thing. And when it stops goin' 'bang,' jest give it back to me, and I'll reload fer you."

Then George wheeled and strode back to his army.

"Follow me up the bank," he said, in the M'balla dialect, "we will ambush the men-apes from above as they come down the path. Do not throw your spears until you hear the order. Have no fear—you are being led by your invincible chief, and by Ki-Gor, the Gorilla-man Slayer."

The M'balla looked at each other fearfully, but loyally followed George up the bank. The giant American Negro led the way cautiously through the twisted brush, one hundred yards, two hundred yards. Then he halted, abruptly, and pointed. Ki-Gor, beside him in instant, followed the pointing finger with his eyes and felt the hairs on the back of his neck stiffen.

III

THEY were standing on the edge of the brush cover. Before them a wide strip of rubbly, rocky ground sloped gently up to a natural rock palisade. There was no vegetation of any kind on the desolate stretch of shale and rubble, and beyond, the line of low cliffs marked the crest of the ridge. Directly in front of them, there was a cleft in the rock barrier—a narrow cleft that looked to be no more than ten feet wide. Through that cleft, a seemingly endless line of huge black gorillas was moving out to the open ground. And the open ground was already occupied by at least fifty or sixty of the monsters. A low murmur ran through the M'balla.

George whirled, eyes flashing.

"There are your enemies!" he hissed, "the filthy beasts who have terrorized your neighborhood for so many years, who have carried your relatives and friends into a horrible, unknown captivity. Let every man look to his throwing spear."

SLOWLY the gorilla-men began moving down toward them in a disorganized mob. The M'balla, grim-faced, crouched down in the bushes behind George and Ki-Gor. There was something hideously menacing about the way the mass of man-apes ambled down over the rubble. They made no sound, but came on with a sort of contemptuous calmness.

When they were less than a hundred yards away, George fingering his big express rifle, clutched Ki-Gor's arm in glee. The gorilla-men were turning away to the right.

They were going down the path, directly beneath the ambuscade!

George waited until the ravine below them was choked with the black monsters, then he drew a bead on one of them, and bellowed a command. A shower of spears rained down on to the seething mass of hairy bodies. The instant they struck, George fired.

Then pandemonium reigned in the ravine.

With screams of pain and rage, the great man-apes milled around trying to pluck the spears out. George kept on firing into their midst as fast as he could reload.

IN five minutes fully half the gorilla-men lay dead or dying. But as they had originally outnumbered the M'balla by two to one, that merely evened matters up. For the brutes quickly discovered the source of the rain of death, and started clambering up the side of the ravine.

But the M'balla, encouraged by the initial success of the ambush, stood confidently on the edge of the bank. Into their midst, Ki-Gor stepped, an assegai in each hand. After he had emptied the Luger, he had returned the weapon in disgust to George, and had gone back to what seemed to him the more satisfactory method of fighting.

A titanic gorilla-man more agile than the rest, reared its head over the bank at Ki-Gor's feet. The jungle man thrust viciously downward, and impaled the monster by the throat. The beast gave a gurgling bellow and fell backwards.

'Hai! Hai!" the M'balla yelped, and they cut and stabbed as more of the gigantic apes gained the bank. All along the line, huge hairy forms poised for seconds on the brink, great arms thrashing, only to waver and plunge downwards, pierced by a dozen assegais. Here and there, single gorilla-men gained a momentary foothold, crushing out M'balla lives with sledge-hammer blows of their mighty arms. Desperately the tribesman swarmed around, thrusting and hacking. And wherever the M'balla were forced to give ground, Ki-Gor flashed in, muscles rippling, and tawny mane flying.

The fighting was so close now, that George could no longer use his rifle, so he, too, waded in to the combat, the Luger spitting in his left hand, an assegai lifting and dipping in his right. But the rifle had done its job. The monstrous gorilla-men, terrifying as they were, were clearly outnumbered. The struggling line along the bank swayed back and forth, and finally a handful of surviving gorilla-men broke away and leaped down through the shaly gravel to the path below.

But the blood-lust of the M'balla was up, and they followed relentlessly. As Ki-Gor and George leaned panting on their assegais, the tribesman hunted down the dozen or so remaining gorilla-men, ringed each one with a bristling wall of steel, and cut them down.

One-half hour after George had fired the first shot the gorilla-men were completely annihilated. But it was a costly victory.

Among the heaped up dead on the bank, thirty-one M'balla tribesman lay crushed and dying. High up in the sky, the vultures began circling downward to their grisly feast.

The sun was hanging low as the little army, having buried its dead, climbed with Ki-Gor and George up to the Gateway. However, their steps lagged a little across the stony ground. For one thing, they were undergoing a natural reaction from the shock of the battle. For another they felt a nameless dread of what they might find on the other side of the Gateway. They were courageous warriors, as shown by their behaviour against the gorilla-men. But gorilla-men, fearsome though they were were tangible enemies that could be faced and beaten in combat. And this cleft in the mountain bastion they were approaching was the Gateway to the Land of the Living Dead. The fear of the Unknown clutched at the stout hearts of the M'balla.

Ki-Gor's finely tuned senses made him aware of this situation in the ranks of the little army. If the truth be told, he felt a little uneasy himself. But far overshadowing any fears for himself was the determination to penetrate into this awesome place, and find out what had happened to Helene. And if Helene were alive, he would probably need the assistance of the M'balla to rescue her. Therefore he felt a responsibility in maintaining the morale of the army.

So when the little force reached the cleft in the rock, Ki-Gor touched George lightly on the arm, and stepped in front of him. Then looking neither to right nor to left, he marched boldly through the opening.

A broad path lay before him, winding off down-hill to one side. Sheer cliffs towered on either side of the path, so that Ki-Gor could not see beyond the first bend, which was about fifty feet away. But as far as he could see, there was no sign of life anywhere on the path. He shouted encouragingly over his shoulder and went forward.

As he did, he felt a noticeable drop in the temperature, and saw that the sun no longer shone around him. Looking up he observed a pall of mist or clouds stretching eastward from the crest of the ridge. But he pressed on down the path, grim-faced, and the M'balla, quaking with superstitious dread, crept silently after him.

It seem to grow colder and colder, and darker and darker, as they descended the narrow mountain gorge. But still they saw no signs of life. Gradually, the cliffs on either side began to flatten out and disappear, and here and there they saw patches of vegetation, bushes and dwarf trees and stringy vines.

But it was the most extraordinary vegetation any of them had ever seen, and the farther they went, the more extraordinary it became. The bushes were wildly luxuriant, with hundreds of branches, wide leaves and long cruel thorns. And the trees had gnarled trunks, twisted into the most fantastic and grotesque shapes. An eerie silence hung over everything, broken only by the whistling of the chill wind as it whipped shreds of mist across the path.

It was getting so dark, now, that Ki-Gor was unable to see very far. The strange bushes and trees loomed up in terrifying shapes in the gray gloom. The M'balla huddled as close to each other as they could and still walk. From time to time, they peered fearfully around them, and the pace of the march slowed down to a crawl, even though the path sloped downhill.

At the head of the party, Ki-Gor picked his way cautiously, an assegai held ready in his right hand. Although he wouldn't admit it—even to himself—he was feeling extremely uneasy. The supernatural spookiness of the surroundings was having an effect on even his stout heart. And besides, the visibility was so poor that he couldn't tell what kind of a trap he might be walking into. His bare body, too, was chilled to the bone with the clammy, gusty wind.

Shivering, he reflected that a good hot camp-fire would not only revive the sagging spirits of the expedition, but would furnish some valuable protection in this strange and desolate situation. He turned to George just behind him, and suggested that they halt for the night as soon as possible. George agreed to the idea with alacrity, and immediately bellowed a command to the M'balla.

A MURMUR of relief swept through the column, and the tribesmen eagerly bunched up on the path touching shoulders to regain their confidence. A few braver than the rest spread out and began hacking at the bushes with their assegais for fuel.

When some fagots had been piled up, George squatted on the ground to start the fire. Ki-Gor bent over him, watching. The flames were slow in coming. The wood was damp, and the wind increased.

Suddenly, Ki-Gor's scalp began to crawl as he heard a sound from the outer darkness.

"Listen!" he hissed, clutching George's shoulder. But George had heard it, too, and so had the M'balla. They stood transfixed, eyes rolling.

It was a kind of soft, melodious wail that rose and fell with ineffable sweetness. It seemed to come from all directions, or from no direction. There was an almost human quality in the sound, and yet no human ever made a sound like that. Mournfully sweet, it hung on the air and died away, as if some sad, disembodied spirit were wandering disconsolately through the darkness, crooning a tuneless song.

The M'balla looked at Ki-Gor and George, and Ki-Gor and George looked at each other. No one said a word. Then the wind blew strongly on their faces again, and again the ghostly voice rose. This time there were *two voices!* Another melancholy wail, pitched lower than the first, sang out in perfect harmony. Then a third —a fourth! And finally a whole choir of unearthly voices rose and fell in a terribly sweet, terribly sad hymn.

"Ghosts!" a tribesman blurted out, "*Living Ghosts!*"

At that moment there was a distant, menacing rumble, and the ground under their feet seemed to tremble. The rumble grew louder, and far away to one side, the sky grew pale. Starkly outlined against it was a conical mountain peak. Little tongues of green and yellow flame licked upwards from the mountain top, shedding a ghastly light over everything. Underfoot, the ground trembled more violently than ever. The wind blew harder, and the ghostly voices rose to a felonious shriek.

The horrified tribesmen swayed against each other for a moment. Then, with a wild yell, they broke and ran headlong, back up the path. George roared at them to stop, but they didn't even hear him. He ran after the howling, frantic mob, and fired in the air twice, but it did not the slightest good. The M'Balla had had enough.

Trembling, Ki-Gor stood and watched his allies until they disappeared from view. He was badly frightened himself, but it never occurred to him to run. He stood glaring about him, assegai ready. Very soon the ground ceased to shake, and the light from the mountain peak dimmed and died out. The wind lowered and the ghostly voices faded away to a sorrowful moan.

Ki-Gor squatted on the ground and collected his thoughts. So far, he was unharmed in spite of the spectacular and terrifying phenomena that had occurred. But the sturdy little army which was to invade the Land of the Living Dead with him, and help him rescue Helene had vanished into the night. So now, if he was to rescue Helene, he would have to do it himself.

A pebble rattle up the path, above him. He started up, and took two stealthy steps in that direction when he was arrested by the sound of a deep voice speaking very softly.

"Is you there, Mr. Ki-Gor?"

George Spelvin had returned.

"I am in front of you," Ki-Gor whispered, "How many are with you?"

"They ain't nary one with me," George answered dolefully, "I is all by myse'f, Mr. Ki-Gor. Them po' bush niggers is still goin' to be runnin' this time next week, I guess. They was reely scared."

"And you?" said Ki-Gor, "Aren't you afraid?"

"Well, I don't feel so awful good. Seems like they's an awful mess of han'ts around these yere parts, and I don't like han'ts, no suh!"

"Why did you come back?"

"Man, they's an American girl down yere and somebody's got to git her out. An' if I cain't bring muh ahmy, I c'n bring myse'f. I don' know if the two of us c'n pull off this rescue, but we c'n try awful hard."

"George, you are a brave man."

"Well, Mr. Ki-Gor, tha's a real compliment when you say it. Cause I guess, when it comes to bravery, you wrote the book."

Ki-Gor ignored the return compliment—mainly because he didn't understand it—and got down to business.

"This place is not good for a camp," he said, "Let us go farther down the trail."

"You said it, Mr. Ki-Gor," said George, heartily, "Le's git on away from yere. Oh My Lawd there goes them ha'nts again!"

THE jungle man shivered as the mysterious, mournful voices began their lament again. Silently, he offered the butt-end of his assegai for George to hold, and the oddly assorted pair moved slowly down the path.

Enough light from the stars filtered through the clouds to illuminate their way, though very dimly. It was enough, at any rate, to bring Ki-Gor up with a start after they had only gone about fifty yards. The trail suddenly narrowed. On one side—the uphill side—a sheer cliff wall rose and lost itself in the misty darkness. On the other side was—a drop into nothingness! Cautiously, Ki-Gor and George crept down the trail, hugging the cliff.

It was a long and terrible night for the two invaders of the Land of the Living Dead. Inadequately dressed as they were, they nearly perished from the cold winds that whistled against the cliffs. And the almost total absence of light made their progress along the hazardous trail extremely slow. But with the coming of daylight, they found an improvement in their condition.

They were down among trees, now, tall trees that rose from gently sloping park land, free from underbrush. The constant fog and cold winds were left behind, and the two companions hurried along the smooth, hard-packed trail to restore their circulation. The first slanting rays of the sun were pouring through the trees, when they reached a clearing in the forest. It was evidently an open bluff on the mountain side, as they could see the tops of trees peeping up on the other side of the open space. They ran forward to the edge of the bluff, to see what the surrounding country was like. What they saw made them gasp.

They were looking down on a broad, fertile valley that was surrounded on all sides by great mountains. The valley floor was entirely cleared, and looked to be one great green pasture. It was dotted with snow-white cattle grazing peacefully, and through the middle of it ran a placid stream. At the far end, on rising ground, a score or more of buildings was grouped in a symmetrical arrangement. They stretched out on either side of a large, palace-like structure, which seemed to dominate the whole group.

The architecture of all the buildings was uniform. They were all one story high, except for the palace, which had three or four floors. They were all startingly white, and had large, flat, overhanging roofs, also white. As Ki-Gor and George watched the scene, fascinated, the sun's rays touched those roofs. Instantly, they seemed to catch fire. The rays were caught and reflected by billions of tiny diamond-like surfaces that dazzled the eyes of the two men on the bluff.

But, except for the buildings themselves, there was not a sign of a human being.

Suddenly Ki-Gor's nostrils flared and he glanced sharply around.

"I smell gorilla," he stated.

"You do?" said George startled, "My glory, I sho' wish I had muh ahmy around."

He moved down the face of the bluff several feet and peered into the base of the trees.

"Man, your nose don't tell you no lies," he called back, "these yere woods is full of gorilla-men. Le's you an' I get outa yere!"

George scrambled back to the edge of the bluff. Then he and Ki-Gor rapidly retraced their steps across the clearing. Suddenly Ki-Gor halted.

An immense gorilla-man was standing in front of them at the edge of the trees.

George raised his rifle, then lowered it again. A second gorilla-man was coming through the trees to join the first one. And another one, and another one—. A rapid glance around the clearing showed the two men only too plainly that they were completely surrounded by at least thirty of the great man-apes.

"Man, we sho' walked right into a spot," George grunted.

"They were hiding," said Ki-Gor, "waiting for us."

"Whut we goin' to do?" said George, "we cain't lick this many. Kill a few maybe, but when I stop to reload, the rest of 'em will come and git us."

Ki-Gor did not answer for a moment, but stood fingering his assegai, and watching the gorilla-men. He was puzzled by their attitude. The great men-apes were not attempting to come any closer to the two men, but merely stood quietly around the edge of the clearing.

"Let us go slowly in the direction of the valley," Ki-Gor said, finally, "and do not shoot until they attack us."

IV

KI-GOR moved cautiously downhill across the grass, and George followed, his rifle held ready. As they approached the ring of gorilla-men at that point, the shaggy brutes silently gave way to either side, making room for the men to pass. They still showed no inclination to attack. With a fast-beating heart, Ki-Gor stepped past the gorilla-men, his eyes darting from side to side. The oddly human brutes remained motionless.

Not until the two men had gone twenty paces or so, did the gorilla-men move. They then, very deliberately, began to follow at a safe distance to the rear.

"Mr. Ki-Gor, I think you-all got the right idea," George muttered, "I truly b'lieve them big fellers *wants* us to go this way."

And so it seemed. Ki-Gor and George went unmolested down through the forest, and emerged on to the valley floor. Behind them was a silent procession of giant man-apes.

The two men hesitated a moment, and then Ki-Gor said, "To the houses." Apparently it was what the gorilla-men wanted. They continued to follow at a respectable distance as the jungle man and his Negro companion traversed the long green fields to the dazzling white houses.

The valley had an extraordinary beauty. The grass was lush and unbelievably green. Here and there, wild flowers, brilliantly colored, grew in profusion. And in every direction, mountains reached majestically to the sky.

As the adventurers approached the houses, the gorilla-men behind them spread out fanwise, and one of them uttered a great roar. Ki-Gor and George whirled about. Was it the sign for a sudden attack?

Apparently not, as none of the monsters came any closer. It was a signal, though. From every direction of the valley, and from the houses, hordes of gorilla-men came running. Ki-Gor and George stood back to back, bewildered, as hundreds of clattering brutes gathered and formed a vast ring around them. Still there was no hostile move.

Just then, a piercing whistle shrilled from the direction of the houses. Immediately the man-apes on that side of the ring separated from each other, and formed a broad avenue straight up to the steps of the palace. And at the head of the steps stood a man.

Wonderingly, Ki-Gor and George walked between the two lines of gorilla-men to the foot of the steps where they halted and scrutinized the man standing above them. He was an erect, handsome man, dressed in white flowing robes. He was middle-aged, judging from the long, gray mustache and the long gray hair that fell to his shoulders, framing an aquiline, brown face. But the most remarkable feature about him was his eyes. They were large and luminous, and had a disturbing penetrating quality. He smiled down at the two adventurers and spoke.

"Welcome! thrice welcome, Ki-Gor," he said, in perfect English. "Welcome to Nirvana. I expected you sooner than this, and I expected that you would come alone. Who is this black man?"

The tone was friendly, but Ki-Gor didn't like it, for some reason. And how did this King of the Gorilla-men know his name? Then it came to him. From Helene, of course! Eyes flashing and fists clenched, Ki-Gor moved forward a step and spoke. As he did, the man-apes stirred restlessly.

"Where is my woman? Is she safe?"

The King of the Gorilla-men made a discreet motion with his right hand.

"Your woman is unhurt," he said, quietly, "She was tired and a little hysterical from her long journey so I put her her to sleep. You will see her soon. In the meantime, let me warn you against making any threatening gestures. These large, hairy creatures are my subjects. They adore and reverence me, and if they ever got the idea that you meant to do me harm, I could not be responsible for their actions."

"Well, jes' a minute now, King," George broke in with a careless drawl, "I'm pointin' a high-powered gun right straight at your guts. You jes' *better* be responsible fer the way these yere babies act, or you-all jes' ain' gonna *live* very long."

The King's eyelids flickered ever so slightly in surprise.

"You are an American black," he observed, "How very interesting. I was going to send you to the mines, but I will reconsider. I will ask you to come into the Palace with Ki-Gor. Very interesting."

THE King gathered up one side of his robe and stepped down the white stairs with immense dignity. When he reached the ground in front of Ki-Gor and George he extended his right hand, and inclined his head, eyes half-closed.

"Let us not talk of fighting and shooting," he said, gently, "Believe me, if you kill me, my subjects will destroy you instantly. No. Let us be friends."

As Ki-Gor watched suspiciously, the King looked at George sleepily, and smiled. Suddenly, the huge brown eyes flew open and glittered at the big Negro.

"You are very tired," he said, in a low voice, "You are extremely tired from your long march. You need to rest—rest. Just relax all your muscles and—rest. You need to sleep more than anything else in the world. Sleep. Why don't you go to sleep? Just close your eyes and sleep. Don't try to hold your eyelids open. Let them fall, and—go to sleep. Go to sleep on your feet —standing up. Go to sleep."

At those last words, George swayed like a tree in a high wind. Ki-Gor, in amazement, saw the big Negro was fighting to keep his eyes open. The King backed up the steps slowly, and George staggered forward after him. Suddenly, the King's right hand flicked out, seized the lowered barrel of George's rifle, and wrested it away. As Ki-Gor leaped forward, the King sprang agilely up the steps and leveled the rifle at the jungle man's breast.

"Carefully, Ki-Gor," said the King, "I now have the gun."

Ki-Gor stood bewildered. He couldn't understand what had happened to George, that he should allow himself to be disarmed so easily. The big Negro groaned beside him and shook his head.

"Look out for the King," George croaked, "Man, he sho-nough almost had me laid out cold. I ain't never been hypnotized befo', but I nearly was this time."

Ki-Gor reached out to steady George, thinking fast. He didn't know what "hypnotize" meant, but he had seen George almost go to sleep on his feet, and he felt a sense of terrible danger from the cool, composed person of the King. More than ever, he wanted to find Helene, and see for himself whether she was safe. The King's voice interrupted his thoughts.

"Now, shall we be friends?"

Ki-Gor and George looked helplessly at the man in the white robe, and nodded slowly.

"Then, be so kind as to follow me into the Palace," said the King, "and we will start getting better acquainted."

He reached the top of the steps and backed across the wide portico, gun still leveled. Then he pulled a whistle from the folds of his robe, and blew two shrill blasts. It was evidently a signal of dismissal to the gorilla-men, and the vast crowd of them began to break up and move away. Ki-Gor and George hesitated a moment, then leaped up the white stone steps after the King.

He was standing at one side of a wide-doorway, and with an ironic smile, he waved his two prisoners through the doorway ahead of him. They proceeded through a spacious hallway, and at the King's command, turned to the right, through another doorway, and found themselves in a large, high-ceilinged room. The white walls of the room were unadorned, but a deep, rich looking carpet covered the floor, and low tables, chairs and divans made up the furniture.

Ki-Gor pivoted on his heel and addressed the King humbly.

"Helene," he said, "My woman. Where is she?"

"She is coming to join us now," the King replied with an inscrutable smile, "In fact, here she is."

At that moment, Ki-Gor's heart leaped within him as Helene walked into the room at the opposite end. He started down the room toward her, but stopped half way with a thrill of horror.

It was Helene, all right, but something was terribly wrong. She was clothed in a white robe, sandals on her feet. Her face was deathly pale, and her eyes looked straight ahead, unfocused on anything in the room.

She walked carefully around the furniture without seeming to see it.

"Here is Ki-Gor," said the King, "You may recognize him, Helene."

Helene swayed a moment, uncertainly, then she turned a perfectly blank face toward the jungle man.

"Hello, Ki-Gor," she said in a hollow voice.

"Helene!" cried Ki-Gor in anguished tones, "What is the matter? Are you all right?"

THERE was a dreadful moment of silence. Then the King's voice broke in gently.

"Tell him, Helene," he said, "Tell him how you feel."

Monotonously, as if she were repeating lesson, Helene said, "I am all right, Ki-Gor. I am very happy here in Nirvana—happy to be with Krishna, King of the Living Dead."

Ki-Gor swung around, his face contorted in an uncontrollable snarl. Disregarding the rifle aimed at him, he sprang at the King. So sudden and so swift was his movement that the King had not time to pull the trigger, before the jungle man was upon him.

"Mr. Ki-Gor!" cried George,"Don't kill him! Don't kill him yet!" He's got the woman hypnotized, an' she won't ever recover until he snaps her out of it."

But Ki-Gor had the King on the floor choking the life out of him in a blind rage. The powerful Negro bent over and wrenched him away from the supine figure in the white robe.

"Now, hold on, Mr. Ki-Gor," George sputtered, as the jungle man spun out of his grasp, "If you kill the King now, tha's just the same as killing Miss Helene, yere."

Ki-Gor hesitated, eyes blazing.

"What do you mean?" he cried, hoarsely.

"Jes' whut I said," replied George. "He's done put her into a hypnotic trance, an' he's the only one can bring her out of it. If you kill him, she jes' ain' never goin' to wake up."

Ki-Gor whirled around at Krishna, King of the Living Dead.

"Wake her up!" Ki-Gor said savagely.

Krishna drew himself up to a sitting position, and brushed the long gray hair out of his eyes.

"I will release her," he said, with a cool smile, "as soon as you two hand your weapons over to me."

"Now, listen yere, King," George bit out, "I wouldn't kid you-all. Don' go tryin' to drive a bargain, because you'll never be closer to dyin' than you is, right this minute. You better wake her up, and wake her up quick, or Ki-Gor'll kill you, and he'll kill you slow."

Krishna's dark face grew paler. He reflected a moment, then smiled again.

"Very well," he said, pleasantly, "I will do as you say."

"You better do a smooth job," George warned, as Krishna got to his feet and approached Helene, "because if she comes out cryin' an' hysterical, they's no power on earth could stop you from bein' beaten to a pulp."

Krishna nodded, and passed his hand over Helene's eyes.

"I am going to release you from my control," he said quietly. "You will wake up, and you will remember nothing of what happened while you were asleep. Now. You are no longer under my control. Wake up!"

He stepped backward and watched the girl. Helene's eyes were tight shut, and she held herself rigid. Krishna paled.

"Wake up!" he said, sharply, and reaching out a hand, snapped his fingers beside her ear.

Helene shivered. Slowly her eyes opened. She stared uncomprehendingly about her, and then saw Ki-Gor. She gave a glad cry and rushed into his arms.

"Ki-Gor!" she exclaimed, "You came after me! Oh, I'm so happy! I've never been so frightened in my life as when the gorilla-man snatched me away from the camp. But he didn't hurt me at all. And when he brought me here, Krishna was so kind. I think this is a heavenly place, don't you?"

Ki-Gor held her tightly to him for a moment, without speaking. Then he released one arm and pointed to George Spelvin, one-time Pullman porter, ship's cook, and Chief of the M'Balla.

"This is George," said Ki-Gor, "He is a Bantu, but he is a brave man, and he is our friend."

"Pleased to meet you-all, Ma'am," said George, with a grin. "I may be a Bantu, but fust of all, I is an American, an I's real proud to be your friend."

BEFORE Helene could express her astonishment at meeting an American Negro in this fantastic corner of Africa, Ki-Gor took command of the situation, again.

"This man," he said grimly, and pointed at Krishna, "is not our friend. He is bad. We are going away from here quickly.

"Krishna? Bad?" said Helene, puzzled, "I don't understand. He has been very kind to me."

"He is bad," Ki-Gor reiterated, "and we are going away, right now."

"If you will pardon me," Krishna broke in, with a sleepy smile, "It is not a question of whether I am good or bad. It happens that I am the ruler of this valley, which is sometimes called the Land of the Living Dead. My own name for it is Nirvana. You see, I am a Hindu, and Nirvana is an ancient conception of the Ultimate of human desire. It is not like the Christian Heaven, exactly, it is merely a removal from the world, a complete absence of desire, of illusion. I removed myself from the outer world many years ago, and found a kind of Nirvana here in this secluded valley. Here I remain until I die. But this Nirvana, unlike the spiritual Nirvana of the ancient Bhuddists, is somewhat concerned with matters of the flesh. I like beauty and comfort and good food. At the same time, I require solitude when I feel like it. My solution was to come here and be served by slaves, and remain undiscovered by the outer world. Human beings built this palace and the surrounding buildings. Human beings grow my food, tend my cattle—I have discarded the Hindu tabu on beef. My soldiers, however, are these curious man-apes. They are considerably more trustworthy than any human warriors I have ever known."

"But, Krishna," Helene interrupted, "how can you be sure that one of your human slaves won't escape, someday, and reveal the secret of your Nirvana?"

"For one thing," Krishna replied, "I hypnotize them. For another if any attempted to leave the Valley, he would immediately be killed by my soldiers. You see, these are no ordinary gorillas. You may have noticed that they are astonishingly human in some ways. They are the product of highly intensive selective breeding."

"Selective breeding!" Helene exclaimer, "I thought that was impossible. I thought that gorillas could not reproduce in captivity."

"The original specimens which I brought here from West Africa years ago, were given the illusion of freedom. They had the run of the valley. But they learned to eat food which I left out for them, and frequently the food was drugged. In that way I had opportunities to observe them closely, control their mating, and sometimes to experiment with their ductless glands. The second generation was more tractable. From then on, I bred them for size, intelligence and docility. These giant creatures you see around here are the result."

"Good Heavens!" gasped Helene. "Where did you get your education?"

"At the University of Cambridge," Krishna smiled, "and later at the University of Bonn. It was at the German university that I became interested in racial evolution and, what might be termed, constructive anthropology. Some bullet-headed Prussian students were busy with a racial theory concerning their Aryan origin. That was vastly amusing to me, who come from the only true Aryan race left in the world—the high-caste Brahmans of Northern India. The appearance of those Prussians indicated to me that they were more likely to be descended from Neanderthal Man. And from that, I conceived the idea of trying to create modern Neanderthalers. Hence the experiment with the gorillas. The experiment is not yet complete, but my man-apes are many times more intelligent than their original progenitors. And the one thing they have learned thoroughly, is that anyone may enter the Valley, *but no one may leave! That is one of the voodoos I have placed upon this land. There are six others. You know, I sometimes call my home* Nirvana of the Seven Voodoos."

"You mean we are prisoners here?" said Helene.

"For the rest of your lives," said Krishna, simply. "And, as I have already told your companions, it will do no good to kill me. Because whether I am alive or not, the man-apes will not permit you to get out of the valley. And with me dead, their master, the probabilities are that they would destroy every human being they could find."

"Oh!" Helene shuddered with loathing. "I thought you were so charming at first. I can't believe that you are such a monster."

"I am not a monster at all," Krishna smiled, "I am just a very practical man who does the things that please him. In this comfortable domain of mine, I let no wish go ungratified. My own happiness is my chiefest concern. Surely, that is not a monster, is it?"

HELENE made no answer, and for a while there was an electric silence. Finally George broke it.

"Man!" he said, heavily. "We sho'ly caught ourse'ves a cold fish!"

"You know," said Krishna, "there is no reason why you should take this situation so gravely. Only technically, will you be prisoners. In a sense you will be freer than you could ever be outside the boundaries of my Lotus Land. By the time you have been here six months, I am quite sure you will feel not the slightest desire ever to go away."

Helene cast a frightened glance at Ki-Gor, who, up to now, had taken no part in the conversation. The jungle man frowned and spoke abruptly.

"How is it that you are master of the gorilla-men? How do you do that?"

"I drug them, my dear Ki-Gor," Krishna replied, candidly, "with a rare substance which I distill from a rare plant that grows in this valley in great quantity. The drug puts them into a deep sleep, and when they wake up, they are especially susceptible to hypnosis. I then hypnotize them. I have hypnotized so many of them so often, that the merest suggestion that they prevent people from leaving acts now as a perpetual command to all of them. In the meantime, of course, they have become strong addicts of this drug, and I have to give them a daily portion of it. If this sounds hard to believe, just come out with me now and I will arrange to give them their ration for the day. You may see with your own eyes that I am telling you the truth."

"No funny business, now, King," warned George.

"There would be no purpose in my doing any funny business," Krishna replied, blandly, "I could have you killed, but I don't want you killed. I want you alive. You see, I have many hobbies, of all kinds. And, for a time now, I intend to make a hobby of you three. You interest me. Therefore, instead of sending you to work my mines, which is my usual procedure with newcomers, I shall keep you near me in the palace. No, there will be no funny business. Besides, you have guns which you might be foolish enough to kill me with. Follow me now, and you will see a strange sight."

Krishna stood up and walked briskly toward the doorway. George followed him closely, covering him with the rifle. Ki-Gor dropped back with Helene and whispered into her ear.

"What does 'hypnotize' mean?"

Helene thought for a moment and shook her head.

"It's a little too complicated to explain right now, Ki-Gor," she said, "Wait until we are alone, and I'll try to straighten it out for you."

Krishna led them out of the palace, down the white steps, and across the great square of the settlement to a long narrow building, which had small, heavily barred windows along its length, and two doors, a small one and a large one, at one end. Several gorilla-men appeared from other buildings moved over to the large door and stood there, hopefully.

"This is my drug laboratory and dispensary," Krishna explained, as he led the way to the smaller door. "Slaves gather the plants and bring them here where I extract the drug and produce it in crystalline form by a formula known only to me."

He opened the smaller door with a small key and motioned them to follow him.

"Then more slaves," Krishna continued, "place quantities of the drug tablets in a long trough on one side of a corridor which extends the length of this building on the inside. I open the large door and the gorilla-men file through and pick up the drug tablets as they go along. And here you see some of the slaves preparing the feast for my simian warriors."

Helene, Ki-Gor, and George found themselves in a long room which looked like a chemical laboratory. A dozen or more blacks moved slowly around emptying sacks into a long bin that stretched along the inside wall.

"The tablets fall through a slit in the wall into the trough on the other side," Krishna explained. "In that way, the anthropoids get all they need of the drug without having access to the source of supply."

But Helene hardly heard him. She was staring in horrified fascination at the slaves. They were every one, unbelievably gaunt and emaciated. They moved with dragging steps. Their eyes were lack-lustre, and they seemed to be walking in a stupor.

"In heaven's name, what is the matter with these poor men?" Helene cried, "Are they victims of a disease?"

"Oh, no," said Krishna, matter-of-factly, "They are drug-addicts. Everybody in the valley, except myself, is a habitual user of the drug. For some reason, it seems not to have an ill-effects on the gorilla-men, but it destroys human tissue inevitably in course of time. That is why I need constant replacements for my slaves, and have to send my man-apes out of the valley on kidnapping expeditions."

George Spelvin exploded.

"Man, you is jes' plain bad an' nothin' else!"

KRISHNA smiled, blandly.

"You are the most interesting black man I have ever seen," he said, "You are going to provide me with a fascinating subject of investigation. You have something, a quality I have never seen in a Negro before."

"Well, I'll tell you this," said George, and his voice had a dangerous edge, "I ain' awful good slave material."

"No, I can see that," Krishna replied with an amused glance, "compared to these specimens in here. But, perhaps I should explain that these men are the dregs of the valley. They are so far gone in the drug habit, that I put them in here where the work is light, and where they can eat all they want of the tablets. They die off very quickly, after they come in here."

"Oh!" Helene cried, impatiently, "I can't understand why your slaves haven't long ago rebelled or run away."

"Only because of my incorruptible apes," said Krishna, imperturbably. "Here, I will give you an example."

He called to one of the slaves. The creature crawled over to him on hands and knees and looked up dully into the King's face. With a careless wave of a hand, Krishna quickly threw the slave into a trance. He got up slowly on his skinny legs and tottered to the door. Mechanically, he opened it and walked outside.

"Come and watch this," said Krishna, "it's great sport. I have hypnotized him with the suggestion that he try to escape from the valley."

With faces expressive of the dreadful premonition in their minds, Helene and George went to the door and looked out. After a minute, Ki-Gor joined them.

Outside, the gorilla-men were massing in the square, waiting for the door to open to admit them to the supply of the drug they craved. The wretched slave was picking his way through the crowd. They looked at him uncuriously and seemed to pay little attention. But when he emerged from the crowd on the other side and walked slowly out on the green pasture, two hulking man-apes were following him.

Farther and farther, the doomed creature went across the lovely green valley floor. And behind him, inevitably, stalked his sinister escort. When the slave was about a quarter of a mile away, he suddenly broke into a staggering run. And as Helene gasped, the man-apes started after him. The first one overtook him in ten steps, seized him by the arm, and flung him high in the air. As the poor creature landed, both gorilla-men pounced on him. Helene closed her eyes to the rest of the spectacle.

"Ah! that is excellent sport!" Krishna exclaimed, eyes gleaming, "Now, you see, perhaps, why nobody tries to leave the Valley. And why, *you three* will never leave the valley."

"We will leave the Valley, Krishna," said Ki-Gor, quietly, "and when we do, *you* will be killed by your own gorillas—torn to pieces like the slave out there."

"Your optimism is delightful, Ki-Gor," replied Krishna, "You forget that the gorilla-men regard me, and me alone, as the source of the drug that they crave. Step outside the door with me, and I will demonstrate the truth of that statement, too."

The throngs of ape-men crowded eagerly around Krishna as he strolled over to the large door. Avidly their little eyes watched him insert the big key, and when he swung the door open, there was a concerted dash for the corridor. Krishna stepped back with a smile as the gorilla-men jammed themselves into the doorway.

"How do they get out?" Ki-Gor asked.

"They go out the other end of the building," Krishna replied. "The door at that end swings outward under the pressure of their weight and springs back into position afterward. There is no handle on the outside of it, and it cannot swing inwards. So they have learned always to go through the building this way.

Ki-Gor grunted, then was lost in thought for a moment. Abruptly he asked another question.

"How soon do they go to sleep, after they eat the drug?"

"Almost immediately," was the answer. "They walk out of the door at the other end, find some spot of ground they like, and lie down and sleep for about four hours."

Again Ki-Gor grunted and bent his head in thought.

"If you are planning," said Krishna, with a sardonic smile, "to strike at me while the gorilla-men are asleep, you may abandon the idea. There are always latecomers to the feast—gorilla-men, who come down from their posts on the mountain sides. I shall lock this door before they get here. So that while most of the anthropoids will be in a stupor, there will still be plenty around here in full possesion of their faculties—more than enough to protect me."

KI-GOR appeared not to have heard the warning. He drew George aside and talked to him in low tones. Krishna gave the pair a narrow look, and then shook his head with a pitying smile.

"Fools!" he said, contemptuously, to Helene. "It is doubly stupid to contemplate escape. For not only is it impossible, but it should be highly undesirable. Life here is extremely pleasant, and also very interesting. I have, by no means, confined my scientific activities to the creation of gorilla-men. Besides this laboratory, I have three others, and in all of them, I am conducting fascinating experiments. At the moment, I am especially absorbed in a study of the endocrines—the ductless glands. As a matter of fact, I have wished for a new subject of experimentation for a long time. One like yourself, a lovely white woman. With what I already know, I could change you in two weeks' time, from a fair lithe Nordic, to an obese, swarthy Latin type. I could make your hair fall out. I could grow a beard on your smooth face. And, I assure you the operations would be completely painless to yourself. The only thing I am not quite sure of yet, is whether, after making these changes in you, I could change you back to your original self. *That* is what we will find out."

Helene shrank back against the wall of the laboratory, eyes dilated with horror, and unable to say a word in reply to the grotesque suggestions she had been forced to hear. Krishna calmly turned his attention the gorilla-men.

V

THE crowd of them around the doorway was rapidly growing smaller, as more and more of them filed through the corridor of the building. Off to either side, other gorilla-men could be seen wandering aimlessly around, on their faces, fatuous expressions of sleepy ecstasy. One by one, these dropped to the ground, curled up and went to sleep.

Krishna moved toward the door cautiously. There was only a handful of the man-apes left, now, clamoring to get into the dispensary. Krishna waited, his hand on the door, until there was room enough for this rear-guard to get inside. His eyes swept the green fields, and a crafty smile came over his dark face, as two little knots of late-coming gorilla-men could be seen running in from the mountain slopes. As the last man-ape in the square crowded into the dispensary, Krishna slammed the door, hid the key in the folds of his robe, and walked toward Ki-Gor and George, smiling.

But the smile died on his face, as Ki-Gor swung around and started for him. He looked around wildly, but the late-arriving gorilla-men were still a hundred yards away out in the field. His hand fumbled for the cord at his throat on which the whistle hung. He ran two steps, blowing a shrill blast, as Ki-Gor hit him.

Frantically, Krishna tried to fight off the jungle man, but he was over-matched. Ki-Gor slung the screaming King over his shoulder and ran back to the doorway of the laboratory. One or two of the drugged man-apes tried to sit up, then fell back in drowsy disgust.

Helene was holding the laboratory door open and George was standing beside her, rifle held ready. Ki-Gor flashed through inside with his struggling burden, and Helene and George ducked in after him. George slammed the door shut and bolted it just as the fresh gorilla-men thundered into the square.

The gaunt slaves shrank back against the wall of the laboratory as Ki-Gor flung Krishna crashing to the floor. Outside a dozen gorilla-men hammered against the door.

"Fools!" Krishna screamed, struggling up from the floor. "You have signed your death warrant by this action! The minute I open that door, my warriors will come in and tear you to pieces!"

"But you will not open the door," said Ki-Gor.

"Somebody will have to open it, some time or other," Krishna shouted, "or do you intend to stay in here until you starve to death?"

"No," said Ki-Gor, with lowered brows, "we will not stay here long. We will go away and *you*, Krishna, will go with us!"

"You are mad! Absolutely mad!" Krishna yelled.

"Watch him," Ki-Gor directed George, and walked over to one of the slaves who was holding a sack full of the drug tablets in his hand. The jungle man took the sack from the unresisting hand of the slave, went to one of the barred windows, and began throwing handfuls of the tablets out between the bars.

It took the gorilla-men outside the door a very few minutes to discover that the coveted tables were being dispensed in an unusual way. With glad cries they pounced on the little white cubes and stuffed them into their huge mouths.

Krishna turned gray, as the full consequences of the stratagem were borne in on him. He staggered back, then flung himself at George. The big Negro swung his left hand at Krishna's chin, and the King of the gorilla-men fell inert to the floor. He did not move.

Outside the barred windows, the gorilla-men finished up the drug tablets, and stood around, gaping expectantly. Ki-Gor obligingly threw another sackful out, and a few minutes later, not one of the man-apes in the square was left on his feet.

Swiftly Ki-Gor set to work, knotting several of the sacks containing the drug together on a piece of rope. As he was finishing this task, Krishna groaned and opened his eyes.

"Stand up," Ki-Gor commanded, "we are going now. We are leaving the Valley and you are going with us."

Krishna fell to his knees.

"Ki-Gor," he pleaded, "it is sure death. You are bound to run into more gorilla-men along the trail. They will kill you even if I am with you. Not even my commands could save you if they catch you leaving the Valley."

"We are wasting time talking," said Ki-Gor, sternly, "get up and walk out of the door or George will shoot you through the head.

Whimpering, Krishna picked himself up under the watchful eye of George and walked slowly to the door.

Ki-Gor slung the sacks over his shoulder and paused to address the forlorn slaves in Swahili.

"O miserable ones," he said, "You are free. Go and collect your fellows, and join us. We will take you out of this accursed Valley, and once more you may see your homes again."

There was a heavy silence. The slaves looked stupidly at one another, and looked back at Ki-Gor. Finally one of them spoke.

"A thousand thanks, O Madman," he said, haltingly, "but this is our home, now. We know no other place. If we went away, how would we find a supply of the drug which we must have now, or die? Go, Madman, hasten, and may luck attend you."

Ki-Gor stared at them incredulously, and spun on his heel.

"So be it," he said, "A thousand pities that we cannot spare the time to stay and persuade you out of this mode of life, which is but a living death. But we must go. Farewell, O miserable ones."

GEORGE snapped the bolt back on the door, swung it open, and pushed Krishna out ahead of him. Then Helene and Ki-Gor followed and the journey out of the Land of the Living Dead was begun.

They threaded their way among the recumbent bodies of the snoring gorilla-men, and struck out across the great pasture. They headed straight for the edge of the forest, and when they reached it, skirted it until they picked up the broad trail which led up the mountain.

As they turned on to the trail, Krishna once more rebelled.

"This is madness!" he cried, "I tell you if we meet any gorilla-men, and we will, I can't save you. They will not obey me!"

"If we meet any gorilla-men," Ki-Gor retorted, "and they do not obey you, George will shoot at them with the rifle. But he will shoot you first."

Krishna gave the jungle man a long look. Then a crafty gleam came into his eyes. He raised his hands, palm upward in resignation, and said, "Very well. I have warned you." And the strange quartet began the ascent from the Valley.

It was a long, nerve-wracking climb. At any moment a great hairy monster might rise up in the path and challenge the way. Ki-Gor's normal alertness was doubled, his keen eyes searching the surrounding forest ceaselessly. And George held the rifle ever ready.

But hours and miles went by without incident. The trees grew less tall, and the air grew cooler. Now and then the travelers could look up through openings in in the foliage and see above them their destination—the rocky ridge, partly obscured by its perpetual mists.

It was late afternoon, and the travelers were climbing into the region of weird vegetation, when they first ran into danger. Some sixth sense prompted Ki-Gor, who was in the lead, to look backwards as he rounded a bend in the trail. A huge gorilla-man was shuffling rapidly up the path behind George who was bringing up the rear. There was hardly time to warn the big Negro, and give him an opporunity to swing around with the gun.

Automatically, Ki-Gor ripped one of the drug-sacks loose from the rope on his shoulder. He shouted at George to duck, and then flung the sack full in the face of the charging man-ape. As the sack hit, it burst and spilled its contents all over the path. The gorilla-man staggered momentarily, and uttered a smothered roar. It started forward again, but suddenly caught sight of the familiar little white cubes, and halted. A hairy arm reached down and scooped up a handful of the drug tablets. As the man-ape crushed them into his mouth a foolish expression of ecstacy came over his savage face. And as the travelers watched, the gorilla-man completely harmless, sat down on the spot and proceeded to eat all the tablets he could find. In a very few minutes the hairy brute fell over backwards in a stupor, and the travelers resumed their journey.

"You wasted a valuable quantity of the drug, Krishna commented, "Six of those tablets are enough to subdue one of the man-apes, and you threw a whole sackful at him. If we meet more of them in any large numbers, you will only have five sacks left to deal with them."

Although Ki-Gor wouldn't admit it, he was worried about that very thing. But there was nothing to be done about it. It was the only way he could have saved George's life. And aside from the fact that George was a powerful friend and ally, Ki-Gor had come to regard the burly Negro with a strong affection. Ki-Gor hoped fervently that they would meet no more gorilla-men.

In a short while they climbed in to the mists, and Ki-Gor called a halt as they arrived at what appeared to be a fork in the trail. He did not remember seeing the fork on the way down, although, he reflected that it had been so dark that he could easily have missed it.

"Which way?" he asked Krishna.

"The way to the right is the way you came in'" was the answer. "Just above here it gets very narrow for a short distance as it crosses the face of a cliff. After that it goes on up to the Western Gateway, the cleft in the rock."

"And the way to the left?" said Ki-Gor.

"It is a perilous trail which the gorilla-men don't bother to guard, for the reason that it leads you to the crater of an active volcano. Once you traverse that crater, you are safe, but your chances are a hundred to one against crossing it alive."

"Volcayno, huh?" said George, coming up. "So that's what all that spooky rumblin' was, and earthquakin', and fire shootin' up out of the top of the mountain. Hoo-wee! An' we thought it was ha'nts! But still that don't explain the singin'."

"Singing?" said Krishna.

"Yeh, they was a whole mess of banshees all wailin' together."

"Oh, yes," said Krishna, "of course. I once had a set of Aeolian harps set up in a particularly windy spot. I thought that the peculiar quality of the instruments might set up superstitious dread in the minds of unwelcome visitors."

"Come, we must go," said Ki-Gor, "and we will take the right fork. The smoking mountain is more dangerous than gorilla-men. We cannot give white tablets to a mountain."

A FEW paces farther on, the trail narrowed, and Ki-Gor hesitated before embarking on the passage across the face of the cliff. The wind in their faces swirled the mist around the rocks terrifyingly.

All of a sudden, through some freak of wind currents, the mist lifted. The travelers could see four or five hundred yards ahead, past the cliff, above which the trail broadened again as it climbed toward the crest of the ridge and safety.

And there, less than four hundred yards away, a company of at least forty gorilla-men was standing.

As yet they were unaware of the presence of the travelers, but Ki-Gor shivered a little as he thought of trying to pacify that many of the brutes with the limited supply of the drug that remained. But it had to be done, somehow. The idea of crossing the crater of the volcano was unthinkable.

As if he had read his mind, Krishna came up and stood beside the jungle man.

"Unless you give them the tablets by hand, six at a time," Krishna said, "you will not have enough to go around. And if you get close enough to give them the tablets by hand, they will kill you."

"Then what are we going to do?" said Ki-Gor.

"There is only one thing to do," said the King of the Gorilla-men, "Give me the drug and I will walk on ahead and feed it to them by hand. I, alone, have the authority to go among them unmolested."

"I do not trust you Krishna," said Ki-Gor, "you are an evil man."

"Very well, then. Die," said Krishna with a shrug. "As soon as they see you, they will come down here and kill you. And I could not stop them."

"Mm," Ki-Gor bit his lip. "All right. Take the drug and give it to every gorilla-man. George will be watching you with the gun, and he will kill you if you do not do as you promise."

"Give me the sacks," said Krishna, and bent his head to hide the light of triumph in his eyes.

The mist stayed lifted as Krishna, King of the Gorilla-men, set forth on the narrow path across the face of the cliff. Over his shoulders he carried the sacks containing the drug tablets. Silently, Ki-Gor, Helene and George watched him gain the other side of the cliff and hesitate. A tall boulder stood beside the trail where it began to broaden again.

With a quick movement, Krishna slipped the sacks off his shoulders. And before the watchers down the trail realized what was happening, he tossed the sacks over the edge of the cliffs, and dodged behind the boulder. Ki-Gor shouted, and George fired, but not in time. The bullet ricochetted off the protecting boulder, and a second later, three shrill blasts of a whistle were heard.

"He's betrayed us!" Helene screamed. "He's commanding the gorilla-men to come down and kill us!"

"We'll have to run!" George shouted. "I haven't got enough ammunition lef' to hold 'em off. We'll have to go across the crater of the volcano!"

"But there's only one chance in a hundred of our making it alive!" Helen cried.

"Well, we ain't got even one chance, if we stay yere," George replied.

The gorilla-men were swarming down the trail, moving incredibly fast. The whistle kept summoning them from behind the boulder.

"You run back to the fork," George shouted, "and I'll try an' hold 'em back long enough for you-all to git up to the crater."

"No!" said Ki-Gor, "We three are friends. We stay together."

The gorilla-men had reached the boulder, and George drew a bead on the monster in the lead. But before he could fire, there was a shrill scream of terror. It was the agonized voice of Krishna, the King of the Gorillas. He had transgressed his own Law, and his subjects were visiting the familiar punishment on him. Two great simians appeared around the boulder. Each had one of Krishna's arms as he struggled between them, pealing shriek after shriek. Then each gorilla pulled . . .

Even Ki-Gor's hardened nerves quivered, as the mist descended, drawing a veil over the scene.

"Come!" said Ki-Gor, in a hoarse whisper, "they may not have seen us. Let us run for the volcano crater, while there is time!"

THE three turned and fled down the path. Ki-Gor hesitated a fraction of a second when they reached the fork, then plunged up the volcano trail.

It was rough going, and steep, and after a while, Helene stumbled and gasped. Ki-Gor picked her up like a baby, and the flight was resumed. Soon the mist lifted and they found themselves hurrying over black laval rock. The ground underneath their feet trembled constantly. Eventually, even Ki-Gor's tremendous endurance sagged, and they paused to get their breath.

George clutched Ki-Gor's arm and pointed. Not far down the bleak mountain side, the gorilla-men were patiently climbing after them.

The big Negro lifted his rifle and sighted down the barrel. But his first shot had no effect. The difficult downhill angle had resulted in the bullet going over the head of the target. George lowered his sights, and a moment later the gorilla-man in the lead toppled over.

Still panting from the exertion of the uphill flight, the three fugitives wearily continued their climb over the rough lava. They were about a half mile from the top, the rim of the crater. The pursuing gorilla-men were less than a quarter of a mile behind them. How long, thought Helene with a sob, could she and her protectors stay ahead of the relentless man-apes?

Up and up they struggled. George paused every now and then to pick off a gorilla-man. But the rest came on resolutely, and slowly the gap between pursuers and pursued narrowed. George had killed nine, but several of his bullets had missed, and his precious supply of ammunition was running dangerously low. There were still twenty-six of the monsters left—many more than there were bullets left in George's pouch.

"If—we—c'n jes' make it—to the top!" the big Negro panted, "Maybe we c'n—hold 'em off fer a little while."

They were a hundred yards from the top now, but the gorilla-men were getting closer and closer. Ki-Gor lifted Helene up in his arms, and, calling on his last reserves of strength, sprinted desperately up the steep incline. This can't be true, Helene thought dully—this is a nightmare. If the gorilla-men don't get us, what will we do when we get to the crater?

Four gigantic man-apes, slavering with rage were only ten yards behind. George whirled and fired point-blank. A scream of pain died out in a gurgle, and George fired again. A second gorilla-man fell. Despairingly, George pulled the trigger again. It was his last bullet. It reached its mark, but the last gorilla-man closed in on the Negro. George eluded a swinging blow of the giant arm and pumped his aching legs uphill. Above him, Ki-Gor was just gaining the crater's edge. The jungle man shouted down a warning. George threw an agonized look over his shoulder. The gorilla-man was almost upon him.

Gripping the rifle far down on the barrel, the Negro whirled and swung the gun like a baseball bat. The butt crashed into the gorilla-man's black face, and the monster reeled back. Lungs fighting for air, George staggered toward the top, still gripping the shattered rifle. He looked once more over his shoulder and groaned. He knew now that he was never going to make it.

One more brute had come up and was reaching an immense arm out toward him. George struck at it feebly with the rifle barrel, but the monster bared its fangs in a horrible grin. George wanted to close his eyes to death, but he couldn't.

Suddenly Ki-Gor was beside him, hacking and stabbing with the assegai. Blood spouted from the gorilla-man's neck, as the jungle man struck with the strength of a demon. The monster roared and lurched back. Then slowly and heavily it toppled over.

Ten seconds before the rest of the gorilla-men could reach them Ki-Gor and George struggled over the rim of the crater. With Helene, they poised on the edge of a sharp declivity for a moment. Then with hardly a glance before them, ran, slipped, and slid down into the crater of the volcano.

But that glance had been enough to show them that the volcano was momentarily inactive. When they reached the bottom of the slope, Ki-Gor looked back. Twenty gorilla-men stood in a row on the rim above them. But not one of them made a move to follow.

"They are afraid!" Ki-Gor shouted exultantly, "They are afraid to come down here after us!"

THE three fugitives stood for a moment, dazed. It didn't seem possible that they were, for the moment, safe. Around them stretched the black desolation of the crater floor. Here and there thin columns of smoke spiraled up from black cones—new little volcano craters within the crater. The ground vibrated uneasily under them. But they were safe from the gorillas!

"I can't believe it," Helene said, tremulously, "but we had better hurry across this place before the volcano starts to act up."

"Yes—*ma'am!*" said George, "if you dead, you dead. Don't matter if a gorilla-man kill you, or a volcayno. Hey, and this yere ground is sho hot, too."

Already, Ki-Gor was dancing on the hot dried lava.

"Over there," he pointed to a break in the rim, half a mile across the crater, "We go there and get out through that opening. Let us hurry."

"Wait a minute," said George, and ripped off the once-white shirt he was wearing. Quickly, he tore it into strips. Then he bent down and wrapped Ki-Gor's bare feet in the strips. He, himself, was wearing shoes as was Helene, and he knew that Ki-Gor could not long stand the heat of the crater-floor wthout some kind of foot covering.

With that operation over, the fugitives set forth. Behind them on the rim, the gorilla-men were still standing. George made a last derisive gesture and turned to follow Helene and Ki-Gor.

The ground continued to mutter, and the columns of smoke still stood up from the little cones scattered about the crater, but that was the limit of the volcano's activity. It was as if the mountain had a personality, and was deliberately holding its fires until the weary travelers could safely traverse the crater. Now and then, they had to dodge jets of steam and boiling water that spouted up from cracks in the lava. But by hastening their steps, they made it across the shaking crater-floor in a short time, and climbed safely up through the wedge-shaped opening in the opposite side of the rim. Far back on the other side, the gorilla-men were still standing in a baffled row.

Safe at last!

They were standing on the eastern slope of the volcanic peak, looking eastward at a magnificent panorama of endless ranges of mountains. Behind them the sun was setting in red glory. Suddenly the volcano gave a menacing rumble. A dozen of the little cones in the crater burst into action, shooting flames and black mud high into the air. The trio looked at each other. A few short minutes before, they were walking through the very spots where, now, molten lava and flaming death were raining down. Ki-Gor stood up.

An hour later, the travelers were a safe distance down the mountain side, looking for trees big enough to spend the night in. And the next morning, greatly refreshed after a long night of undisturbed sleep, they breakfasted on fruit, and headed eastward down the mountain.

Late in the afternoon, they stepped out of the forest on to the sandy shore of a vast blue lake.

"Oh! how beautiful!" Helene gasped, "I wonder where we are!"

But Ki-Gor was gripping her shoulder and pointing up the shore.

"What is that?" he exclaimed.

"I be dam' if that ain' a young battleship!" George cried, "Hey, let's hail 'em."

Coming toward them, quite close in to shore, a long white-hulled boat was gliding. Smoke poured from its single tall funnel.

GEORGE ran up the beach, shouting and waving his arms. As the boat came abreast of him, several startled figures appeared on the single deck. The water churned under the stern of the little vessel and it slowed down. The deck swarmed with men in white, and a small boat was lowered away. Ki-Gor watched fascinated as the gig, propelled by four oarsmen, moved rapidly toward shore, and slid up on the beach.

A tall, blue-eyed young man in a white uniform stepped out of the stern holding an automatic in his hand. An expression of bewilderment came over his face as he beheld the white girl in tattered white robe, the tall bronzed man in leopard-skin loincloth, and the huge Nego.

"Lord in Heaven!" said the stranger in English, "Who the deuce are you, and where have you come from?"

Helene felt tears of relief coming into her eyes, and her voice was unsteady as she replied, "We have come a long way. My name is Helene Vaughn and this——"

"Helene Vaughn!" the young man shouted, "The lost American aviatrix!

Oh, I say, dash it all, this is extrawdnry! You've been more or less given up for dead, you know. Oh, I say, this *is* a bit of luck! I'm Sub-Leftenant Tiverton of His Majesty's Sloop 'Rhododendron,' on patrol duty here on Lake Victoria. You must come aboard immediately and we'll make arrangements to get you out to the Coast."

"Thank you," said Helene with a misty smile, "and will you take my companions aboard, too? This is Ki-Gor. And this is George."

"Ki-Gor? George?" said the young officer, passing a hand over his bewildered eyes, and staring first at one and then the other.

"Yassuh, Cap'n" said the Negro, "George Spelvin of Cincinnati, U.S.A. An' I sho' could pile into some civilized vittles right now."

"Extrawdnry!" Sub-Leftenant Tiverton muttered, "Extrawdnry!"

Ki-Gor moved forward and touched the dazed young man on the shoulder.

"Are you N-Glush?" he said, shyly.

"N-Glush?" replied the young man, stupidly, "Oh, *English!* Oh, yes! Rather. You know, I'm awf'ly sorry, old man, but I don't think I quite caught your name."

Ki-Gor stepped back without answering. A smile lighted up his bronzed face. He liked the looks of this blue-eyed young man. And yet even then he knew he would never go back to his people. His home was the jungle, and there he would stay.

THE FUGITIVE

I

THE new Governor looked his secretary squarely in the eye.

"Tarleton," he said, pleasantly enough, "we're strangers to each other just yet. We shall pull very well together, I've no doubt at all—but just as a beginning, and unofficially, I wish you'd forget about all this sort of thing. How long did it take you, by the way?"

He tapped a beautifully typed three or four pages of report and put it down with a smile. Tarleton, a thin-faced man of forty, in neatly tailored drill, caught something of his humor.

"Most of last night, your Excellency," he admitted ruefully. "I wish I could forget about the things just as much as you do. But they're matters of record——"

He waved competent hands in a gesture of hopelessness. Quayle, the Governor, smiled again, the smile that had carried him so far, a twisted, humorous quirk of the facial muscles, accompanied by a sudden warm twinkle of his dark eyes.

"True," he agreed. "Sacred things, records, Tarleton. But in future, and just between ourselves, let's have the meat of

A novelette of a challenge that sounded from a remote corner of the African jungle.

By R. V. GERY

the thing verbally first, and let the phrasing go until later. I like the direct method."

He took up the report again and flicked a glance over it.

"H'm!" he said. "Very nice. Slaving, eh? Now, I suggest you put it in your beloved files, Tarleton, and shut that door. Tell the sentry we're not to be disturbed, and take a cigarette. It's unorthodox, of course, but I'm not altogether an orthodox person. I daresay that's been hinted at here already."

He reached out a brown hand to a cedar lined box of plain silver on his desk. "Go on, smoke," he said. "And let's hear some more about this slaving business. It's on the French border, to begin with?"

Tarleton unrolled a great wall map. On it, a narrow line of civilization, the river and its settlements showed up startlingly clear. The rest of the canvas—nine tenths of it—was blank. An angular red streak, crosswise athwart the upper corner, was the French boundary the Governor had referred to. Tarleton set his palm on it.

"It's there, sir," he said, tactfully dropping the "Excellency." "We've had trouble off and on in that bit of country for years. So've the French. It's a case of passing the buck," he grinned at the expression. "They say we're to blame, and we——"

Quayle nodded. "Yes, I heard," he said. "Diplomatic representations to Paris, and so on and so forth. Damn nuisance all round, Tarleton, and it's got to stop. Well, continue. What's the latest?"

"Something a bit out of the way, sir," said Tarleton. "There are indications that white men are mixed up in it—slave-running, I mean."

THE Governor opened his eyes a trifle wider. "White men, eh?" he asked.

"Very little doubt about it, sir," Tarleton said. "Old Ibn Akarish—he used to be the head local pirate up there; into everything he shouldn't be—was killed last year. Murdered, I rather fancy. Since then we've had a number of pretty strong hints that his successors are white. English speaking, too."

"How d'you know that?"

Tarleton put his hand on the report. "A lot of this, sir," he said, "is what we dug out of a fellow the police picked up up there."

"Where?" Quayle's normally level voice had a sudden little edge to it. His secretary took warning.

"A hundred and fifty miles up-country, sir," he said. "Made his own village too hot for him, it seems, and cleared out. He's a bit of a tough customer."

"Why haven't I seen him?" The Governor's question was matter of fact, ordinary; but the smile had gone from his lips and the twinkle from his eye.

Tarleton knew something about his senior's reputation. Therefore he did not attempt to shuffle.

"Your Excellency," he said, "your predecessor left these things a great deal to subordinates. The Inspector General of Police——"

"Listen to me, Tarleton," said the Governor decisively. "We'll settle this point now, once for all. I don't believe in decentralization. Nor am I a figurehead, Tarleton. I'll see for myself—always. What's this man's name?"

"M'Laka, your Excellency. He's a ——"

"Fellata," said Quayle curtly. "Yes, I know that. I've been this way before, Tarleton, remember. All my working life. Briggs hadn't. That's where you're going to find me different to him. Where's this M'Laka now?"

THE secretary hesitated. "I imagine the Inspector General will be holding him, your Excellency," he said finally. "We might want him again."

"We might indeed," said Quayle, a shade grimly. "Will you be good enough to go and get him—and while you're about it, get the Inspector General as well. I'll wait."

He sat back in his desk chair, lost in thought, twirling a heavy gold ring on the third finger of his right hand. The secretary left the room, in rather more of a hurry than was entirely dignified.

M'LAKA," said the Governor, "look at me!"

He spoke in a guttural singsong dialect of the Bantu, and the black man standing straight as a ramrod across the desk started a little. So also did Colonel Mobbs, the big Inspector General, who was at attention just behind the Governor's chair. This language business was a new accomplishment to a Governor; one that the estimable Briggs had not possessed—most eminently not.

M'Laka stared obediently at the slight figure in the chair. Quayle set his chin in his cupped hand and watched him for a full minute.

"Who am I, M'Laka?" he asked mildly.

The black showed his brilliant teeth in a skull-dividing grin.

"A Great One, lord," he said with fervor.

Mobbs permitted himself a faint smile, which faded almost instantly. Nevertheless there was something not without its humor in M'Laka's applying the title to a governor not a month in office—even if he had had a certain amount of experience out here already. It had been the prerogative of men whose names were even now almost legendary, the men who had carved the Province out of its seething aboriginal confusion.

Quayle, however, seemed to take it as a matter of course. He resumed his close inspection of M'Laka.

"So?" he said, after another interval.

"A Great One? Then you shall tell me the truth, M'Laka."

The native waited impassively for where this might lead to. He had, at the back of his dim mind, one or two well developed ideas, one of which was that anyone who regarded you in the gimlet fashion of the Governor was not any person to lie to. He therefore refrained from speaking until further questioned. Men had been known to be hung, expeditiously, for incautious statements to this type of being.

"And there are slaves in your country, M'Laka?" Quayle's voice was very calm. "Now you shall tell me of this—and thereafter will come not punishment, M'Laka, but a reward. Show your hands!"

M'Laka stretched them out. He was handcuffed, with a steel chain preventing him from separating his wrists by more than a foot or so. Quayle frowned at the sight.

"Knock those off, please," he said to Mobbs.

A sergeant of the police escort, trim in yellow khaki and with a red *tarboosh,* importantly produced a key and unlocked the bonds. M'Laka's eyes gleamed as he rubbed his chafed wrists.

"Speak," said the Governor.

FOR perhaps ten minutes M'Laka spoke in his clucking, gobbling tongue. He told of matters up on the shadowy border, two hundred miles and more from Administration Headquarters, and the recital was not a pretty one. According to it, slaving was very much alive up there, despite the decease of Ibn Akarish the Arab. It had been merely a change of devils, that was all, and villages in the forest clearings were still raided, with horrid accompaniments, and women and children swept off across the border into the edges of the great desert, there to be formed into caravans and, under Arab escort, hustled away into the unknown. Only, said M'Laka, now the raiders were commissioned by white men, not Arabs or local profiteers. Of this M'Laka had heard much.

"You have seen these lords?" Quayle asked.

M'Laka nodded his head in immediate dissent. He had not.

Mobbs interrupted with a disciplined apology. "That's the point, your Excellency. We know——"

"Just a moment, Colonel," the Governor's thin hand waved him down. "We'll go into all this later." He swung back to the black. "Yet there is the talk, M'Laka. What manner of men are these?"

"One lord is a fat lord—and the other skinny, like a monkey or the Great One himself."

Quayle accepted the description without a flicker of amusement. "So," he said. "These are Franki lords?"

M'Laka thought not. "Their tongue is as the Great One's," he believed.

"And their house?"

M'Laka did not know. It seemed that no one knew. Up in the many hundreds of miles of green forest from which he had come, that was perfectly possible, Quayle and the rest were aware. It was in the last degree unlikely that men engaged in slave running would advertise their headquarters.

Quayle changed his line. "And why are you here, M'Laka?" he inquired.

M'Laka shuffled his feet. "Lord," said he, "there was a killing palaver. N'Kema——" He clapped a fist to his mouth, as if in terror of having said too much.

"And who," Quayle asked, "is N'Kema?"

IT TOOK a great deal of persuading to get anything further out of M'Laka about this individual. Tarleton came to the rescue finally, with what was known of him. He was, Tarleton explained, the headman—chief, if the term was to be preferred—of a village deep in the forest, almost inaccessible behind mountains and swamps. There were rumors, said the secretary, that he had traveled more than was usual for a native and picked up a smattering of Western civilization. Consequently he had a formidable reputation as a trafficker in mysteries and something of a wizard; and there was no reasonable doubt that he was a party to any slave driving there might be in his neighborhood. M'Laka evinced a great disinclination to discuss him at all.

"A killing palaver," said Quayle thoughtfully at last. "I have a rope for killers, M'Laka. You shall tell me of this palaver."

"Lord," said the black, "N'Kema would chop me."

"And why?"

"He stole my fine wife," said M'Laka, "and sold her as a slave. Therefore I had it in my stomach to complain to the Great One. Therefore N'Kema sent his killing men for me. Therefore," he added simply, "I ran away."

"Very wise," said Quayle in English. Then, "And N'Kema walks with the white lords?"

"This was so," said M'Laka. N'Kema and the two white men were said to be more than friendly. Nevertheless—and here his teeth began to chatter—there were matters about this N'Kema that wise men did not discuss. He shut down tighter than a clam.

"Speak, O man!" The Inspector General threatened. "There are whips. . . ."

Quayle turned over his shoulder. "Colonel," he said very politely, "I am conducting this investigation. M'Laka," he resumed his staring at the native, "one day you shall tell me more of this N'Kema. Meanwhile, you shall sit here. There is my service, if you desire—pay, and a uniform even as this man here," he flicked a finger at the resplendent escort, "and a hut. Do you wish that?"

For a moment M'Laka gaped alternately at the man behind the desk and the trim sergeant. Then, with his eyes goggling in his head, he choked out a delighted assent. Quayle watched him follow his future companion in arms out, his head once more cleft in two by a huge gape of pleasure.

"Now, gentlemen," the Governor said to Mobbs and Tarleton, "let's go into this affair."

COLONEL MOBBS, the Inspector General, and commander of the native troops in the Province, was a large officer with a great fund of assurance. For the several years of his service at Administration Headquarters he had enjoyed himself a great deal with governors who were excellent ornaments, genial superiors, and strong supporters of anyone who would shoulder a little responsibility. Briggs had been an excellent case in point, and under his regime Mobbs had accumulated not a little extra prestige.

He had now and again in his time encountered the other type—the dry, lean expert such as Quayle—and disliked them heartily. They knew too much, he reflected, or thought they did; in either event they were an inconvenience.

"But, your Excellency," he said after a quarter of an hour's discussion, "I don't see where the difficulty lies. If you'll authorize it, I'll clean up the situation in a couple of weeks. It'd only need a small flying column, and I'd go myself. M'Laka knows where these men are—I've no doubt about that—and he'd talk all right if he was made to. He might even act as a guide, since your Excellency" the Colonel was growing heavily sarcastic, "has seen fit to enlist him."

Quayle heard him out patiently.

"Your men would be over the French border at the first whisper of anything like that, Colonel," he pointed out. "And we can't have any international complications over this business. Moreover, I'm not so sure that M'Laka does know anything more than he told us. He'd come out with it if he did."

He paused, fingering his ring, while Mobbs looked disgruntled. Tarleton said nothing. He was watching Quayle interestedly.

The Governor spoke once more. "No," he said. "I'm sorry, Colonel, but I'm afraid I don't see it your way. In the first place, you've no evidence whatever at present but hearsay, and native hearsay at that. That's fatal. You might go up there and find these chaps, and they'd be innocently washing tin or prospecting. True, we could chuck them out of the Province for being there at all without permits, but that's not quite what we want. They're slaving all right—no serious doubt about that. It's up to us to catch them at it. It's a lesson that's wanted—not a mere ejection."

Mobbs rose. "Then I'm to await instructions, your Excellency?" he inquired, with disciplined insolence.

"Please," said Quayle. "I'd like time to think this over. It doesn't at present seem to me to be a matter for military action. I may be wrong, of course," he flashed his disarming smile once more, "but let me have a day to consider. I'll let you know tomorrow."

THE Colonel saluted regimentally, and clanked out with much dignity. Quayle turned to Tarleton with the merest suggestion of a grin.

"Pity," said he. "I hate having to deflate a chap. But you see my point, Tarleton. These fellows, whoever they are would be out of it and over the French line five minutes after there was a whisper of activity from down here. They're not fools—and they've got their wires out all right, I've no doubt. No, this is another affair."

He got up and went to the window—a slim, spare figure, with the dry wiry look of the trained athlete and careful liver. Tarleton mentally contrasted him with his predecessor, Briggs, that bluff and hearty hedonist whom arteries, plus a hankering after the fleshpots of civilization, had sent home a month before.

The secretary waited, while Quayle walked up and down, whistling tunelessly under his breath. For ten minutes he paced thus. Then suddenly, "Who's that hospital doctor I met the other night?"

"Willoughby," said Tarleton.

"Good man?"

"Splendid. Old stager up here—longer than any of us. Knows the ropes."

"H'm. Send for him, will you, Tarleton?"

The secretary went to the door and spoke to the sentry; then he came back into the room to find Quayle back in his chair again, regarding him quizzically.

"Tarleton," he said, "can you keep your mouth shut?" Then, as Tarleton looked surprised, "No, don't be hurt. I mean shut—shut tight. I know you've the ordinary service tact, and a lot more, of course. But are you a real expert in silence?"

"I've been in the service sixteen years, sir," he said. "Most of it out here. It's good training."

The Governor pointed to a chair. "Sit down, then," he said. "Here's a trial for you."

When Doctor Willoughby was announced, the Governor was just saying, "You speak and write Arabic, of course?"

"Pretty fluently, sir. I was up in Darfur for five years."

"Yes, I knew. Queer country, isn't it? I'd quite a little out-of-the-way work there myself once. Well, that's all right. Now—what about this business? Are you on? Volunteer, of course."

"Certainly I'm on, sir," Tarleton said.

"All right. That's settled. Hullo, Doctor—come in! How's the hospital? Need any help?"

Willoughby, a tubby little man with a black mustache, looked slightly surprised.

"Your Excellency," he said, "there are always things——"

"I've no doubt," said Quayle. "Well, count on me if you want anything." He held out his wrist. "Feel that," he said astonishingly.

The doctor pulled out his watch and took the pulse. "Nothing wrong there, your Excellency," he said. "Might I ask——"

"Do you know," said Quayle, and winked solemnly, "it's a very remarkable thing, Doctor, but you're wrong. That's a very sick pulse. If you've a nice private ward in that hospital of yours, I think you'd better be looking it over. It'll be needed." He pulled the corners of his mouth down in a comic grimace.

"But—but—" the doctor stammered.

The Governor chuckled. "All right, Doctor," he said. "I've already shocked Tarleton here into something like heart failure. Now it's your turn. Just take this in, will you?"

II

INGLEBY and Slade went about their daily routine in a clearing of the deep forest.

Slade, the smaller of the pair, a man so emaciated that his ribs almost showed through his sweat stained shirt, was methodically checking over tusks of ivory laid out on the trampled grass. Ingleby sat in the shadow of a crazy mat veranda, and sipped gin with the passionate absorption of an alcoholic virtuoso.

Their conversation was mainly confined to monosyllabic grunts, which had lately been growing less frequent and a great deal more irritable. Now and again Slade would swear viciously, as a tooth turned out to be cracked, or when one of the darting insects stung him more painfully than usual. Ingleby would thereupon laugh throatily, as if his companion's discomfiture pleased him. And once, when Ingleby's limp shaky hand dislodged his tin mug from the elbow of the home made chair he sat in, Slade looked up from his counting with a sneer.

"Lushed again, eh, Tom?" he asked unkindly.

Ingleby hiccuped, and refilled his mug from a square bottle under the chair. There was a pile of cases in the shade, and a mixed assortment of tins—meat, preserves, soups, the usual prospector's chop. The gin came through devious channels across the French border; so did the supplies. For excellent reasons, Ingleby and Slade preferred to have few dealings with the Province at their backs.

The fat man gulped his liquor once more and picked up a crumpled newspaper on his knee.

"Well," he said, "we haven't come to any conclusion about this."

"No, we 'aven't," Slade said with a strong cockney accent. "An' what's more, me boy, we shan't. Not if you go on bein' so bloomin' comfortable about it."

The paper had filtered through here, taking six weeks about it, and passing through all kinds of hands and all manner of odd places. Unlike the gin, however, it had come from the rear of them, held gingerly in a cleft stick by a goggle-eyed native, to whom papers with devil marks upon them were a matter that savored strongly of Duppy. It was the weekly sheet produced at Administration Headquarters for the benefit of the Province's handful of whites, and its immediate interest for Ingleby and Slade lay in the fact that it contained a smudgy announcement of Quayle's appointment as Governor.

"Comfortable?" Ingleby queried. "Don't see any reason to be anything else. Do us good, as likely as not, this new man coming in. He'll be so busy making himself a pest he'll have no time for us."

"Bloomin' cocksure, ain't yer? Well, I ain't, Tom Ingleby. I've 'eard of this bloke before, I'm pretty sure. It was him that strung up MacKenzie and Dysart down in the Charaka country five years ago. And that was a gun-runnin' business."

"Well?" Ingleby grunted. "I daresay he did. But this isn't the Charaka country, Joe, and we're not gun-running. And he's got to find us before he can hang us. No one has yet. I don't believe there's a soul of this lot," he indicated the paper, "has the first real idea where we are. Or even who we are. Might even not know anything about us at all."

"Oh, come off it!" Slade sneered. "There's about as much chanst of us and our little doin's not bein' known as there is o' me preachin' a sermon. Whatcher think slavin' is—Sunday School picnic? You know damn well it isn't, Tom Ingleby, and you know damn well there's been things done that'll get about as long as there's men with tongues up here. Yus, and you c'n lay to that! I don't like it, cully, and I don't care 'oo knows it. We've 'ad enough of it—and we'll swing if we ain't careful. Ivory now——"

HE COCKED his head on one side at the row of teeth. "Look at 'em!" he said admiringly. "Only three out of twenty cracked—and not a rat among 'em. Here's the game, Tom Ingleby."

"You always were a coward, Joe," Ingleby told him dispassionately. "There's no real money in that stuff there. Trouble with you is, your liver's the wrong color—like your ivory. Black ivory's what pays."

"Yus," said Slade, "until we're nabbed. Then it'll be chokey first, if it ain't the rope. There's too much bloody risk in it for me."

"No more than there is in that stuff of yours."

"Try again, mister. We 'aven't got any N'Kema mixed up in this, anyway. That swine'd sell his grandmother for a plug o' tobacco."

"N'Kema's all right. He knows where he is. He's made a fortune with us in a twelvemonth."

"Yus. 'E 'as. And when 'e's got all 'e can out of us, 'e'll make another fortune out of our bloomin' skins. You see if 'e don't."

Ingleby suddenly flung the paper down and staggered to his feet. His temper was beginning to fray.

"Oh, shut up," he exclaimed. "You're enough to make a man cry with your whining, Joe."

He lurched unsteadily into the hut, and Slade watched him go.

THEY were an oddly assorted pair. Ingleby, in his lethargic alcohol-soaked way, was the brains and daring of the partnership. Once he had been a rising barrister at home, until the coming to light of an unsavory scandal had revealed him at its heart, and he had served eighteen months in jail. Released, he had made for West Africa—since, as he professed to himself, it was possible there to kill oneself rapidly, enjoyably and more or less cheaply. Ingleby, like many another of his kind, rather dramatized his remorse; on the day he left the Mersey he had honestly made up his mind to see to it that he was a dead man inside three months.

That he was still alive, four years later, was due to no want of earnestness in his attempts. He began to drink with wholehearted abandon, but unfortunately for his purpose his was one of those uncommon constitutions that gin seems to preserve and pickle rather than disintegrate. He throve on it and kindred tipple, grew gross and bloated, looked about him with new eyes, and commenced once again to hunt employment for the brains he had so prematurely condemned to

the grave. Unable to keep out of shady businesses, he was ejected from three or four coast ports in rapid succession, narrowly missed serving a second sentence in Accra jail, and finally, with the uncomfortable memory of that escape before him, struck inland.

There he met Slade, a down at heels cockney with just the qualities of experience he lacked himself. Slade knew the hinterland well, and its possibilities. It was he who had suggested striking far out into the wilds, and there, on the edge of French territory, setting up in the slaving game. He had heard of Ibn Akarish, the Arab, who, so to speak, owned the slaving concession thereabouts; and he knew where to go, spoke the local dialects well, and had some time previously had dealings with N'Kema, the educated aboriginal who had gone back to his wildernesses to carve out a little kingdom for himself there. In his way, Slade was very accomplished.

Thus, it was Ingleby who had suggested the removal of Ibn Akarish as a preliminary step, and Slade who had carried it out, by means of a .303 bullet through the body at a range of some six hundred yards. One of the cockney's talents was that of crack shot, and he had spent a week making his preparations for the Arab's undoing, calculating windage, atmospheric pressures, and drift. Ibn Akarish duly received his quietus as he sat peaceably at meat beneath a tree; and the bullet was ingeniously poisoned, at Ingleby's suggestion. The slaver died in picturesque convulsions that evening; and N'Kema with assorted braves rushed his leaderless camp that midnight, and put a neat finish to the affair with stabbing spears.

SO THE firm of Ingleby and Slade came into existence, with N'Kema the monkey chief as a junior partner—vice-president in charge of supply, so to speak. It was he and his white-bedaubed ring-straked followers who went forth to distant villages and brought in the goods; the young women and striplings that were the cream of the trade. Slade acted as jailer, interpreter, and bargainer in chief with N'Kema; and Ingleby, crasser than ever, but to all appearances lined within with sheet steel, periodically slipped over the border, and in a mixture of bad Arabic and Parisian French, interviewed the solemn desert sheikhs who represented the consumer.

Their camp was a curiosity. It took Slade a month's hard work to discover a location for it—tucked away in a green-clad valley in the foothills of a mountain range, almost undiscoverable to one who did not know the secret. They had a man of N'Kema's for attendant, with the fear of N'Kema's spears perpetually before him to keep him trustworthy; and for more than a year now they had been busily shipping cargoes of living souls.

It paid. In the year, Ingleby and Slade had accumulated a sum—in British or French gold, for they accepted nothing else—that made them lick their lips at thought of it. Slade had, out of his own imagination, evolved the subsidiary traffic in illicit ivory—rather to Ingleby's scorn. The big man's financial outlook was that of the city of London, and he had small patience with side lines. Slaves paid best; therefore slaves it should be, Ingleby held. If Slade liked to fool with ivory, well and good; but it was not Ingleby's affair.

NATURALLY, they had threshed out in great detail the ultimate chances of their being hunted down; but, as Ingleby pointed out, things were in their favor—distance and seclusion. Moreover, N'Kema had his ear to the ground for suspicious activity down the Province, and three hours' trek would take them into the French sphere of influence. Besides, at Headquarters sat the estimable Briggs. Ingleby, chuckling, recollected that in his earlier days he had several times sat at dinner with that genial public servant; and by applying his cynical mind to the Governor's personality he had evolved a theory of probabilities, as far as serious action on his part was concerned, that was very close to the truth.

Then two things happened, almost together. M'Laka, one of the monkey chief's young men from an outlying village, had a young wife inadvertently picked up and sold into slavery. His reactions to this mishap were so pronounced that the chief came to the conclusion that he would be better in another world. M'Laka, however, had long legs and a stout heart; and his escape ended ultimately in an interview with authority itself in the person of Quayle.

Secondly, the estimable Briggs went home, and Quayle reigned in his stead. It was just this occurrence that had been providing Ingleby and Slade with food for heated argument ever since the arrival of the crumpled and tattered *Gazette* the day before.

EVENING fell on the forest glade. Ingleby, careless of the insects, had dropped asleep in his chair. The cockney, a tidy soul, had been for an hour house cleaning; the earth floor was swept, the ramshackle table set with tin spoons and forks, a meal was in preparation. He called through the doorway to his companion.

Ingleby stirred, shook himself, and came in through the screens, blinking muzzily at the kerosene lamp. He sat down and began his meal.

The cockney ate in moody silence. The brush with Ingleby during the last day had hit him harder than he cared to own. Thanks to the big man and his brains, so Slade held, he had set hands on money such as he had never dreamt of before, and he did not at all desire just now to see matters run into a quarrel. Nevertheless, he was desperately anxious about this new Governor.

At last Ingleby spoke. The food had sobered him a little. "You're a surly little animal, Joe," he said. "What's the trouble? Same thing?"

"Well, I ain't 'appy, an' that's a fact," Slade admitted. "We don't know nothin' about this bloke, excep' what I told you about MacKenzie an' Dysart, an' that's not so good. Briggs was different. You 'ad 'im sized up, all correck an' proper, and a good job you made of it, Tom. This feller you ain't—that's all."

Ingleby scowled. "Oh?" he said. "You think so, do you? Well, if it's going to do you any good, I can make as good a guess at this chap as at Briggs. I'll tell you just what he'll do. Like to hear?"

"Go on," said Slade. "Seems to amuse you."

"First of all," said Ingleby, "he'll point out to everyone there that he's not Briggs. That he's been up to here before, and that he's not going to stand for any damn slack nonsense. He's going to run the show as it ought to be run, and anyone who crosses him will get into trouble. Then he'll start off with a campaign of remedying what he'll call his predecessor's abuses. That'll just about drive everyone crazy, trying to catch up with him, and it'll take a month or more before he's decided that it'll be better to leave things as they are. It'll take another month getting them back there. Then he'll begin complaining that he's misunderstood—and it's quite likely he'll hunt about for some congenial feminine society to tell his troubles to. Women, I mean."

"Any there?" Slade asked.

"Can't say, I'm sure. But if the place is anything like other places of the sort, no. Quayle'll make that another grievance. Then he'll start annoying the government at home about things. Then he'll get the Province into some nice little diplomatic mess through not leaving things alone. And then—if he hasn't taken to the bottle by this time—he'll go home."

He leant back in his chair and wrinkled up his fat face in a contented smile. "That's why, my good Joe, I don't think there's much danger in this Quayle. You see, I know the type. They're all the same. Give them a bit of authority and they'll choke themselves with it. You'll see. In six months Quayle'll be home."

He checked, listening. From outside in

the blanketing darkness a sound came, clear and well-defined, like the irregular beating of an artery. *Tok-a-tok, tok-a-tok, tok-a-tok-tok-tok,* it went, monotonously repeated. Ingleby and the cockney looked at each other. In these forests of N'Kema's the *lokali*—the hollow-log signalling drum beaten with two sticks—was not encouraged save in matters of utmost urgency.

THE two men went outside. Makombo, the black servant, was already listening, his stork-like neck craned in an attitude of acute attention. Neither Ingleby nor Slade interrupted him as he picked up the message of the hammering sticks.

"Well?" said Ingleby at last, as the boy relaxed.

"Lord," Makombo said, "the Great One is dying in the house of many windows."

Ingleby stared. "Good Gad!" he said. "Hear that, Joe? Quayle's dying—already."

"I ain't sorry," said Slade with a sniff.

"Think it's true?"

"I ain't known the drum to lie yet," said Slade. "Damn bad *ju-ju* for a drummer to send a lie. He'd be chopped one time if 'e was found out."

"Well, so much for Quayle, then. You'll be able to sleep at nights now, Joe."

"'Ope so," grinned Slade. Ingleby picked up the paper again.

"So that's that!" he said, half to himself. "Another Governor retires, eh? Wonder if he's gone yet."

The drum rattled again. Makombo called from outside. "That One is dead," he announced.

Ingleby shrugged and poured himself a tot. *"Prosit,* Quayle," he said with cynical humor. "Good hunting!"

The remark seemed to irritate the cockney. "What's the matter with you?" he demanded. "Can't yer speak Henglish?"

"Oh, sometimes," said Ingleby lightly. "One gets out of practice, though, living with you, Joe."

His speech was one of Slade's sore points. "Stow that!" he said flushing. "We ain't all of us been toffs and come a mucker, y'know!"

"True enough," said Ingleby with deliberate composure. "Still, I wish you'd try and moderate that accent of yours now and then."

"Oh, yer do, do yer! All right, Mister bloomin' Tom Ingleby—s'pose you try moderatin' that lush o' yours you're so free with. Dirty guzzlin' hog!"

"What's that?" It was Ingleby's turn to flush. Both men's nerves were on edge. "You be careful, my man. One day you'll go too far."

"Ho!" The cockney thrust his triangular face within a foot of Ingleby's. "So that's the way of it, eh? Be careful, huh! Well, you look at this——"

He whipped out a skinning knife from its sheath. Ingleby stepped back and grabbed the rifle leaning against the wall.

For a moment the pair stood thus, Slade with his knife poised, Ingleby with the .303. Another instant, and things might have happened in that hut; but there was a sound of stumbling feet in the darkness outside and a man, panting, lacerated, and streaked with blood, fell headlong into the room.

III

SLADE was the first to recover himself. "Cripes!" he said fervently. "Wot the 'ell's all this?"

The man on the floor appeared to be half conscious. He lay there, sobbing for breath, the picture of desperation. His clothing was in rags and festoons about him, his shoes in ribbons, and he was drenched and dripping with sweat and exhaustion. But he was a white man.

Ingleby stooped over him. "Here," he said. "Get up! Let's have a look at you."

He took the man by a shoulder, and raised him to a sitting position.

"Try some of that," he said, handing him his own mug of gin.

The stranger drank thirstily, choking over the raw spirit.

"Lord, that's good!" he gasped. "Much obliged, whoever you are."

Ingleby pushed and dragged him into a chair, where he sat slumped in a heap, utter weariness personified. He was a little man, thin and wiry; but the battering he had received from falls and stumbles—he did not seem to be wounded—made him difficult to size up. Beyond the fact that he was white and spoke English there was little that could be said of him with any certainty as yet.

Slade looked at him with suspicion. "'Oo are you, cully?" he said. "And where d'ye come from? This ain't an 'otel."

The man had a pair of dark eyes in which there still remained the spark of boldness. He looked Slade up and down.

"Easy, there," he said. "One question at a time, please!"

"'Oo are you, then? Come on—out with it!"

"This French territory still?" The man parried the question with another, anxiously.

"No," said Ingleby. "You're over the line."

The stranger gave a gasp of relief. "Then I'm safe for a while," he said. "Might I have another tot of that gin?"

INGLEBY poured him out a stiff dose. "When you're quite ready," he said, "we'd like to hear from you. As my friend here says—where d'you come from, what's your name, and what are you doing here? This is by way of being private property, I might add."

The man's composure was returning to him with his breath.

"Private, eh?" he said. "Well, you're safe with me. I've got enough private affairs of my own just at present to keep me occupied, gentlemen. My name's Mason, if you want it. And I'm on the run from the French."

"Wot for?" demanded the practical Slade.

"Murder." The newcomer spoke coolly. "Any objection?"

"Didja do it?"

"Oh, come!" The tattered Mason waved a deprecating hand. "You can't expect me to tell you just like that. Perfect strangers, you know. Let's say there was an accident. 'Twasn't much else, as a matter of fact—but the French won't see it that way. They've been after me with a rope, and a lot closer than I cared for. I must have crossed the line today, I suppose."

Ingleby inclined his head. "Probably," he said drily. "Mind telling us a bit more?"

The fugitive looked at his two hosts speculatively. "Why, no, Mr.——" he said.

"Let names alone," said Ingleby. "That can come later. What was the trouble?"

"I told you," said Mason. "I got into a mess over there and killed a man—a Frenchman. So I had to cut and run for it. That's all. Why?"

"Pretty thin, so far," said Ingleby. "I'm afraid you'll have to be a bit more explicit, Mason. What did you kill him for?"

"Usual reason, of course," said Mason. "It was one or the other of us. Any more cross-examination? You must have been a lawyer in your time."

Ingleby ignored the close shot. "Never mind that," he said. "You're a pretty unsatisfactory witness, at all events. What were you doing over there?"

"Here, that's enough!" The little man spoke with asperity. "I've told you all I'm going to. You can't make me talk."

"Can we, by crimes!" Slade spoke through his teeth. "You'd be surprised, now, mister. Come on—out with it! What was you doin' across there? Somethin' crooked, o' course. Was it booze?"

Mason laughed. "No," he said.

"Rubber? Interferin' with the French concessions? They're mighty touchy about that."

"No!"

"Ivory, then? You'd better tell, cocky, or I'll twist it out of you."

Ingleby suddenly jumped to his feet with an oath, upsetting his chair.

"Slaves, by Gad!" he roared.

MASON preserved a sullen silence and for a while no one spoke. Then Ingleby laughed harshly.

"Well," he said, "you've run into something this time, Mason. Happen to know any prayers?"

"Why?" Mason asked. "Going to knock me off? You'd not dare do it."

"Without any more fuss than a chicken," said Ingleby. "You're trespassing, Mason. In our way. Poaching, if you like."

"Why, dammit!" Mason's face was a study. "You—you don't mean to tell me you're in the business, too."

"Very much so," said Ingleby. "So you'll quite realize that we aren't any too friendly with anyone—let alone a stranger who comes along, finds out where we live, and then admits he's in our own line of trade. I'm sure you'll see that."

His tone was bantering, but there was a tense note in it, and he fingered the .303. Mason's dark eyes roved from him to Slade and found little comfort there.

"Well," he said, "this is a surprise, gentlemen. Any chance of making a deal with you?"

"Deal? What d'you mean by that? You don't imagine we're going to let you out of this, do you?"

"Possibly not," said Mason. "But—seeing that we're in the same boat—I might be of some use to you."

"Go on," said Ingleby, still in his softly urbane manner.

Mason appeared to consider for a moment. "If I'm not impertinent," he said, "how d'you find markets over there?"

"That's our own affair," Ingleby said. "Why? Know any better ones? Is that what you're driving at?"

"It is—exactly," said Mason. "Cut short, d'you want any other connections?"

Slade broke in. "Bribery, eh? Don't you listen to 'im, Tom. Put a bullet into 'im and 'ave done with it. 'E's foolin' you."

Ingleby had been considering the fugitive carefully. "Wait a bit, Joe," he said. "Let's look into this a bit further. Go on, Mason."

"Did you ever hear," Mason said slowly, "of Abu Hussein?"

Both Ingleby and Slade jumped. "What about Abu Hussein?" Ingleby demanded. "He's not up here. He's down round the Tchad."

"He was," said Mason. "So was I. But—if I told you he was up here, now, looking for trade——"

"I shouldn't believe you, for one," said Ingleby. "Abu Hussein's too well known as a slaver for us not to have heard about him if he was within a hundred miles of this."

"He's not thirty at this minute."

"Very interesting, Mason. I'm afraid it's a little too tall, though. Try again."

Mason felt in a pocket. "Like me to demonstrate a bit more clearly?" he asked.

"Of course."

"Look at these, then." He handed Ingleby a scrap of paper and a curious gold ring.

THE paper was covered with spidery Arabic script, and Ingleby turned it over doubtfully.

"I don't read the stuff," he admitted. "It's beyond me. Beyond my partner here, too."

"Like me to translate?" Mason offered. "No—hardly, I imagine. Well, that's a pity. Without that the ring won't go for much with you, I presume."

"Nothing at all," said Ingleby.

Mason sat upright. "Too bad," said he.

"I could have put you gentlemen in the way of a biggish job. You see, I'm representing Abu Hussein, as this paper would tell you if you read Arabic. However," he shrugged, "what can't be, can't be, and I see your friend here looking pretty wolfish. You'd better shoot and have done with it."

Ingleby thought for a long time. "What about it, Joe?" he said.

"You know what I think—finish him off. Don't take any chances."

"I won't," said Ingleby. "Still, there's this thing. I'd like to find out—look here, doesn't N'Kema read Arabic?"

"Says he does," Slade growled. "Dunno if it's true."

"I shouldn't be surprised if it was," Ingleby said. "He's a queer stick, N'Kema."

"Well," said Slade, "that don't make any difference to this bloke 'ere. Put 'im out o' the way first—and if there's anything in this stuff, we can swing the deal ourselves with Abu Hussein."

"And have him making awkward inquiries about his friend Mason?" Ingleby snorted. "Joe, you're a fool, sometimes. No, if there is anything in this, Mason's right. He's too valuable to lose. You say Abu Hussein's out there?" He spoke to the fugitive, with a nod at the darkness.

"About thirty miles away, I should say," Mason's voice was entirely level. "Just where, of course, I don't know, but he'd be easily enough found. He's probably in French territory yet. But he'd come across here if I told him. He's alone."

"Alone? Abu Hussein? Expect us to believe that?"

MASON shrugged once more. "Just as you like," he said. "Look here. You get your friend What's-his-name to translate that for you. Then you send across to Abu Hussein with a note from me—yes, your friend can read that, too. If Abu Hussein isn't here within twenty-four hours, you can go ahead. That's fair enough, isn't it?"

Ingleby rose. "Come outside, Joe," he said. Then, a thought seeming to strike him, "Just a minute, though. I'm not going to leave you like this, Mason. We can hardly have you loose about the place. You'll have to forgive us, if you're what you say you are."

He produced a length of rope and strapped Mason to his seat. The newcomer merely chuckled.

"Don't mention it," he said. "I quite see your point."

In the darkness outside, Ingleby handed the paper and ring to Slade.

"Now," he said, "you slip across to N'Kema. Find out from him what's the meaning of all this—then come back here. You ought to be in by dawn. I'll look after Mason in the meantime."

"Yus, you will!" Slade grumbled. "You'll be sittin' on 'is knee as like as not, time I'm back. There's too much jenny-have-a-cup-o'-tea with you all round, Tom Ingleby!"

The big man gripped his arm. "You damn little fool!" he said savagely. "D'you think I'm done with him yet? Not by a mile. We'll use him—and then I'll put paid to him one way or another. He's dynamite, Joe. I know that as well as you do."

FOR long hours of the night, Ingleby and the stranger sat in the hut. To begin with, although he released him from his bonds with a half-humorous apology, Ingleby was inclined to be reserved and cautious; but as the night wore on he insensibly relaxed from a jailer into a host, and in time he and Mason were chatting more or less amicably.

The little man proved quite ready to talk. He had, it appeared, had an even more checkered career in Africa than Ingleby himself. He talked at first hand of the continent from Suez to Mozambique, and from the highlands of Abyssinia to the frightful heats of Gaboon. Ingleby was given to boasting of his great days in the past, before his fall; Mason quite frankly gloried in his African doings, and their recital lost little in the telling. By his own account, there were few queer occupations and borderline avocations in which he had not been from time to time involved; and Ingleby listened to him with increasing interest. The man obviously knew his Dark Continent.

He told of his killing of the Frenchman two days before. The man—a bush trader—had resented Mason's presence there, it appeared, and told him to get back whence he came. Abu Hussein had not revealed himself yet, and Mason had remained to argue the point with the Frenchman, who had suddenly drawn a gun on him.

"Of course," Mason said casually, "after that there wasn't anything to do but *mafish* him. I did, and so I had to bolt for it, with the French after me. A pretty dance they led me, too. I'm about all in."

He certainly looked it. He was obviously almost worn out, but there was something about his wary dark eye and the little twisted smile that kept Ingleby still close to his resolve of finishing him off when he should have served his turn. Ingleby knew a dangerous man when he saw one.

He tried to pump Mason about Abu Hussein. The trader's name was common property wherever the slave trade was mentioned; Ingleby had heard of him many times before, always as a mysterious but deeply interesting personality. He had the reputation of dealing in larger numbers of slaves and paying higher prices than any of the desert men; and there were strange tales about his acquaintanceship with the great ones of the world, and his influence on that involved tangle, African politics.

But Mason was very reticent about him. "You'll see him in person tomorrow," was all he would say, and Ingleby had to be content with that.

Gradually the talk veered to London and the original haunts of both men, and here Ingleby shone. Vanity, like gin, was one of his obsessions, and after a year of the mocking Slade he found this Mason a welcome subject on which to practice. He was perfectly ready to admit his past, now, and to lift the curtain from at least one kind of high society.

Mason took it all in, interestedly. He too had heard the chimes at midnight in the old land, and had left it for its good. However, in contradistinction to the boasting Ingleby, he seemed to have a general grouch against society, which he developed at some length while Ingleby drank steadily and nodded in owlish comprehension. Surprisingly, Ingleby found that he was enjoying himself more than for many a long month. Dangerous or not, this Mason spoke his own language.

THE turn of the night came. It was stiflingly hot, and Slade could not be expected for some hours yet. The ceaseless drone of the insect life made a drowsy undertone to the two men's conversation. Little by little it grew desultory, the sentences fewer and farther between.

Ingleby nodded—roused himself with a jerk. Across the table Mason had dropped his head on his arms, and was snoring softly and regularly. Poor devil, Ingleby thought in maudlin sympathy. He tilted another jorum of the gin into his mug, tremulously, and swallowed it at a gulp. Then he closed his eyes for a moment. In five minutes he was fast asleep.

Mason continued to snore realistically. Then, with extreme caution, he opened an eye. Ingleby's head had fallen on his chest; he was fathoms deep in hoggish slumber. Inch by inch Mason sat up. He looked about him, bright eyed for all his weariness. After a minute's careful inspection of the room and its clumsy furnishings, he rose to his feet and began a swift methodical search. Ingleby slept on as the fugitive's deft fingers explored, rummaging here and there silently and unhurried.

At last, in a rough chest, he discovered an object which seemed to please him. He looked at it a moment, and then stuffed it down his ragged shirt. Foot by foot he stole back to his chair, and resumed his previous position, head on arms, making the night melodious with his snores.

IV

SIX of N'Kema's young men, doing sentry-go outside the village, stopped Slade and with broad grins of welcome conducted him to the monkey chief's hut.

N'Kema was still waking. He sat on a mat of skins, a gleaming leopard cloak about him, fringed with monkey tails. A stuffed monkey head grimaced from each of his shoulders. Although contact with Western civilization had taught him enough to keep a couple of very well tended rifles on the wall of his hut, he still carried the two broad-bladed stabbing spears, for intimidation, and as a symbol of authority. He was a middle-aged man, with an enormous paunch and legs that were already growing too weak to support his great weight.

He rose with some difficulty to his feet as he saw Slade.

"I see you, lord!" he rumbled in conventional welcome. N'Kema spoke English of the coast brand as well as Arabic, but it suited his book best to confine himself in conversation to his own clicking dialect.

Slade handed him the paper. "Wot's this, N'Kema?" he asked.

The chief took it, and turned it over in the light of his guttering oil lamp. Slade, watching him narrowly, saw him give a start as he read it, scratching himself the while. A frown appeared on his hideous face—a frown of puzzlement. He looked up at Slade.

"Lord," he said, "this is a book of Abu Hussein the trader."

" 'Ow d'yer know?" Slade demanded.

N'Kema sat down again and commenced to deliver a recital. "Long ago," he announced, "before the little monkeys that are my people" he gestured towards the grinning heads on his shoulders, "whispered in my ears that I was the chief of this place, Abu Hussein the trader loved

me, saying, 'N'Kema, we are brothers, you and I.' Therefore, lord, I marched in his caravan many moons, speaking much fine talk with him, as brother to brother, and learning the reading of these devil marks. And the name of Abu Hussein here, lord, is as he was used to write it. But where, lord, is Abu Hussein?"

Slade gaped at him. This looked very like confirmation—startling confirmation—of Mason's claim. He pulled out the ring.

"Seen this before?" he asked.

N'Kema goggled at it. "Lord," he gasped, "it is the ring of Abu Hussein himself, for I have seen it on his finger." He moved closer in obvious trepidation and scrutinized the chasing. "This is a great wonder, lord!" he said under his breath.

"You're sure, N'Kema?" Slade queried.

N'Kema protested that he was completely certain. He did not tell Slade that as a youth he had been Abu Hussein's body servant in his caravan—in other words, one of the very slaves he was now trafficking in himself; but such was the fact, and it was so that he had come by his knowledge, small enough but sufficient for this purpose, of written Arabic and familiarity with Abu Hussein's signet.

Luckily, perhaps, for him, Slade was convinced and did not demand a translation of the writing. It was merely an order signed by Abu Hussein—half a continent knows that flourishing scrawl—commending the *sidi* Mason to all comers; but N'Kema would have been hard enough put to decipher that in its completeness. He did, however, point out Mason's name, completing Slade's conquest.

"Now look 'ere," said the cockney to him earnestly, "you keep this thing quiet, savvy? There's a big deal goin' through, and you'll get yer share, just as usual, if you're good. 'Ow many've you got in 'and just now?"

N'Kema had sixty, he asseverated. He could, if necessary, find as many more in a couple of days, since even then a raiding party of his young men was expected back from a distant and hitherto virgin village.

Slade swore to himself. "Gawd!" he breathed. "A 'undred an' twenty—and at Abu Hussein's prices! This is a job for Tom."

He left N'Kema with renewed instructions as to silence and went off back through the night. The monkey chieftain watched him as he left the circle of the village fires, and scratched himself in an agony of perturbation. There were excellent reasons, even at this distance in time, why he was not anxious to encounter Abu Hussein.

DAWN was already breaking when Slade hurried through the wet grass of the glade. Ingleby, rubbing gummy eyes, was standing in front of the house, and advanced at sight of the cockney.

"Well?" he asked.

Slade gave a swift and excited account of his mission. The big man nodded in a satisfied manner.

"Thought so," he said briefly. "Well—what's next?"

"Better 'urry up an' get this Hussein feller over 'ere," said Slade. "Ain't no use wastin' time—there's N'Kema with a 'undred 'ead an' more all ready to do a deal. I'd 'ave Mason bring 'im across one time. Where's 'e now—Mason, I mean?"

"Sleeping inside," said Ingleby. "He's beat to the wide world."

Slade glanced at him oddly. "Still think the same about doin' 'im in?" he enquired. "Ain't gone moony about 'im, 'ave yer?"

"No!" Ingleby's voice was harsh. "I've not. What's all the fuss, Joe? You've not found me moony, as you call it, about other things—Ibn Akarish, for instance."

"No, I 'aven't," Slade said. "But this feller 'ere's a toff—easy to see that. 'E's your own sort, Tom. But if you let 'im off, because o' that, you're a bigger fool than I gave you credit for, that's all."

"Don't you worry about that," said Ingleby. "I'll cook his goose all right when the time comes."

He made as if to re-enter the house, but stopped again. "Look here, Joe—there's another thing. This fellow's going to take us to Abu Hussein—not he come to us. I won't have him here. There've been quite enough people about the place as it is."

"Think he'll do it?"

"Oh, he'll do it all right. Why not? He and I'll go over there—by appointment, as he suggests. Tomorrow, I suppose. You can go down to N'Kema and get the stuff ready for shipment. Then we'll do our bit of haggling with Abu Hussein, slip the goods across—we'll have to find escorts until Abu Hussein's own people come up—and then, well, I'd not be surprised to see some kind of accident happen to Mister Mason. Eh?"

"Sounds all right," Slade said. "But don't you go forgettin' the accident part, or our number's up, unless I'm a Dutchman."

INGLEBY laughed good humoredly and went in. Mason still slept, his head on the table. The fat man shook him awake.

"'Morning!" he said cheerfully. "Well, I'm glad to say you were right about Abu Hussein, and we owe you an apology. Put it there, Mason—shake hands with him, Joe. Now, we'll just have a little refresher to open our eyes a bit, and then breakfast. Afterwards you can drop your line to Abu Hussein, and we'll have N'Kema—nice fellow, N'Kema; you'll like him—deliver it. By the way, I suppose there's no objection to our going to meet Abu Hussein instead of his coming here. You'll appreciate why, I've no doubt."

Mason considered. "Why, no, I don't think so," he said. "In fact, it might be just as well if we did go to him. He's a dignified kind of a josser, as you may have heard and he'd take it as a compliment. Yes, we'll go to him, if that suits you all right."

"Then that's settled," said Ingleby cheerfully. "Joe, tell that black devil outside to get something to eat—and meantime, Mason, here's how. Drink hearty, man! It's the only thing to do up here."

All that sweltering day the three men spent in the house, stretched on chairs, drinking and talking. Once more Mason proved himself to be a born narrator of his own adventures up and down Africa. Ingleby retailed more of his tales of London at its most civilized, and Slade, not to be outdone, told of his own lurid youth.

Mason had written his letter to the Arab, and Makombo, the black boy, had been entrusted with it for delivery to N'Kema, and thence to its destination. Neither Ingleby nor Slade had any doubt of the monkey chief's ability to find Abu Hussein in the forest. His young men would comb the place until they came upon him.

The anticipation proved correct. Late that night a runner came in, tired and travel stained, but with Abu Hussein's answer. The Arab would expect them on the morrow, at a place to which the bearer of the missive would guide them.

"We'll sleep," said Ingleby. "There's a big trek before us."

The three curled up in more or less ungraceful positions about the house. As Mason rolled over, he felt inside his shirt the hard square object he had looted from the chest the night before. He smiled in the darkness at its touch—a queer twisted little smile.

V

ABU HUSSEIN the trader puffed gravely on a little silver water pipe and turned his slow glance from Ingleby to Mason and back again.

They were seated in the shade of a group of giant ironwoods, putting the final touches to a deal that made even Ingleby swell with anticipation. Starting at dawn, he and Mason, with N'Kema's black for a guide, had come upon the Arab at evening; and now, with the light beginning to fail and the trees flinging long shadows across the open ground before them, they smoked and talked with the placidity and good humor of a task half accomplished.

Ingleby in particular seemed impressed with the Arab. To begin with, Abu Hussein, although he had a reputation for taciturn dignity, had expanded rapidly after the first exchanges of courtesy; surprisingly to Ingleby, he spoke English, fluently if brokenly, and was a man of very obvious culture. The big man discovered yet another audience for his own narratives, and Abu Hussein listened with polite sounds of incredulity to tales of London in the great days when Ingleby had been one of its ornaments.

The Arab was a tall man, with slightly sunken cheeks covered with a small beard, and shoulders bowed a little, as if with age. He was probably fifty or more, thought Ingleby; but once, when he rose and went to his leather traveling sack for tobacco, he seemed to display an activity and wiriness not in keeping with the flecks of gray in his beard and the tiny crows feet at his eye corners.

Ingleby, sitting with his rifle across his

knees and Mason at his side, conducted the negotiations with the tact and bargaining capacity of the man of business he was. The Arab, on his carpet with a roughly devised canopy overhead, spoke briefly and to the point when it came to the question of slaves. He knew what he wanted, and was prepared to pay a price substantially higher than usual. Ingleby, curious, attempted to discover his ultimate markets for the goods; but the Arab with a humorous little gesture passed the question by.

"Well," said Ingleby finally, "that settles it, I suppose. I—we can deliver something over a hundred, at any time you like. Would here do for the place? We'll supply escort, of course, until you can hand them over to your own people."

Abu Hussein took his pipe out of his mouth and nodded. "In the name of Allah!" he murmured, "Let them be here at dawn tomorrow. Then I will pay."

Ingleby spoke to Mason, who had kept in the background of the conversation so far. "I'll send this fellow," he pointed to N'Kema's runner, "across to Slade at once. He and N'Kema can bring the party across here by that time. We'll wait for them."

He scribbled a note on the back of an old envelope, and the man went off with it at a steady lope. Then he fumbled in a canvas bag at his side and drew out a couple of square bottles.

"After business, pleasure," he said. "Can't tempt you, Abu Hussein, I suppose?"

The Arab declined courteously, but remained sitting on his carpet, while Ingleby and Mason drank.

"By the way," Ingleby said, "Mason here's in some sort of a mess with the French, he says. Murder, wasn't it, Mason?"

"Unfortunately, yes," said the fugitive. "When this deal is over, I'll have to make myself scarce. Well, it won't be the first time—eh, Abu Hussein? We've been in some tight places together," he added reminiscently.

"I don't doubt it," Ingleby said. "I wonder you're not a bit leary of sitting here. We must be over the line now."

"I'm not so absolutely sure about that. Maps aren't any too accurate, as you'll know well enough—and I've not taken a bearing. Might be either side; at any rate I'm taking the chance. But when I do get out of this it'll have to be back through the Province, all the same. The other side's too hot just now. Abu Hussein here can slip through them all right with a little palm greasing; but a killing's another matter. I'll find my way out all right, though."

Ingleby stroked his rifle thoughtfully. There might be two views of that question.

THEY ate at nightfall, a rough meal cooked for them by a lanky black, who was, it appeared, the trader's sole attendant on this expedition. His main body, the big armed caravan with which he normally moved, was four days' march away, beyond the strip of French ground. It was caution that had dictated this single-handed reconnaissance with Mason, he explained. Even his assurance did not run, he said smiling, to a full-dress parade through the French posts.

Ingleby turned the subject, speaking of Quayle and his swift death. The Arab had heard of Quayle by reputation, and told of some of his exploits down in the Tchad country and on the edges of the desert. He evinced something like regret at hearing Ingleby's news, and muttered an Arabic text under his breath. It seemed to Ingleby, listening to his account, that Slade's estimate of the Governor might after all have been the right one. It was just as well, after all, that Quayle had been thus early removed.

The black erected shelters for the night for Mason and Ingleby, and towards ten o'clock Abu Hussein signified his intention of retiring. He had a tiny tent of silk, and wrapping himself in his cloak entered it after ceremonious salutation; the flaps closed after him and the two white men were left alone.

For a while they sat chatting in the darkness. Then Ingleby yawned.

"Let's turn in," he said. "Tomorrow's liable to be a day when we'll want our wits about us."

He crept into his shelter, and Mason followed suit. Silence fell on the clump of trees, and darkness, except where a faint flicker of light showed from Abu Hussein's tent, withdrawn a little from the rest. The black got up, stretching enormously, and moved out to a lair he had scooped for himself at the wood's edge. He lay down, as if for slumber; but his eyes did not close, and he was very wide awake indeed, listening.

INSIDE his tent, Abu Hussein was occupied in an odd manner. He was also wakeful; and lying on the floor, out of range of the rays of his tiny lamp, he was industriously cleaning and oiling a remarkably serviceable pair of flat automatics. The gravity had fallen from him, and his face muscles had been allowed to relax; from time to time he rubbed irritatedly at his beard.

His task done to his satisfaction, he turned the light out and rolled over, still with the cloak about him, and the two pistols strapped to his waist beneath it by a leather belt. Like the black outside, however, he remained awake, hour after hour of the slow night.

It was well after two o'clock in the morning, and the moon was on the point of rising, when the crouching black pricked up his ears, and emitted a little hiss through his teeth. Out in front of him, low on the open ground, something moved stealthily; as he watched it it vanished, then reappeared closer to him. He lay perfectly still until a head arose from the earth not a foot from his and he found himself staring into rolling white eyeballs like his own.

The stranger's dress was invisible against his background, but Abu Hussein's retainer appeared entirely incurious. A few hoarse whispers, the passing of something from one black paw to another, and the man was gone, vanishing as silently and expeditiously as he had come.

Abu Hussein, open-eyed and alert, was aware of a faint scratching low down on the silk wall of his tent. Cautiously, and in the manner of one who was prepared for something of the sort, he thrust a hand underneath the curtain. A folded paper was slipped into it, and the trader heard the man outside edging foot by foot away through the dark.

He felt at his side and took up a pencil-sized electric torch. Sheltering its flash with the half-closed palm of his hand, he scanned the message thus secretly delivered. Then with a little grunt of satisfaction he turned over and slept.

THE gray of dawn was in the sky when he awoke, and thrusting the flaps aside looked out. Ingleby was still sleeping, his feet protruding from the bivouac; but Mason was already up and about, and Abu Hussein beckoned to him in silence.

For a few moments the two conversed in whispers, earnestly and as if on some matter of importance. Then Abu Hussein turned away with a gesture that was half a salute, while Mason strolled down to the wood's edge and looked about him.

The trader had, it appeared, chosen his position with considerable care. In front of the tall clump the ground fell away for two hundred yards or so, open save for an occasional low bush. On each side, the forest swung round in almost impenetrable horns of green growth, forming a kind of amphitheater; and in the rear of the clump itself it stretched away until it merged in the great solitudes of leaf and colonnaded tree trunk, back and back into the utter wilderness.

Mason stood, hands in pockets, letting his quick dark eyes rove over the prospect. He was still in rags, torn by his flight through the undergrowth, begrimed with dirt and sweat. Nevertheless, there was an alert decision in his attitude, speculative and aware, until Ingleby stirred under his covering and thrust his head out.

"Gad!" he said lugubriously. "What a head! Must have been that cold salmon at supper."

He winked at Mason, as if in admiration of his own clumsy humor. Then staggering to his feet with a groan, he took up his rifle and was ready for the day.

Abu Hussein came from behind his tent, where he had been performing his morning's devotions. He greeted Ingleby with his usual serious civility, and clapped his hands for the black, who had a pot of coffee boiling over a little fire of sticks. The three men drank standing, while Abu Hussein's canopy was erected and his carpet spread.

The east was yellow with approaching sunrise by now, and Slade with N'Kema might be expected at any moment. The Arab took his seat impassively, and waved to Ingleby to take the post of honor at his right; rifle still in hand, the fat man complied, not without a sideways glance at Mason. He intended to keep an eye on the fugitive until this piece of business was over and he had served his turn; and then his mind was made up as to his course of action. Mason at any rate would not see the sunset; for Abu Hussein, that was perhaps another matter. It might not be a paying affair to wipe him out as well. Too many strings were attached to his name. But as far as Mason was concerned, there were no such difficulties. One scalawag white man more or less up here hardly mattered; and an accident was easily enough devised.

MEANWHILE Mason was unsuspicious enough. He sat on his heels, chewing the stem of his pipe, talking generalities with Abu Hussein, and now and again including Ingleby in his conversation. For some reason he appeared to have Quayle's death much in his mind, and plied Abu Hussein for more information about him. Ingleby, whose nerves were beginning to feel the strain, found the subject supremely irritating; and after a quarter of an hour of it, he broke in with brutal suddenness.

"What's the use of talking about the fellow, Mason?" he complained. "He's dead, and good riddance. Might have been damned inconvenient up here. You can never tell what these jacks in office are liable to do next."

"And yet," said Abu Hussein, fingering his lip, "I have heard that the *Mudir* was a wise and excellent governor."

Mason turned his head away to peer over the open ground as Ingleby exploded.

" 'Wise and excellent governor', eh? Infernal prying busybody, more like. He'd have been up here—it's quite likely—seeing for himself in six months from now; and that wouldn't have been pleasant for any of us."

Gin, heat, and the waiting were affecting Ingleby, and he held Quayle up to bitter ridicule for minutes on end. His attitude of tolerance for the new Governor had vanished, and he was viciously triumphant at the chance that had now removed him.

Abu Hussein and Mason allowed him to run on without interruption. Mason still seemed absorbed in watching for Slade and N'Kema, and the Arab continued to fondle his beard, to hide an occasional twitch of his sensitive mouth. Above them, the black had climbed into the branches of the ironwoods, and from that watch tower kept vigil.

At last Ingleby worked himself up into a passion. "You, Mason!" he said savagely. "Why can't you say something? Might try and be polite, anyway. Or was this scum Quayle, and damn him, a friend of yours?"

No one answered him for a moment, save that Abu Hussein smiled outright.

Ingleby cursed restlessly. "Come on, Mason," he taunted. "Out with it!"

He fingered his rifle ominously. Abu Hussein shifted ever so little as he sat.

"Lord," said the black from above, "they come!"

VI

IT WAS nearing midnight when Ingleby's scribbled envelope was delivered to Slade in N'Kema's village.

The cockney had been having a disturbing time with the monkey-caparisoned chieftain. N'Kema, at the last moment, had shown an utter disinclination to have anything personally to do with Abu Hussein. To all Slade's remonstrances and oaths he turned a deaf ear, retiring into his shell of aboriginal stupidity.

Once again he kept his thumb on essential truths. His real reason for being shy of the Arab was that away back in his "long ago, when Abu Hussein loved him," he had abruptly left the trader's service, taking with him as loot whatever his black hands could grasp. Fleeing precipitately, he had not gone so fast that rumors of the trader's fury had not overtaken him, and for many months he had skulked in seclusion down at the coast, with terror riding him day and night. It was not until he had come into his own up here behind the hills that he had felt safe. And now Abu Hussein was just across the road from him, so to speak, expecting him to deliver a drive of slaves.

N'Kema would rather not. He told Slade so in a dozen fashions, and the cockney, blaspheming sulphurously, could not budge him an inch.

"You damn black animal!" he told him. "Just you wait until this affair's through. I'll cut the 'ide off of you, chief or no bloomin' chief. Strike me pretty if I don't!"

He pulled out a turnip of an old silver watch and glanced at it in the firelight.

"Gawd!" he said to himself. It was nearly one. "Look 'ere, you black *barn-shoot,* if you won't take 'em across, I'm goin' to. So that's flat, ugly-face, and you better come down an' pick 'em out. 'Op it, now!"

N'Kema had no possible objection to this. Anything rather than face Abu Hussein, was his attitude; and if he could get rid of this little wasp of a white man as well—and at the same time sell goods —he was more than contented.

He shambled to his feet, and Slade and he went down the village street to the pens outside where the miserable victims of three men's avarice were corraled.

They were sheeplike with fear and suspense, herded together in a shrinking mob within fences of notched logs, with N'Kema's spearmen on guard. A fire burnt at the only entrance to the place, and its flickering light shone weirdly through the chinks upon staring eyes. As Slade and N'Kema came into the illuminated circle, a babble of terror arose.

"'Ow many've got 'ere?" Slade demanded. "First chop stuff, I mean?"

N'Kema was of opinion, after consulting with the head of his raiding party, that the eyen hundred would about represent it—sixty girls and forty young men and boys. With half a dozen of his braves he went into the pen and cut them out from the crowd, seeing them shackled, mute now with the final agony of dismay, to a long chain. The process took an hour and Slade stood by, watching and smoking composedly; he had seen all this too often before to be in the least put about at the spectacle.

At last it was done, and the cockney's watch made it a scant two hours to dawn. He turned on N'Kema angrily with a final appeal.

"You comin' along?" he asked. "It'll be the worse for you if you don't, me lad!"

N'Kema shook his head, European fashion, to express his extreme unwillingness, and fell to agonized scratching once more. Slade cursed him again, fluently and with gusto, and gave the order to move.

The convoy, a stumbling mass of linked

misery, tottered away into the dark, shepherded by the ready spears. Behind it swaggered Slade, pipe in mouth, his yellow teeth showing in a smirk of anticipation.

N'KEMA went back to his hut and sat by the fire, meditating in disgust on this thing that had befallen him. Of all people in the wide world, Abu Hussein was the last he had ever expected to set eyes on up here. The trader's beat was six hundred miles to the south-eastward—many, many days' journey. He had hoped never to have heard the name again, and to have lived and waxed fat in this nook of the forest he had made his own, without any skeletons resurrecting themselves from his past to confront him.

Now, however, all was changed. There was the faint possibility that Abu Hussein might take this convoy and depart; but there was a far better chance that he would come again and again for more. N'Kema knew the ways of Arab slavers very well. And then, sooner or later, there would be the meeting — inevitably he saw it ahead of him. The meeting, and then Abu Hussein would spit him like a chicken or as likely as not blow daylight into him.

N'Kema went through all the tortures of the coward, and his gloomy thoughts were not cheered by the prospect of what he had anyhow to face at Slade's hands on the morrow. He had a lively dread of the uncompromising little cockney, and he knew exceedingly well that he had men in his own village who would be only too delighted to see him in difficulties. Indeed, without the rifles of the two white men to back him, it would be a spear-thrust in the back for N'Kema some night, and a new chief wearing the monkey tails and dealing in slaves with Ingleby and Slade. The picture was not a pleasant one.

He sat huddled there until dawn was bright in the sky. Then he went inside, still deep in thought, and kicked one of his wives awake, with the order to cook him food.

Meanwhile he revolved affairs once again, seeking for a solution to his troubles and not finding one. The woman crouched at the door, grinding corn in a bowl.

SUNRISE came, and the village street began to stir. A sudden shadow—two of them—fell abruptly across N'Kema's dark meditations. He looked up. Surprise shot into his hideous face and was instantly driven from it by consternation. In the doorway, neat but forbidding in their khaki shorts, cocked *tarbooshes,* and crossed belts, stood a bullet-headed pair of King's Houssas; and in the hands of each of them, levelled directly at N'Kema's heart, was a wicked looking service rifle and a gleaming, deadly bayonet.

They took him forth, unresisting as his own prisoners of the slave-corral, his teeth rattling like castanets, his voice stuck in his gullet. The village street was full of the soldiers, and a big man, perspiring profusely and most obviously in no pleasant temper, was walking down the middle of it.

"I see you, N'Kema!" he said with cold venom.

The monkey chief's knees turned to water beneath him, and his stove-polish face went a livid shade of gray. Abu Hussein had been a calamity, no doubt—but in his wildest dreams of disaster N'Kema had never envisaged anything so appalling as this. He knew that yellow uniform, and with it went noosed ropes. He had seen plenty of them in his time. And he was caught in staring guilt, without even the time to take spearmen and put the remainder of his prisoners where they would not be evidence against him. He sagged between his captors, a pitiable spectacle.

Colonel Mobbs was in no mood for trifling, after a five-day march through frightful country and a night dash of fifteen miles to climax it.

"You hang, N'Kema," was all he said, and N'Kema thought it highly likely.

Mobbs glanced at the watch on his wrist and blew a whistle. The Houssas rapidly fell in line, and leaving the sergeant and ten men to clear up the village, the Colonel struck into the bush. At the head of column marched N'Kema, enthusiastically assisted by bayonets.

VII

SLADE emerged from the cover of the wood, and saw with relief the three men sitting together under the tall trees opposite. He turned and gave the command to his guards to hurry the wretched convoy across the open, and make them lie down awhile in the shade, while he reported to Ingleby. The few moments' rest would bring them before Abu Hussein fresher and therefore a better bargain.

Ingleby had risen at sight of him, and walked out across the clearing, leaving Mason and Abu Hussein to themselves for the time. Abu Hussein moved slightly once more, so as to free the belt at his waist; and Mason grinned at him peculiarly, but without speaking. The tension that had fallen on the two during Ingleby's last outburst relaxed.

The fat man addressed Slade. "How many?" he asked, running an eye over the limping prisoners.

"'Undred, all told," said Slade. "Good stuff, too. That's Abu Hussein, I s'pose."

"Yes," said Ingleby. "Where's N'Kema?"

"Cut up rough," Slade responded indignantly. "Said 'e wasn't comin', and I couldn't make 'im. 'E's scared of Abu Hussein, I b'lieve."

"Scared, is he? I'll give him scared. Still, it doesn't matter. You'd better come up and we'll close the deal. And while we're about it," he added under his breath, "you stand by for that accident soon. Mr. Mason's just about ripe for it."

He flung the rifle carelessly across one arm, and together the two went back to Abu Hussein's seat. Ingleby introduced the cockney and the Arab bowed with his usual grave politeness.

"Now, Mason," said Ingleby briskly, "there's the goods for you. We're ready to talk business when you are."

Mason had been idly contemplating the risen sun. "Very well," he said slowly. "We'll have to have a look over them first, of course."

"Why not?" Ingleby said. "Take your time. No hurry, gentlemen."

VERY leisurely, and with great care, Abu Hussein went over the huddling crowd of slaves. Limbs, teeth, muscles, were inspected and reinspected; a second line was formed from the first, of those for whose bodies the Arab was prepared to pay a price. One by one the chosen were unshackled, and re-shackled afresh; the line of bought men and girls grew little by little.

Slade and Ingleby followed the trader, Ingleby doing the bargaining, and Slade making memoranda in a dirty note book. Mason stood aside, an elbow supported by one hand, the other stroking his unshaven chin. He seemed to be more or less indifferent to the deal taking place and looked about him a good deal. Neither Ingleby nor Slade took a great deal of notice of him.

It was a full hour before Abu Hussein was satisfied. He glanced at the immobile Mason as he passed the last slave. Then he walked solemnly back to his carpet, where the black had now laid the heavy traveling sack.

"In the name of Allah!" he said sententiously once more, and produced a small bag of gold.

"'Ow much, cully?" The cockney's impatience got the better of him.

Ingleby scowled at his eagerness, but the Arab smiled gently. With deliberation he calculated, counting the prisoners over again and figuring with his fingers in the palm of one hand.

"Three hundred pounds English!" he said, and Ingleby's, "Done with you!" drowned Slade's gasp of amazed gratification. Mason had moved in closer, and was standing behind the pair. Abu Hussein began to count the gold, dropping it piece by piece into another bag in Ingleby's hand.

The glittering coins fell one by one with a faint clicking sound. Slade, fairly dancing with impatience, caught Ingleby's eye. The big man motioned with his head, almost imperceptibly, towards Mason. Slade fell back in silence, watching the dropping gold pieces with fascinated eyes and holding his breath.

The last vanished, and Ingleby closed the bag with a click. Then he stooped suddenly and reached for his rifle. Slade saw him, and ducked instinctively out of the way of possible trouble. And as Ingleby rose again Abu Hussein whipped out an automatic and thrust it under his nose.

"Put your hands up, Ingleby!" he snapped.

THE cockney gaped open mouthed for a split second. Then he too found himself with a blue muzzle within a foot of his eyes, and Mason's hard little face behind it. Behind him again, there was the glitter of arms among the undergrowth. Mobbs and his Houssas broke from cover and swept across the open at a run. Ingleby and Slade were seized, unprotesting. Neither of them had recovered enough to say a word when Mason spoke to the Arab.

"You are evidence," he said, "that these men sold a convoy of slaves for three hundred pounds gold."

The tall man nodded. He was engaged in some mysterious operation with his beard. Mobbs saluted.

"There's another of them here, sir," he said. "We got N'Kema. There are more slaves in his village."

He was interrupted. N'Kema was pointing to the tall Arab with a shaking forefinger.

"Lord," he babbled wildly to Ingleby, "that is not Abu Hussein!"

The disclosure seemed to shake the fat man out of his lethargy. "Then what's the meaning of all this? What the devil d'you think you're playing at, you?" he roared, struggling with the two stout Houssas that held him. "Who the hell are you, that officer there? You can't lay hands on me this way—I'm the wrong man to play games like that with. Let me go—at once, sir! And then you'll explain, unless you want questions asked in Parliament."

Mobbs was talking in undertones to Mason. "Very good, sir," he said, saluting again. Ingleby, foaming, turned his attention to the little man.

"You there—Mason!" he stuttered. "What's this game? Have a care, you! You're a murderer on your own confession. I'll have you handed over to the French—and this officer broke as well. Just let me have five minutes with the Governor——"

Mason looked at him. "I am the Governor," he said.

There was a dead, stricken silence. Slade shrieked suddenly. "You're a bloody liar! He's dead! Quayle's dead!"

"I am Quayle," said Mason.

THEY hung N'Kema even as he had foreseen, expeditiously and without fuss. Quayle watched the corpse jiggling from the ironwoods in the bight of a rope, his mouth set into a tight line. Ingleby and Slade, with shocked faces, waited in handcuffs for what might fall next, and Quayle went over to them.

"There's what comes of slaving, Ingleby," he said. "Know any good reason why you two shouldn't be up there too? I don't, except that there's one justice for the black and one for the white. You're not a jot better than N'Kema there—rather worse, as a matter of fact. So I've got to take you down and try you, and your precious lives aren't in any danger."

He paused; neither of the two could meet his eyes. "I can't hang you," he went on. "But I can see to it that you don't forget this. I think the court will endeavor to prove to you that laws aren't made to be played with—and you'll have some considerable leisure to think about it. And by the way," he smiled an icy little smile, "I'm inclined to think you're a lawyer, Ingleby. Well, you'll be allowed counsel—but I wouldn't bank too much on his shaking my own witness against you, or Mr. Tarleton's. By the way, Mr. Tarleton's your Abu Hussein—the real man's still down in the Tchad. No, Ingleby—I've got you better than that. Recognize this?"

He reached down into the breast of his lamentable shirt and drew out a flat black ledger.

"It's a pity," he said, "Ingleby. Sometimes it's as well to keep no accounts, even for a good man of business like you. Also, it's a mistake to leave your records where they can be found."

HE LEFT them and went across to where Tarleton was still struggling with his beard.

"O M'Laka," he called to the secretary's black, "you shall go to my fine bag and bring me the bottle that is there."

He handed it to Tarleton. "Spirits of wine," he said. "That'll take it off. I've been infernally sorry for you this last day or two—I know what it means, wearing one of those things. I've had to wear one or two in my own time."

Mobbs came up, while Tarleton, grimacing, rubbed the hair from his itching face. Quayle addressed him.

"Colonel," he said heartily, "a very neat bit of work, that of yours. I was beginning to be a bit afraid of the timing till M'Laka gave me your note in the small hours this morning. However, it worked out excellently."

Mobbs saluted once more, and this time there was no trace of irony in his manner.

"May I move off, your excellency?" he asked. "I'd like to clean things up in M'Laka's village before night."

"Yes, you'd better," Quayle said. Then, "Oh, by the way, Colonel," he went on, "one of those men has a ring of mine on him somewhere. I wish you'd tell someone to get it for me. I'd sooner not lose it—it's a present Abu Hussein gave me years ago. I'm by way of being a blood brother of his; and if he knew how we'd been using his name up here, he'd have apoplexy. I'll have to write and tell him, all the same."

A none too gentle corporal went through their pockets and from Slade took the ring. Quayle slipped it on his finger, and as he did so Ingleby's eye met his. A flush of crimson, whether of repentance or mere fury, crept over the ex-barrister's face.

"Very well, Colonel," said Quayle. Mobbs fell his men in, and with Ingleby and Slade in its center the little column moved rapidly across the open ground.

The PHANTOM DETECTIVE

SUBSCRIPTION

Due to popular demand, we are now offering a 6-issue subscription to THE PHANTOM DETECTIVE.

$70

6 Issue Subscription, not necessarily consecutive issues. Cannot use subscription to pay for issues already published.

Regularly $14.95 each, now get 6 issue subscription for only $70.00. More than 20% off the retail price, with free shipping.

Adventure House
914 Laredo Rd
Silver Spring, MD 20901
www.adventurehouse.com
sales@adventurehouse.com
301-754-1589

Check - Money Order - Paypal - Visa - Mastercard - Amex

Adventure House Darrell Richardson Postcards - Set One

10 - 4x6 Cards
Full Color - Glossy
Each Card A Scarce Cover Reproduction!

NOW ONLY $5.00

sales@adventurehouse.com
www.adventurehouse.com

914 Laredo Rd - Silver Spring MD 20901
301-754-1589

Our Tenth Year!

WINDY CITY PULP AND PAPER CONVENTION

April 23rd-25th 2010

Adventure

Art Show
Movies
Con Suite
and more.

Celebrating the 100th Anniversary of Adventure Magazine

Pulps
Paperbacks
Original Art
Movie Memorabilia
Old Time Radio
Science Fiction
Popular Culture
Mystery
Good Old Stuff!

Westin Lombard Yorktown Ctr
70 Yorktown Shopping Ctr
Lombard, IL 60148
630-719-8000

For more information:
Windy City Pulp and Paper Convention, LLC
13 Spring Ln - Barrington Hills, IL - 60010
847-217-4241
info@windycitypulpandpaper.com
www.windycitypulpandpaper.com

Gold and Silver Medal Winner
ForeWord Magazine's Book Of
The Year Awards.
ADVENTURE
HOUSE
PRESENTS:
CAPTAIN FUTURE
MAN OF TOMORROW
MAGICIAN OF MARS
A Complete Book-Length Scientifiction Novel
By EDMOND HAMILTON
PHANTOM DETECTIVE
THE ISLAND OF DEATH
The LONE RANGER Magazine
May
10 CENTS
The Masked Rider's Justice
A COMPLETE NOVEL featuring The Lone Ranger
ADVENTURE
HOUSE
ADVENTURE HOUSE
sales@adventurehouse.com
www.adventurehouse.com

#112

Black Bat
Dbl Issue
May 2010

#113

Jim
Anthony
Jul. 2010

#114

Ki-Gor
Dbl Issue
Sept. 2010

Made in the USA
Charleston, SC
13 April 2010